Siren in the City

Other Books By Lexi Blake

ROMANTIC SUSPENSE

Masters And Mercenaries
The Dom Who Loved Me
The Men With The Golden Cuffs
A Dom is Forever
On Her Master's Secret Service
Sanctum: A Masters and Mercenaries Novella
Love and Let Die
Unconditional: A Masters and Mercenaries Novella
Dungeon Royale
Dungeon Games: A Masters and Mercenaries Novella
A View to a Thrill
Cherished: A Masters and Mercenaries Novella
You Only Love Twice
Luscious: Masters and Mercenaries~Topped
Adored: A Masters and Mercenaries Novella
Master No
Just One Taste: Masters and Mercenaries~Topped 2
From Sanctum with Love
Devoted: A Masters and Mercenaries Novella
Dominance Never Dies
Submission is Not Enough
Master Bits and Mercenary Bites~The Secret Recipes of Topped
Perfectly Paired: Masters and Mercenaries~Topped 3
For His Eyes Only
Arranged: A Masters and Mercenaries Novella
Love Another Day
At Your Service: Masters and Mercenaries~Topped 4
Master Bits and Mercenary Bites~Girls Night
Nobody Does It Better, Coming February 20, 2018
Close Cover, Coming April 10, 2018
Protected, Coming July 31, 2018

Lawless
Ruthless
Satisfaction
Revenge

Courting Justice
Order of Protection, Coming June 5, 2018

Masters Of Ménage (by Shayla Black and Lexi Blake)
Their Virgin Captive
Their Virgin's Secret
Their Virgin Concubine
Their Virgin Princess
Their Virgin Hostage
Their Virgin Secretary
Their Virgin Mistress

The Perfect Gentlemen (by Shayla Black and Lexi Blake)
Scandal Never Sleeps
Seduction in Session
Big Easy Temptation
Smoke and Sin
At the Pleasure of the President, Coming Fall 2018

URBAN FANTASY

Thieves
Steal the Light
Steal the Day
Steal the Moon
Steal the Sun
Steal the Night
Ripper
Addict
Sleeper
Outcast, Coming 2018

LEXI BLAKE WRITING AS SOPHIE OAK

Small Town Siren
Siren in the City
Away From Me, Coming February 6, 2018
Three to Ride, Coming March 13, 2018
Siren Enslaved, Coming Spring 2018

Siren in the City

Texas Sirens Book 2

Lexi Blake

writing as

Sophie Oak

Siren in the City
Texas Sirens Book 2

Published by DLZ Entertainment LLC

Copyright 2018 DLZ Entertainment LLC
Edited by Chloe Vale
ISBN: 978-1-937608-74-3

Dedication

To my first readers, that amazing group of women who never flinch when I ask them to read my books. Kim, Mindy, Britta, and Maggie—I couldn't ask for a better group of friends. Thanks for everything.

Special thanks to Shayla Black for making this a better book than it was in the beginning.

Updated dedication: to my team on the second edition—Kim, Rich, Dylan, Liz, Stormy, Riane, and Danielle Sanchez and the InkSlinger family. And Margarita Coale, without whom this edition doesn't exist.

Author Foreword

I've had readers ask me why write a second book for Jack and Abby and Sam. I mean, come on, Lexi, they're happy. Let them be happy. It's funny how stuff happens in the background the reader doesn't see. If you look at the publication schedule, *Siren in the City* is my second published book, but the truth is I wrote *Three to Ride*, *Bound*, *The Dom Who Loved Me*, and *Away From Me* between *Small Town Siren* and *Siren in the City*. I wrote *Siren in the City* because I missed the characters. I also wrote it because I realized that my lovely threesome was left undone. While Abby had her happily ever after, Sam had only begun to truly find his.

I didn't actually plan Sam's confession in the first book. It was one of those things that surprised me as I typed the words. Those are the best surprises—the ones that take the author to a new place she hadn't expected to go and forces her to look at the characters again. Even in reworking this book, I've gotten to take another look at the characters who so shaped the beginning of my career. Though you might not notice it because one is paranormal and this one is contemporary, *Siren in the City* has a lot in common with *Steal the Light*. At the heart of both is a hero dealing with trauma by pulling away from his loved ones. This happened to my husband and me. I won't go into the hows and whys, but I was still dealing with it at the time. My books are my therapy. Like all my characters they are a little bit me, a lot of my husband, and ultimately, they show you who I want to be. Strong like Jack. Brave like Abby. As loyal as Sam. Seven years later, I'm still working on it.

I hope you enjoy this new edition. It's got insights on how my Texas Sirens characters fit into the Lexiverse, but remember the timing of these books. *Siren in the City* takes place as a small startup security company is just getting its feet on the ground. So don't be surprised if this new version includes a young Viking or another twosome who will someday look for one woman to love.

Much love,

Lexi

Sign up for Lexi Blake's newsletter
and be entered to win a $25 gift certificate
to the bookseller of your choice.

Join us for news, fun, and exclusive content
including free short stories.

There's a new contest every month!

Go to www.LexiBlake.net to subscribe.

Chapter One

"Open, Abigail." Sam Fleetwood's voice had gone dangerously low.

Abby Barnes sat back. That deep tone of his was a sure sign that her husband number two was rapidly getting irritated with her refusal, but it didn't matter. She was done taking his crap. It had been going on for far too long. He'd been shoving stuff in her mouth for days. She simply wasn't taking it anymore. This was her bedroom, not some prison cell. He was her husband, not her jailer. Her hand toyed with the magazine lying on top of the comforter.

She had to figure out how to handle Sam. Then she could figure out how to handle the real problem in her life.

"No." There was really only one way to handle Sam. He had to be handled head on. She eyed him, giving him the sternest look in her repertoire. She crossed her arms and sat back against the headboard of the bed. It was time to make a stand. She wasn't spending one more day with him like this. She was done obeying him.

"I swear to god, Abby, if you don't open that pretty mouth of yours and let me inside, I'm going to turn you over my knee," Sam promised. His gorgeous face was turning an amusing shade of red.

It would be a bad idea to laugh though.

Abby primly pulled up the comforter. She was settled in for a nice long fight. "I don't think Jack will like the idea of you turning me over your knee. You're supposed to be taking care of me."

Jack Barnes was her legal husband. They had married in a civil ceremony six months before. Together with Sam, they'd formed a happy threesome. Jack was an alpha male, and beyond that, he was a Dom in every sense of the word. Abby was more than happy to be his wife and his submissive. Jack took very good care of her, and he also took care of Sam.

Well, he had.

Sam's blue eyes narrowed, and he cocked his head to the side, studying her for a moment. "That's what I'm trying to do. I'm trying to take care of you like Jack requested. You're the one being extremely stubborn. Come on, baby. Don't you want to be full?"

The last question was asked with a low growl.

She rolled her eyes. She wasn't giving in simply because he used his sexy voice. "I'm full enough. I don't need you to fill me up. I'm fine. I'm perfectly satisfied, so you've done your duty. Why don't you go see if Jack needs help? You've been in bed with me for three days. I can't take anymore." And if Jack Barnes didn't agree, he could come and tell her himself.

"You'll take as much as I give you." Sam leaned forward aggressively. "Now, Benita made this chicken soup, and you're going to eat it. It's supposed to be good for colds." He held out the spoon once more. "Open up."

"No." She was sick of eating no matter how delicious the soup was. She wasn't sure what Sam's health care plan was here, but it definitely had something to do with stuffing her way past full. She. went back to reading her magazine.

The way she viewed it, she was well on the path to recovery. The bacterial infection that had settled into her lungs was almost gone thanks to antibiotics. It wasn't as though she didn't have some skill in this case. She was a registered nurse who'd served over a decade in trauma ERs. She wasn't coughing anymore, and her head felt clear. She was tired but feeling better.

Now she just had to convince Sam to get off her back. He'd been playing nurse for days, and it was starting to drive her crazy. She'd been a nurse for ten years and never once had she ridden herd on a patient the way Sam did.

Sam stood up. He moved the tray off the bed and stood over her. Abby glanced up at the man she thought of as husband number two. Though she was annoyed with him at the moment, she couldn't help but sigh. Sam Fleetwood was a gorgeous man. He had sandy blond hair that curled around his ears. His blue eyes were the most prominent features on a handsome face that also boasted sensual lips. His chest was what had her attention now, though. He was wearing nothing but a faded pair of Levi's, and it left his perfectly cut torso on heart-stopping display. She wanted to reach out and run her hands down those muscles to his six-pack and lower, but she had a point to make.

"Go away, Sam," she said dismissively, as if she didn't want to throw him down on the bed and have her way with him. That would only reward his overbearing behavior.

Sam's Texas accent was thick as he explained his world view to her. "You don't seem to understand the order of things. Let me explain a little geometry to you. You seem to think we're a triangle, with Jack at the top and you and me on equal planes at the bottom. We aren't a triangle. We're a straight line, baby. Jack might be at the head of this household of ours, but I'm on top of you, and that's exactly the way I like it. Jack gives the orders to me, and I give the orders to you."

Now Abby felt her eyes narrow. She loved him. Oh, how she loved that man, but Sam didn't have a dominant bone in his body. Jack might be at the head of the household, but she would be damned if Sam wasn't on the same level she was. Sam was her playmate. Sam was her best friend. He was not her keeper.

Abby got to her knees on the big bed. She was wearing a cute set of green baby doll pajamas, which proved beyond a shadow of a doubt that she was feeling distinctly better. If she hadn't she wouldn't have put on some sexy lingerie. As she leaned forward, she couldn't help but notice Sam's distinct interest in her breasts, bouncing without the support of her bra. She kept her voice low so he would know she was serious. "Is that right, Samuel Fleetwood? Do you think simply having been born with man parts gives you the right to top me?"

That seemed to give him pause. His hands went to his lean hips and his handsome face screwed up into what she liked to think of as his thinking face. Yes, she watched as he thought about his answer,

15

and then still got it all wrong. "Yes, Abby, yes I do. I'm the man in this relationship, and you should obey me."

She hurled a pillow toward his head. "You're the man? Who are you kidding? Jack's the man. You're the…" She struggled to find a word to describe him. Sam was fun and playful. He wasn't demanding in any way except sexually. Sam was the indulgent one. She settled for truth. "You're the Sam in this relationship, and that means you follow Jack's orders just like I do."

They did follow Jack's orders, when they couldn't find a way around them. Though lately there hadn't been all that many orders to follow.

Sam's blue eyes lost some of their luster as he broke contact with her and seemed to suddenly find the comforter endlessly interesting. Shit. She'd handled this morning's confrontation all wrong. Her heart softened toward the man who formed one half of her world.

"Baby, that didn't come out right," she tried.

Sam took a step back, his handsome face marred by a frown. He waved off her worry. "It's no big deal, darlin'. I get the message. You're feeling better. You don't need a keeper. I'll go get dressed and find some work to do. Jack's been on his own for days."

He turned to leave.

She was off the bed in a shot. There was no way she could allow him to leave like that. He was sensitive. Oh, he would say he wasn't, but when it came to her, Sam Fleetwood was one big teddy bear and she'd hurt him.

She wound her arms around Sam's waist, knowing he would never do anything so impolite as break her hug. He stood still for a moment, and then all of his instincts took over. He relaxed against her as his hands curled around her body and found her backside.

"You honestly feeling better?"

Abby didn't bite, not yet. "I feel like crap, Sam, and not in a physical sense. I shouldn't have talked to you that way. You are so important to me. You know I love you."

He laughed softly. "I know you love me. You wouldn't put up with me if you didn't love me."

There was the trouble. She kissed the well-defined muscles of his shoulders softly. He smelled like soap and some masculine smell she couldn't quite define. "You aren't hard to put up with. I love you, Sam. Jack loves you, too."

She knew exactly where Sam's insecurities lay.

Though there was no legal way to marry Sam, she considered herself his wife as well. Jack and Sam owned a highly lucrative cattle ranch together. They'd been friends and partners for years. Jack had grown up in foster care. Sam had spent a portion of his teen years in the same group home Jack had been assigned to. From the day they met, they'd been inseparable. They shared a home, a business, and now a wife.

And Sam wanted more. He wanted to be a true threesome, not merely a pair of friends sharing a woman. Sam wanted Jack, wanted him in every way a human being could want another.

"I know," he said, but she could hear the sadness in his voice.

It made her ache for him. Made her ache for them. She'd thought the day they'd married they'd become complete, but something was missing. Something deep.

If only they'd been able to go on their honeymoon like normal people. If only the day hadn't ended the way it had…

On their wedding day, Jack had taken a bullet meant for her. A woman with a long-held grudge against Abby had shown up as they were walking out of the courthouse and taken a shot at her. She could still remember how it felt to look down and see a hole in Jack's strong chest, to know how close he was to death. To know that she could lose him just when she'd found him.

It was funny how the world worked. The same woman who'd shot her husband had been the one who'd sent her out into the world alone at seventeen and pregnant. It had been Ruby Echols who'd fueled her desire to prove her hometown wrong. If Ruby hadn't driven her out of town, she didn't think she would have chosen nursing as a profession, wouldn't have been so deeply determined to reach the top of her field.

Her skill had saved Jack that day, and oddly her skill was wrapped up in Ruby Echols.

Jack had spent time in the hospital and his recovery period had been long and hard. Physically, he'd come out stronger than ever.

She wasn't so sure he'd recovered emotionally yet. He'd been very close to death. As a nurse, she'd seen what facing your own mortality could do to a person.

For some people, it was a wake-up call. The revelation that they weren't immortal spurred them to do things they never would have before.

There was another portion of the population that retreated into themselves. It was as though they'd never thought of themselves as fragile and couldn't handle it even though they'd come back. Jack had been a bit like that.

It wasn't that he held himself apart. He was generous with everything. He told her he loved her. He made love to her most nights and a whole lot of the mornings, too. But there was something missing. The outrageous dominance Jack had always brought to the bedroom before had disappeared. Jack liked to be in charge, but coming close to death and being weak for so long seemed to have humbled him in a way she didn't like. It had also caused him to stop the playful experiment he and Sam shared before the incident. Sam had been close to getting what he wanted, and now it seemed a million miles away.

When they were in bed together, Jack avoided Sam physically, and it was starting to wear on them all. Cracks were forming where she would have sworn there was a solid concrete foundation.

"He needs some time," Sam said quietly.

"Or he needs a good, swift kick in the ass." She rubbed against Sam's back, the warmth of his skin comforting. Of course there was something else that was comforting, too. Something they hadn't done for a couple of days. She ran her hands down his chest to the front of his jeans. His cock was already erect, but that wasn't surprising. A slight breeze could get Sam erect. It was one of the things she loved about him. He was always ready to go. She cupped that big cock of Sam's and felt him sigh.

"You going to give it to him, baby?" Sam's voice went low and husky. He pressed himself into her hands.

She could feel the heat coming off Sam's body. "I think our Dom needs to be reminded of who he is. When was the last time he punished me? I stayed out until three in the morning at Christa's

18

three weeks ago and forgot to call. He was panicked by the time he found me. Did he toss me over his knee and spank my ass? No, he very politely requested that next time I text him when I'm going to be out late. Seriously? That is not the man I married. He walks like Jack, and he looks like Jack, but I want the real Jack back."

Sam shook his head. "I tried to talk to him, but he always says he's fine. We haven't been in the playroom for months. I bitched about it, and he said we're married now and should show you more respect. I married you because I wanted to do all sorts of dirty things to you. I love you, and I respect the hell out of you. I respect how smart you are and how funny you can be, and I also respect your blow job skills."

"Good to know." She sobered quickly as she considered the problem. Jack was wrestling with something. He wasn't willing to talk about it yet. Maybe what he needed was a shake-up. Though he wouldn't admit it, Jack considered Sam his own, just as he believed she belonged to him. Sam was as much Jack's sub as she was, but he didn't feel it. When the Dom lost control, it was up to the subs to force him to take it back. None of them were truly content with the current situation, and they wouldn't be until things got back to their weird version of normal.

"See, you are a bad girl, Abigail Barnes." Sam groaned as he gave her cheeks a good squeeze. "I can feel you plotting from here. This better be good, baby. When he comes back to us, I don't think he'll come back quietly."

"Oh, I intend to make that man roar." She stopped rubbing him and walked around so she could look into his eyes.

They were at a crossroads and she could see her choices so clearly. One road led to more of the same. Maybe Jack would come out of it. Maybe he wouldn't and his new, quieter personality would become permanent and something precious would be lost between the three of them.

She could face him and give him an ultimatum. They all went into therapy or she would have to think about leaving. But that wasn't fair and she couldn't travel down that road. Ever.

Or she could gamble. Sometimes a wake-up call was needed. Sometimes a woman had to push the boundaries and see what happened. He would explode and they would at least talk about what was happening. Or he would do nothing and she would know.

"I've been thinking, and I came up with a few things." She dropped to her knees in front of Sam. It was time to prove to him that she was definitely worthy of his respect. Sick time was over. She was also done with sitting around waiting for Jack to get over whatever he needed to get over. She was walking a dangerous line and was probably in for the spanking of a lifetime. Luckily, she liked spankings. Her hands ran up Sam's thighs to play with the fly of his jeans. "I'll handle everything. But first, you promised to fill me up."

Sam tore open his jeans. He shoved them to his knees, freeing his big, beautiful dick. She took it in her hand and stroked the soft skin covering his hardness. It was already weeping. There was a pearly drop of him right there waiting for her. She gathered it on her tongue and sighed.

"You know me." Sam thrust his hands in her hair. "I never like to disappoint a lady."

* * * *

Jack Barnes wiped his boots off on the mat before he walked into the house. It was March, and it had been raining nonstop for a week. The weather outside matched his general mood, though he had no one incident to tie his malaise to. It was a general restlessness that he couldn't get rid of. He pulled off his light jacket and hung up his hat before shutting the door.

"You're early, Mr. Barnes." A familiar voice greeted him. Benita, his longtime housekeeper, stood in the doorway that led to the kitchen. She had a carrot in one hand and a knife in the other. It was his habit to come in for lunch at noon. He would sit with his best friend and their wife. Today he'd knocked off a bit early because of a message on his cell. He couldn't return it until he reached the quiet of the house. It was far too noisy to call someone from the back of a horse in the middle of a storm.

"Don't worry about me, Benita." Jack nodded to her as he moved through the house. He wouldn't have time to sit and eat

20

today. "I'll get a sandwich later." He stopped and backed up. "Is Abby eating better?"

He hated that cough she'd had a few days ago, hated any time she was sick.

The older woman smiled brightly. Jack knew she genuinely liked the new mistress of the house. "I believe you'll find your wife is feeling much better this morning. She's been giving Mr. Fleetwood hell. You won't be able to keep her in bed for much longer."

Jack nodded. She would be up and about before he felt good about it. A thought floated through his mind.

She wouldn't be up and about if you tied her to the bed.

Instantly, his cock hardened at the thought of her spread out and naked. Then he winced and let it go. It might be what he wanted, but it wasn't what she needed. He was a selfish ass. She'd been sick and he was thinking about his cock. Marriage changed things. Getting older changed things. He had to adapt or he would lose them both. "As long as she finishes out those antibiotics, it should be fine."

That was what the doctor had told him. He should listen to people who went to medical school. He started back toward his office.

"Now how do you feel about triangles, Sam?" He heard Abby's laughter as he turned down the hallway.

Sam groaned, and Jack could guess what his partner was doing. "I love 'em, baby doll. Triangles are the best. Don't stop. God, Abby, you feel so good…"

He went still and listened for a moment. His cock got harder as he listened to the sweet sound of their wife sucking and Sam enjoying the ride. It was the kind of thing he ached to join in on. He should walk into that room and demand that Abigail remove his clothes and see to him, too. It had been days since he sank into his wife's tight pussy. Since then, she'd been too sick for play. Now, he could walk in that room and calmly explain that he wanted them both to join him in the playroom. He wanted Sam to tie Abigail up, and then he would tie Sam up. Both of his subs would be bound and trussed for his pleasure. He could spend the rainy afternoon disciplining them and then rewarding them for their submission. He

21

wanted it so badly, he almost couldn't catch his breath.

Jack dragged air into his lungs and shook the thought off. When had he started thinking of Sam in those terms? Sam had always been the follower to Jack's leader, but getting married had changed something in Jack. In fact, a lot of things had changed.

And what the hell would he do if Abigail didn't want things to change like that? Sure she'd been the one to ask him to kiss Sam that night long ago, but kissing was different from sex.

He wanted Sam, wasn't sure how much longer he could hold out without taking him, and then everything would change and he wasn't sure it would be for the better.

He turned away from the bedroom and forced himself to walk down the hall. He could still hear Sam and Abby's lovemaking. He wanted to join them, but he knew what would happen if he did. He would burst in and start making demands and take over, just the way he always did. He was a selfish bastard, and he knew it. It was better to let them have their fun.

It was better to not push boundaries.

Sam practically bounced out of the room. Jack's heart seized a little at the sight of his oldest friend in nothing but a pair of blue jeans.

Sam's head was turned as he shut the door. "I'll be back, baby." He stopped and stared at Jack. "Hey. Abby needs some water."

Jack nodded and turned away. It was easy for Sam to be happy. He didn't have all the responsibility in the world on his shoulders. Jack wanted the responsibility. He needed it, craved it, but sometimes it was hard to make the decisions. It was hard to shoulder everything alone, but he couldn't, wouldn't burden his submissives with his problems. "Then you should take care of her. Is she feeling better?"

Sam's hand came up and almost made it to Jack's shoulder before he pulled it back down. Playful Sam seemed almost subdued. He shook his head, and there was a sunny smile on his face again. "She's fine. Hell, she's downright frisky. Come join us. You know it takes more than me to keep that woman satisfied."

Jack's hand was on the door. Damn it, he couldn't. He hadn't slept in days and his control was shot. He would take over and possibly hurt his wife. He would wreck everything by asking too much of Sam. At the very least, his demanding behavior would drive them away eventually. He had to remember how fragile she was. There was a popping sound as Benita slammed the door to the kitchen. That door needed fixing and had for months, but it didn't stop him from jumping.

Every time he heard a sound like that, he saw the gun in Ruby Echols's hand and felt the bullet slam into his chest. The world seemed to go hazy, his peripheral vision fading. He needed to breathe but something was wrong with his damn lungs.

"Come on, Jack, let's have some fun," Sam cajoled.

"No, damn it." The words came out far harsher than he intended, but he was sweating now, panic close to the surface. He needed to be alone, to calm down, to figure out how he was going to gently make love to his wife and respect his partner. He had to ignore this craving to utterly dominate them both. "Some of us have work to do."

Sam's mouth slammed shut, forming a stubborn line. "Well, we wouldn't want to keep you from your precious work. I'll take care of Abby. It's all I seem to be able to do these days."

"See that you do." He practically ran into his office. He hated himself for the look on Sam's face, but he couldn't call him back.

His office was cool and dark. He didn't bother to open the curtains. He sat down at his desk and pulled out his cell phone, needing to think about anything other than how pissed off Sam must be. His jaw tightened.

Maybe he was the one who should be pissed. While Sam rolled around with their wife, Jack was the one who couldn't fucking sleep at night. While Sam got Abigail's kisses, Jack got her worried glances. Anger felt better than the pity party playing in his head. He punched in the number on speed dial while thinking about the message Julian Lodge had left on his voice mail. It had been cryptic, with no greeting other than, "Call me yesterday, Jackson."

Julian's voice had been terse and tight with irritation. On the edge. A little like Jack felt.

And it wasn't like the man would respond to a text. If Julian asked him to call, a call was what he wanted. Despite the fact that

Julian had the best of everything—including technology—he was also slightly paranoid about how he used it. A simple text would have saved Jack so much time, but he knew that if Julian thought the conversation would be important, he wouldn't allow it to be sent up to the "cloud."

Julian Lodge had been the man to pull him off the street. Jack had been introduced to the wealthy club owner through a lover who appreciated his control. She'd thought he would fit right in at the underground establishment known only as The Club. After an interview and what felt like endless training sessions, Julian brought Jack in as one of the resident Doms.

It was a job he'd enjoyed, especially in those days. He'd quickly become a leader in the place. The Club catered to a clientele dedicated to the D/s lifestyle and ménage. Jack learned everything he knew about how to pleasure a lover from years of working there. He'd gained more than mere sexual knowledge. Though Julian was only a few years older, the man had been a mentor to him. Julian had taught him how to handle himself both in business situations and in personal ones. He'd taken a rough street kid and taught him that ruthlessness involved far more than one's fists.

From Julian, Jack had learned the fine art of revenge.

His father had been the first recipient of Jack's newly acquired knowledge. Julian had aided the young Jack in finding the biological father who knowingly left him to the wolves of foster care at the tender age of six. Senator Allen Cameron had a bright political future, and a love child who worked in a sex club could ruin everything. He had promptly found himself the satisfied owner of five million dollars in exchange for signing away any rights to future inheritance. He'd taken Sam to small-town Willow Fork, Texas, and bought his spread. Ten years and a whole bunch of natural gas reserve later, Jack was a very wealthy man.

"This is Lodge." A tense voice interrupted his thoughts. Just the fact that Julian's usually smooth voice was rough gave Jack pause. "Is that you, Jackson?"

"Yes," Jack replied calmly. "I'm sorry I didn't get back to you sooner. I was on the range. I had to get back to the house before I could call. What can I help you with? It sounded urgent."

"You can get your ass up here and handle your business, Jackson. I need you here tomorrow. I'll expect you sometime in the afternoon." There was no mistaking the fine edge of Julian's temper.

Jack found himself sitting up straight. He didn't like anyone, including his old mentor, speaking to him in such a fashion. It brought out the alpha in him. He ruthlessly shoved the irritation down. "Would you like to explain yourself, Julian?"

There was silence and then a short laugh from the other end of the line. "Yes, that should do it. Use that exact tone on the little asshole, and it should have him crapping his pants."

Jack took a deep breath. "Which asshole might you be referring to?"

"His name is Lucas Cameron," Julian said with a sigh. "Jackson, he's your brother, and he's intent on blackmailing all of us."

Chapter Two

The next day, Sam leaned in to hear Abby talk over the sounds of diners at Christa's Café. The clatter of dishes and people talking made it hard to have an intimate conversation.

"What do you mean he left a note?" Abby asked a second time.

He shrugged, wondering exactly what to say to her. He should have known something was up with Jack. He'd been preoccupied the night before. Now that he really thought about it, Jack had acted pretty odd even for lately. He hadn't listened to anything Abby had said and barely touched his supper. He'd gone to bed without saying a word to the two of them.

This morning Jack had skipped breakfast. When he asked Jack about it, he'd been evasive, saying something about work.

Then shortly afterward, Sam had found that damn note.

He looked at Abby from his place across the booth. All around them the lunch crowd at Christa's Café was moving and talking. Sam ignored them all. The town still loved to gossip about him. Marrying Abby had lent fuel to that particular fire, but he had bigger things to worry about now.

If it had just been him, Sam would have shrugged it all off as Jack brooding. Abby deserved more from Jack. "He left a note. I was working in the barn, and when I got back to remind him we were meeting you in town for lunch, the truck was gone. He left this note on the refrigerator."

Sam passed it across the table to their wife. He watched her hazel eyes widen as she read the terse note Jack had left behind. It was on the ranch's stationary, but at least it was handwritten.

Something came up and I need to go out of town. I'll be back in a few days. Love you, Jack.

Abby's pretty mouth tightened. She reached into her purse and pulled out her cell. There was a certain righteous indignation that went along with pressing the number that called Jack.

"He's not answering, baby." He'd already tried it several times. He'd called and sent a couple of texts. There was a big part of him that was scared Jack would pick up. If Jack picked up for Abby, then he would know exactly where his place was in this family.

"Damn it, Jack," Abby growled into the receiver. "Call me. This note is bullshit, and you know it. You call me and tell me where you are. Sam and I are worried about you."

She pushed the button to end the call, and Sam relaxed slightly. At least Jack was ignoring them both. Sam reached across the table and stroked Abby's hand. Out of long habit, he made excuses for the man he'd lived with for years. "He doesn't like to talk while he's driving. You know that."

"He didn't even tell us where he was going." Abby drummed her free hand along the top of the booth.

Sam caught his breath. Even though he was concerned about the state of his household, he couldn't help but love the way looking at Abby made him feel. She was a stunning woman with red hair and a killer body. She was forever bemoaning her weight, but Sam loved her every curve. There was a time when she would have been spanked for disparaging herself. The last time she'd called herself fat, Jack had told her not to be so hard on herself.

Sam missed the real Jack.

Christa Wade walked up carrying a platter of food. The brunette was wearing her usual uniform of jeans and a Western shirt, though all the other waitresses wore pink uniforms. Sam smiled, thinking about the uniform Abby had kept from her short period as a waitress here. It was in the back of the closet with her French maid's uniform and the hot nurse costume he bought her for Halloween the year before. Abby tried to explain that she'd never have worn that in a hospital, but Sam wasn't going to let her ruin his fantasy. She'd worked all those years in tiny miniskirts and high heels with a little nurse hat on her head.

"Here you go, guys," Christa said with a smile. She started chatting about things going on in Willow Fork while Sam thought about his stomach.

Abby had ordered for him, and he fought the urge to close his eyes against what she thought of as a proper lunch. Abby firmly believed the word wholesome and food should go together. Sam had never met a cow he didn't want to eat. It was a food chain thing.

Christa laughed as she set the burger in front of him. "She's not cruel, Sam."

He winced as he noted there were no fries. Christa set down a mound of green stuff alongside the burger. Christa asked if there was anything else she could get them. It took everything Sam had not to respond with fries and ketchup and maybe a hot dog on the side. Christa winked at him as she walked away. He pushed the bowl of salad around with the side of his fork.

"It's called compromise," Abby explained. All she had in front of her was green stuff. With Jack distracted, she'd gone on another diet. She'd been eating like a bird, and it was starting to worry Sam. "You get your burger, exactly the way you like it, and I get the satisfaction of knowing you ate something today that didn't used to have a face."

Sam sighed and gave the lettuce a tentative try. His wife had some strange ideas about eating. He suspected she got it from years of big-city living.

"Where do you think he went?"

Sam hated the sadness in Abby's voice. He silently cursed his partner for putting it there. He and Jack were going to have it out and soon. Sam could handle being ignored, but he wasn't about to let Abby get hurt. He had no idea what was bugging Jack, but he meant to find out. As to where his partner had gotten off to, he did have an idea. He simply wasn't certain he should tell their wife.

"You know, don't you?" Abby let her fork drop. Those hazel eyes became laser beams shooting through him. Abby, for all the submission she showed in the bedroom, could be damn bossy when she wanted to be. "Samuel, you better tell me what you know right now."

"Fine." He knew there was no real way to keep her from finding out. He wasn't able to keep things from Abby. "I might know the password to his voice mail, and I might have listened to his messages."

Abby's mouth dropped open. Then a slow, appreciative smile crossed her face. "You little sneak. I love you so much right now."

He winked at her. The day was looking up. She appeared properly impressed with his more criminally inclined talents. He might be able to convince her to spend some time in Christa's office. He had fond memories of the desk in there. He wouldn't mention to her that he'd figured out her password, too. He always kept tabs on those he loved. "I checked his voice mail. There was one he'd already listened to, but hadn't erased. It was a message from Julian."

"Why do I know that name?" Abby asked as she took a long drink of iced tea.

This was the part he was pretty sure she wouldn't like. "He's the man who runs The Club."

"That's right," she said, obviously remembering. Jack had told her about the time they had spent in Dallas. Sam was pretty sure she'd gotten a nicely sanitized version of what went on there. "Julian Lodge. He's Jack's old mentor. He sent that lovely bouquet to the hospital when Jack was there. What did he need?"

"He didn't say exactly." Sam took a bite of the burger but everything tasted like cardboard to him today. He put it down. "He told Jack to call him in that voice of his."

Abby leaned in and glanced around, as though worried someone was listening in. He knew she had a lot of questions about the time he and Jack had spent at the BDSM club in Dallas. While Jack had worked there as a resident Dom, Sam had tended bar.

"Which voice is that?" She gasped as she answered her own question. "He's a Dom like Jack, isn't he?"

Sam nodded and fought off his shiver. Julian Lodge scared the crap out of him sometimes. "He's the Dom of Doms, baby. You know how Jack gets when he's really in control? That voice he gets that you just can't disobey?"

A smile crossed her face, likely because she was remembering some good times. Hell, he couldn't stop thinking about it either. Jack would growl in that voice of his, and Abby would be on her knees at his feet, her clothes lost in a flurry of obedience. He loved watching her submit. He wanted so fucking badly to kneel next to her, to know his turn was going to come.

"I know the voice, Sam." Her tone was husky with remembered pleasure.

"Well, multiply it by a hundred and know that Julian Lodge uses it twenty-four seven."

She flushed, her skin turning a pretty pink. "Wow, and he taught Jack?"

"Yep, though Jack doesn't take it as far as Julian does," Sam explained. Of course, Jack hadn't been taking it anywhere lately. "Jack likes a sub when it comes to sex."

Abby's smile was wry. "Does he? I couldn't tell. I can't see his face when my ass is in the air waiting for him to spank it."

"Sassy," he tossed at her and continued. "Jack doesn't try to make every decision for you. He's very protective, and he can be overbearing at times."

"Not lately." Her mouth turned down in a glum frown.

He ignored her. It wouldn't help to talk about it. "But for the most part, he's indulgent. That is not the way it is with Julian. Julian's lovers fall into the slave category."

Rather than shirking away in disgust, Abby leaned in closer. She was an adventuresome thing. "Really? So he keeps women around, and he makes all the decisions for them? He chooses their clothes? They have to ask for permission to speak?"

Sam nodded. He left out the part about the collars and absolute obedience Julian Lodge required from his slaves. "Yes, that's about it. Though in all the time I've known him, he's only kept a couple of subs with him at his home, and no one for more than a year. Still, he's gone through a string of casual subs. How exactly do you know so much about slaves?"

"Well, Sam, you know I like to read."

He laughed out loud. Abby liked to read, all right. Abby liked to read erotica. It was her substantial collection that had brought them together in the first place. "I forgot. You're an expert."

She rested her chin in her hand and sighed. "He's going to The Club without us."

"We don't know that." He was pretty sure that was exactly what Jack had done, but he couldn't bring himself to say it out loud.

"Why else would he leave with nothing but a note?" Her eyes were downcast. "I think he's tired of me."

Sam leaned forward, catching her hand in his. His heart ached at the sorrow in her voice. "That's not true, baby. He loves you."

Her laugh was a hollow sound. "He doesn't seem to want me the way he used to. I've got to face the fact that maybe Jack is one of those men who loves the chase more than anything else. Now that I've been caught, someone else will be more interesting to him."

"No," he said fervently. "I've known Jack Barnes my entire adult life. He's never loved anyone the way he loves you. He would never have married you if he didn't know he wanted to spend the rest of his life with you. Something's wrong. We need to find out what it is. When he comes back, we need to confront him. We need to sit down as a family and figure out what's wrong."

Abby thought for a long moment. "I don't know if talking about it will work. He doesn't want to talk. I've tried. You've tried. I don't know how he would handle it if we put together something with a therapist. I can't go on like this. I need to know if it's time for me to walk away."

"Don't even talk like that." He was shocked that she would suggest it. He couldn't imagine his world without Abby in it. He also couldn't imagine a world where he would have to choose between them.

"I hope that's not the reason he's been distant, but I fear that he wouldn't tell me even if it was," she said with grim resolve. "Sometimes a patient needs a shock to the system to get him going again."

"Shock to the system?" He wasn't sure he liked the sound of that.

"I'm only saying that Jack thinks everything is fine and that he can handle whatever is going on in that head of his alone. Part of the reason he thinks that is we've done everything we could to make him comfortable. Maybe it's time to make him uncomfortable."

31

"How do we do that? It's kind of impossible to make him anything if he won't talk to us."

"I think we should go to Dallas." Abby sat up straighter than she had before. "You still have a membership to that club, don't you?"

There was a mixture of horror and excitement flowing through his veins at the thought of what she was saying. It was ninety-nine percent horror, though. He could imagine what Jack would do if they showed up at The Club without his permission. This was a very, very bad idea. "I don't think going to The Club without Jack is a sound plan, baby. The Club is hardcore. It's not a place for normal women."

Her big hazel eyes rolled, and she did that cute little snort she used when he was acting like a dumbass. He thought she used it an awful lot. "Yes, I'm so normal. I'm married to two men. I think I can handle The Club."

He wasn't so sure. Her only experience with the world of kink was through romance novels and two men who loved her enough to marry her. Sam knew that the men who inhabited The Club would eat up a sweet submissive like Abigail. She would be the softest thing any of them had seen, and he worried that without Jack, she would be unprotected. He doubted he could convincingly play the Dom. Sam was honest enough with himself to admit he was every bit as submissive as Abby, maybe more so.

He tried for logic. "Besides, we don't know for sure that Jack went to Dallas. He could be anywhere. We could go up there and be all on our own."

"Then we'll view it as a vacation." Abby picked up her fork again. She smiled, and it melted something in Sam. She seemed more animated than she had in weeks. "We never got our honeymoon and the farthest either one of us has been from the ranch in months is Tyler. If Jack isn't there and he's off doing some sort of ranch work, then we simply indulge in a big-city vacation. Jack's always telling me how I should enjoy my position as the wife of a wealthy man."

"I think he meant you should do more in the community," Sam pointed out. "He was talking about taking on charity work. You know you've been discussing opening a clinic for a while now."

"And I firmly intend to do that. If I'm still in a position to do so. In the meantime, I'm going to apply a very liberal meaning to Jack's words. I'm going to Dallas, and I'm going shopping. Come on, Sam. I know what you want. You've always wanted a motorcycle. Let's get a big, gorgeous hog and drive to Dallas. We'll get a room at The Club, preferably a suite, and tear up Neiman Marcus with Jack's credit cards."

Sam's jaw dropped. "You know Jack won't let me buy a bike. Do you have any idea how long I've been trying to convince him to let me get a motorcycle? He always tells me I'll kill myself on it, and he won't allow it. Besides, I don't want a Harley, baby. I want one of those ninja bikes like Tom Cruise rides in *Mission Impossible*. It's called a Ducati."

"Well, as far as I can see, he's not been in the mood to allow or disallow anything lately," Abby said simply. "You know what they say. When the Dom's away, the subs will play. What do you say we play, Sam?"

He sat back and thought for a moment. Since he'd been fifteen years old, his whole life had revolved around Jack Barnes. He'd never seriously thought about disobeying his friend. Jack always knew what was best, and he always looked out for Sam. In return, Sam did what Jack told him to do.

But Jack didn't know what was best now. Jack was floundering, and he doubted that an intervention would help. Maybe Abby was right. Maybe the only thing that would get through to Jack was a shock to his system. Jack believed in a well-run house. In Jack's mind, a well-run house had one leader—him. What would happen if they questioned that right of his?

Especially since lately he hadn't been leading at all.

Sam pulled out his cell phone and called information. In the end it was easy. While Jack had all the ambition and power in the relationship, he'd given Sam half the money. Money, Sam rapidly discovered, was power all on its own. Twenty minutes later, he hung up with a smile on his face.

"They're going to deliver the Ducati out at the house. Can you imagine? They're going to bring it to us," he said with a little thrill.

Abby's smile was perfectly Cheshire Cat-like. "Yes, Sam, that's what happens when you pay forty-thousand dollars in cash to a salesperson who lives off of commission. He'd probably kiss your feet if you asked him to."

He could picture himself on the back of that sleek bike. Abby would be behind him with her arms wrapped tightly around his waist. He envisioned himself driving up to The Club with her and tossing the keys to the valet before leading his lady in. Yeah, he could do this.

He then envisioned Jack taking him apart piece by piece for allowing their wife on a motorcycle.

"Don't." Abby snapped her fingers and pulled him out of it. "It's going to be fine. We'll have fun, just the two of us. The truth is I don't know if he'll care that we're gone at all."

"He might kill me." He picked up the burger again. If he was going to die, then it would be on a full stomach. It tasted better this time. Perhaps it was the idea of doing something rather than sitting back and waiting that made everything seem better.

She shrugged. "Then we'll know he still cares."

He was going to worry about Jack's revenge later. For now, he would concentrate on the positive. He had Abby to himself, and he was taking her on a road trip. Where it would lead them, he couldn't tell. He knew that with Abby, at least he would enjoy the ride.

* * * *

Four hours later, Sam watched as Abby strapped on her helmet. Sam stood quietly looking at his unbelievably cool new bike as Abby got prepared for the trip. Her hair was pulled back in a low ponytail, and she wore the leather jacket he'd ordered her to wear. He wasn't letting her on a bike without her skin being protected. She was dressed in a leather jacket, T-shirt, heavy denim jeans, gloves, and motorcycle boots.

It was a good thing he wasn't the world's most obedient sub. Though Jack had told him he couldn't buy a motorcycle, Sam rode them as often as he possibly could. He had friends who let him practice on theirs, teaching him the ins and outs of how to handle a bike.

"I feel like a biker mama." She grinned as she settled on the back of the motorcycle. She looked hot sitting on the back of his brand-new Ducati Panigale V4 Speciale. She was so cute, he could eat her up. He leaned over and kissed her, slipping her a bit of tongue before breaking off and sliding in front of her.

He smiled as she leaned against him. Why he hadn't done this a long time ago, he had no idea. He could feel her pressed against his backside. He might never get in his car again.

He started the engine, satisfied with the way it purred to life. "You ready?"

Abby wrapped her arms around his waist in response.

He took off, and they left the ranch behind them.

Chapter Three

Jack was shown to the austere waiting room outside Julian's office by a lovely young woman in her twenties. She kept her head down and her eyes averted, and he realized she probably spent a lot of time in the club downstairs. His eyes briefly skimmed her body. She was dressed conservatively, as Julian would have anyone working in the business end do. She wore a skirt, silk shirt, and a jacket. The only thing that marked her as anything other than an office drone was her shoes. They were a scarlet red, the heels at least five inches of pure stiletto. He had no idea how she managed to walk in them, but he admitted those shoes were hot. They would look nice on his Abby. On the blonde, he was merely able to appreciate them on an aesthetic level. The girl was pretty and obviously submissive. She probably never talked back or disobeyed. Julian wouldn't have it.

He took a seat in one of the antique chairs Julian insisted gave the office an elegant feel. They always made him feel like a hulking beast perched on something fragile. He sighed, stretched, then pulled out his phone. There was one message, and he bet it was a doozy. He could almost hear Abigail tearing him a new asshole for leaving that note. He smiled at the thought of her face flushed with anger. Her whole face went red when she got really mad, and her eyes flashed fire. She was pretty when she was pissed. She could spout some seriously filthy language, too. When she got going, she could rack up the punishment time. He could give her five every time she cursed. That gorgeous ass of hers would get a lovely shade of pink. He frowned and tried to think of something else.

"Sir?"

He glanced up, surprised to see the secretary still there. He'd forgotten about her completely. His mind had been on his wife.

"Yes?" He found himself slightly annoyed. He didn't want to be here in the first place, wanted to deal with Julian's subs even less. There were always at least two, one male and one female. Julian believed in variety.

She sank to her knees, placing her slender body in between his legs. Her hands went to his denim-clad thighs, her perfectly manicured nails sinking in slightly. "Mr. Lodge told me to see to your every need, Mr. Barnes. Might I offer you the comfort of my mouth? Or would you prefer something else?"

"I would prefer it if you took your hands off me." Even he could feel the room's temperature drop by several degrees. He made no move to remove the offending hands. He didn't need to do anything physical to put a sub in her place. "I didn't ask you to put your hands on me, nor do I want your attentions. Do we understand each other?"

Her hands dropped to her thighs, palms up. She looked straight down. "Yes, Sir. I was—"

"Nor did I ask for an explanation." He didn't need one. She was only following orders. She didn't have to spell it out. He also knew that a soft explanation wouldn't work on her. "Move back, sub. You're invading my space, and I do not like it."

The blonde sub quickly moved back, though she found her position again. She remained still and silent.

"You are dismissed." He wanted to be left alone. This was why he hadn't come back in a while. He'd known exactly what he'd be offered the minute he walked into The Club again. Sex. Submission. Drama. So much damn drama.

The blonde's head came up. Her mouth opened and closed as though she wanted to say something but couldn't quite make it happen.

The door to the office opened. Julian took in the scene in front of him and shook his head. "He said you were dismissed, Sally. Are you so improperly trained that you don't obey a direct order?"

37

"No, Master Julian." She gracefully got to her feet and was back at her desk in a moment.

Jack stood up quickly. "And what was that scene about?"

He knew he should give the man who had mentored him some leeway, but he was feeling restless. That anger he held inside him was looking for an outlet, and Julian was a big boy. He could handle it.

Julian Lodge cocked a single aristocratic eyebrow. Jack could tell a lot about Julian's mood from that one brow. Julian could say the same thing in exactly the same voice, but it held a different meaning when that dark brow was climbing off his face. "Am I not allowed to be hospitable, Jackson?"

He was annoyed. Well, good for Julian because Jack was annoyed, too. "I'm a married man. I doubt my wife would appreciate that scene you tried to play out."

Julian shrugged in his custom-made Italian suit. If he followed the habits he'd had while Jack worked for him, Julian went to Milan once a year for a new crop of the slick suits. "As I have yet to be introduced to this paragon of virtue, I have no idea what she would find offensive and what would be acceptable to her. Would you care to join me in my office? Our guest will be here soon."

It was posed as a question, but there was no way to mistake the inherent command behind it. He nodded shortly and followed his former mentor. The door closed behind him. It had been years since he'd been called into Julian's office. He remembered the last time he was here. He had been informing Julian of his decision to quit. He was buying his ranch. He was taking Sam with him.

"Well, of course you are, Jackson," Julian had said. *"A Dom never leaves his favorite sub behind."*

"Please have a seat." Julian indicated the dark leather chair in front of his large mahogany desk. Jack sank into the chair as he continued. "I give you permission to punish my slave. She questioned you. She shouldn't have done that."

That wasn't going to happen. He had zero need to punish some sub he didn't know. "Punish her yourself. I don't intend to be here for long. I need to get home. I want to meet with this guy and hightail it out of here. If I get on the road fast enough, I can be home by midnight."

He'd told them he might be gone a few days. Perhaps they would forgive him faster if he came home early.

Julian sat back in his chair, and his long hands steepled. "You're in a hurry. Tell me, Jackson, why haven't you brought your lovely bride to enjoy all the pleasures our club can provide? Is she not submissive? Do you not share her with Samuel?"

He was taken aback by the question. "Of course I share her with Sam. I wouldn't have married a woman who couldn't love both of us."

He and Sam were a package deal and had been since they met.

"Then I must assume she is either not submissive or you're ashamed of the time you spent here," Julian mused. "Otherwise I can't understand why you turned down my generous offer to host a honeymoon for you."

He softened slightly. "It was a generous offer. I'm not ashamed. Abigail knows about what I did here. She certainly knows what I owe you, Julian. We haven't taken a honeymoon. I was sick, and it's been hard. The recovery…" Jack let the sentence trail off. He really didn't want to go into this.

"Well, you were shot in the chest," Julian pointed out. "You can't expect to recover quickly from that, old friend. You should rest and recuperate."

He shook his head. "It was six months ago. I'm fine."

Silver eyes assessed him. "I doubt that very much. I'm sure you're physically fine, but the emotional aspects of such an injury can have much longer-ranging consequences."

"Like I said, I'm fine." It was something that was best left completely in the past. He needed to work on his future and on controlling his darker impulses.

Julian's long fingers drummed on the top of his desk. "It's just as well you decided not to stay. The Platinum Suite was taken an hour ago. One of my wealthiest clients is bringing his wife in to play." There was a secretive smile on Julian's face that gave him pause. "Tell me, Jackson, how is Samuel?"

"He's fine," Jack responded automatically. He didn't like to think about how annoyed Sam was with him. That restless feeling was back. Maybe he *should* stay the night. He wouldn't have to face Abby and Sam and their questions if he spent the night here. He wouldn't go down to The Club. He would order a bottle of Scotch and try to pass out. He wouldn't sleep. He never slept alone. He'd spent far too long with another body in bed with him. Even Sam, who he didn't cuddle, was a comforting presence in bed.

There was a trill from the phone. Julian pressed a button. "Yes, Sally?"

"Your five o'clock appointment is here, sir." Sally's voice was completely professional over the phone. She sounded nothing like a woman who had offered her boss's old friend a blow job mere moments before.

"Send him in." Julian stood and straightened his silk tie. A look of deep distaste crossed his features.

"Is this Lucas?" Jack asked. He didn't mention the part about Lucas Cameron being his half-brother. He'd disavowed the Camerons a long time ago. He didn't intend to make this a family reunion.

Julian shook his head as he smoothed out his tie. "No, this is Matthew Slater. He's your father's campaign manager."

"Don't call him that." He didn't have a father and never would.

Julian inclined his head in apology. "Of course. He's the senator's campaign manager. Lucas is due in tonight. You'll be late getting home, I fear. Mr. Slater is here to attempt to talk some sense into Lucas. I thought he could shed some light on the situation."

The door opened and a slender man in an immaculately cut suit strode into the office. He was in his prime and obviously a professional in every sense of the word.

He held his hand out to Julian, but Jack could see he didn't want to touch the club owner. Julian's handshake was brief.

"Mr. Lodge, I apologize for the inconvenience." Slater's hair was perfectly cut and graying on the sides. His dark eyes found Jack and immediately registered an awed kind of surprise. "My god, you have to be a Cameron. You look exactly like your father did at that age."

His hands fisted. He didn't like to be reminded that he had a father, much less one who he resembled. "I have no idea what you're talking about. My father died before I was born."

It was all in the paperwork he'd signed when he'd accepted the five million Cameron offered him to keep his mouth shut about his paternity.

Matthew Slater smiled slowly. "Of course, Mr. Barnes. I understand the situation well. I was the senator's aide at the time. I typed up the agreement myself. You've been scrupulous about keeping your end of the bargain."

"I got everything I wanted out of it," Jack allowed.

"And you've made something of yourself." Slater took the seat beside Jack. "Sadly, it seems the senator's most successful offspring is the only one he can't acknowledge."

"He should remember that." Jack checked his watch and wondered how long this was going to take. He didn't want to be acknowledged by anyone, least of all Allen Cameron. "Does someone want to tell me why I got pulled into Senator Cameron's crap?"

Julian shook his head. Yes, it was just as it had always been. Poor Julian, ever despairing of his lack of diplomacy. Julian liked to keep things civilized. Jack refused to act the part. Once, he would have tried for the sake of his job, but he didn't work here anymore. He was a rancher and he would talk like one.

"I believe my associate would like to know a bit about the situation with Lucas Cameron, Mr. Slater." Julian was a master at understatement.

Slater's face became a mask of irritation. "Lucas is the senator's youngest child. He's the youngest of three and, undoubtedly, the most troubled. He's twenty-three, and he barely made it out of college. He seems to have an addictive personality. He can't stay away from booze and women…or men. He really doesn't judge. If it has a pulse, Lucas will jump into bed with it. If there's a camera around, all the better. He has no sense of decorum whatsoever. He's the bane of his father's existence."

Julian smiled grimly. "I'm afraid Jackson doesn't keep up with the latest gossip magazines."

Jack shook his head. He didn't. He couldn't care less. Abigail did, though. She often came home from the grocery store with some ridiculous magazine she'd bought because the headlines were so atrocious. *"Someone has to reward truly outlandish reporting, Jack,"* she would say. She and Sam would laugh about the latest over-the-top hijinks. Jack would hold himself apart. He wondered if Abigail and Sam knew who Lucas Cameron was. "I don't care about his reputation. I want to know why he's decided to ruin mine."

Slater let out a long-suffering sigh. "I'm afraid he's decided to take after his older brother." There was a long pause as Jack refused to take the obvious bait. He gave Slater his best "no bullshit" stare, and the older man caved. "Lucas found out about the deal you made with the senator years ago. He discovered the paperwork and made the proper assumptions. He might be a wretched addict, but he's got a brilliant mind. Anyway, once he got it into his head that his father would cave to blackmail, he came up with this scheme."

"Why is he involving me?" Jack's entire manner was brusque. He couldn't care less that the great Allen Cameron was, once again, being raked over the coals by his unfortunate offspring.

"His father won't give him another dime," Slater admitted. "Senator Cameron is currently in a power play with his son. He's told Lucas that he will admit to the affair with your mother and claim you as his son before he'll give in to blackmail again."

He was out of his chair before he could take his next breath. The implications of that admission made his head want to explode. He could see it now. Reporters everywhere. They would come out to the ranch, besiege him at every turn. "Like hell he will!"

Julian held out a hand, gesturing toward a chair. "Jackson, please." He turned to the older man. "I believe you will find that outcome is unacceptable to Mr. Barnes."

"Damn straight," he said, clenching his teeth. "I will not have my wife barraged by tabloid reporters. The senator and I had a deal. I've kept up my end of the bargain. I expect him to do the same."

"The trouble isn't with the senator." Slater looked as though he was trying to placate a growling beast. He held his hands out in defense. "Lucas is the one pressing forward with his blackmail scheme. When he decided his father was serious, he did some research. It didn't take him long to trace you, Mr. Barnes. It was a bit harder to find Mr. Lodge, but he decided that Lodge would be the easier mark."

Julian snorted and somehow made it elegant. "He's threatening to bring down The Club. He says he has evidence of illegal goings-on here that he intends to hand over to the tabloids."

"What's his asking price?" It didn't matter. Lucas wouldn't be making any money. He intended to take his little brother apart piece by piece. There wouldn't be enough left of Lucas to collect blackmail. He merely asked because he was curious.

Julian sighed. "He wants ten million from me and twenty million from you."

He actually felt his blood pressure tick up. "That little shit isn't getting a dime from me. When does he get here?"

"He's due to arrive at seven p.m. this evening." Julian glanced down at his calendar. "I've sent a car to retrieve him. We'll be dining with him at nine, if that's all right with you."

"I have no intention of sitting down to dinner with a boy who's trying to blackmail me," Jack swore.

"Now, Jackson." Jack recognized the voice. Julian was in full-on teacher mode. "There's no reason to leave civility behind." Julian turned his attention to Slater. "Did you need a room, sir? Or were you planning to return to DC this evening?"

Slater looked slightly horrified at the thought of bunking down in a notorious club. He had to wonder what was going through the other man's head. Did he envision himself sleeping in the equivalency of a bordello? Jack could have told him that Julian owned the entire building. The rooms on the upper floors made most five-star hotels look like a Motel 6.

"No." Slater choked out the word. "I've taken a suite at the Fairmont, thank you. I thought I should be on hand in case I was needed. The senator is making this his top priority."

Jack bet he was. Cameron was up for reelection soon, and he had his eye on the presidency in a couple of years. A scandal involving his sons, one legitimate and one not, wouldn't do the politician any good. "I don't give a crap about the senator, but I will protect my family. Do you understand?"

Slater gave him a nervous glance. "Yes, I believe you will, Mr. Barnes." The campaign manager took a deep breath, and his shoulders came down, relaxing slightly. He stood and straightened his jacket. "I will leave it to you, then."

He passed a card across the desk to Julian and handed one to Jack. Jack glanced down. It contained Slater's contact numbers and the Cameron campaign slogan, "Family First." Jack rolled his eyes as the officious man left the office.

"I'm going to need a room after all." He wasn't leaving until he was sure this mess wouldn't come back to haunt him. Every protective instinct in him was on full alert. He had to make sure that nothing hurt Abigail or Sam.

Julian nodded as he pressed a button on his phone. "Yes, of course. I'll have you settled in one of the smaller rooms."

Sally the sub walked briskly into the room. She had a notebook in her hand, ready to work. "Yes, sir?"

Julian stood, so Jack did as well. He glanced over at the clock on the wall. There were a few hours left before the meeting with his soon-to-be-dead baby brother. He would clean up and call home to apologize. He would come up with some excuse that didn't involve worrying his wife or partner.

"Please get Mr. Barnes checked in to one of the rooms on the fifteenth floor. I think there's one open next to the Platinum Suite," Julian ordered. "I believe he's going to need clothing."

"Sorry, I didn't bring a suit," he groused. Julian insisted on dressing for dinner.

Julian's hands ran down the lapels of his suit. His mouth curved up fondly. "I doubt you wear them often on that ranch of yours." He looked back to his secretary. "Call Neiman's, please."

Sally bounced slightly up and down in her heels. There was an expectant air surrounding her. Julian nodded slightly and her eyes lit up.

"We should have called them sooner. They could have sent the suit over with the stuff the clients in the Platinum Suite ordered," Sally said, a cheerful grin on her face. Her earlier debacle with Jack seemed completely forgotten.

"Have you met our latest guests, pet?" Julian's smile was smooth.

So smooth that Jack wondered for a moment if he might be

missing something.

Sally nodded vigorously. "She's very pretty. She wanted to know where she could buy some hot shoes for tonight. She's never been in The Club before so she's not sure what to wear. She's really nice, though."

"And her husband?"

Jack fought to keep control of his temper. He didn't want to listen to Club gossip. He wanted to get to his room and get Abigail or Sam on the phone. He had some explaining to do.

"He's incredibly hot. The valet was super excited. They roared in on a brand-new motorcycle." Sally's face turned serious for a moment.

Julian watched her, curiosity plain in his expression. "Yes, pet? Do you see a problem?"

She thought for a moment and obviously decided to press on. "She's a sub. At least sexually, she is. She's very soft and gives off an air of innocence that will have every Dom in the club panting after her."

"No Dom in this club will go after a collared sub." He'd worked here for years, and that rule had always been in place.

"She's not wearing a collar, at least not now." Sally tapped her pen against her red lips. "And there's something about her husband."

"Yes," Julian urged her on. He seemed pleased with his sub, as though she were figuring out a problem he already knew the answer to.

"I don't think he's a Dom." She twirled her pen in her hand as she thought. "He's playing at it, but if I had to guess, he's a sub, too."

"Then he's an idiot." Jack was done. "If he walks into the dungeon with a gorgeous sub, he's going to lose her. The Doms here will sense weakness. Hell, the man already proved himself to be a dumbass. He drives a motorcycle. That's a death trap. He lets his wife on that thing? He deserves to lose her. I'm going up to my room. I need to make a call."

He stalked out of the office and into the waiting room. He was surprised to be assaulted by boxes and sacks with the names of

Dallas's most exclusive stores.

"I had them bring it up here," Sally explained.

Julian stared at the bounty crowding out his waiting room. "And why is all this not up in the Platinum Suite?"

Sally's smile was small and secretive. "There's a *Do Not Disturb* sign on the door, sir."

Julian laughed. "Well, after giving her husband's credit card a good workout, she should spend some time pleasing the man."

Jack stared at the ridiculous indulgence around him. Who needed that many pairs of shoes? "That man definitely isn't a Dom, Julian. You're going to have trouble tonight. He has no control over his sub, if this is any indication. She's walking all over him."

"She does seem to be making a statement, doesn't she?" Julian mused. "Perhaps you could speak with him. You used to be excellent at teaching a Dom how to behave. He might need advice from someone who knows how to maintain control over his household."

This man obviously needed some help. "Sure, if I have the time, I'll have a drink with him."

"It's good to have your help, Jackson." Julian's eyes looked a little wistful. "It's good to simply see you again. We'll handle the Lucas Cameron situation."

Jack nodded. He'd definitely handle it.

Chapter Four

Abby stared at herself critically in the bathroom mirror of the suite Sam had checked them into not an hour before. It was a ritual most women approaching forty performed on a regular basis. She snapped the front closure on her brand-new La Perla bra and wished it offered more support. It looked so beautiful in the shop. Sam's eyes had glazed over when he'd seen it. He'd snatched up the emerald green bra and matching thong, saying it would look gorgeous against her fair skin. Now, she wasn't so sure. Her boobs weren't what they used to be. She didn't even want to turn around and be confronted with the sight of her ass in a thong.

It was hard getting old, she thought as she considered herself in the ornate mirror.

The Club's suite was the most decadent room she'd ever been in. It came fully equipped for BDSM play with hooks in the ceiling and walls. The bathroom was bigger than most hotel rooms, and the mirror was something else. It took up one whole wall of the bathroom. Between the wall-sized mirror and the one over the sink, a woman could see herself from every angle.

There was no getting away from it. She was going to be thirty-eight this year. She stared at the small lines around her eyes and thought about the strikingly beautiful woman who had shown them up to their suite. She'd been a lovely blonde and couldn't be older than twenty-five. Abby had a daughter approaching that age. Lexi was twenty.

Though she hated herself for doing it, she'd watched Sam's reaction to Sally. Abby doubted Sam would be able to pick her out of a crowd. He'd paid very little attention to her despite her perfectly toned body.

She wondered if Jack had met the lovely Sally.

"Now, see, I can feel your anxiety from the other room, gorgeous." Sam came up behind her, and his hands curled around her shoulders.

She looked at the two of them in the full-length mirror. Sam was wearing jeans and a tight white T-shirt that molded to his every muscle. He had a boy-next-door sexiness about him that always got to her. Like Jack, he was five years younger than she was. He hadn't even reached his prime, while she was on the other side of hers. It was one of the dirty tricks Mother Nature played on the female of the species. Men got more attractive as they approached forty and women merely got older.

"Do I even want to know what you're thinking?" Sam let his hands find her curves.

His mouth came down on her shoulder, dropping soft kisses across her skin. Everywhere his mouth touched, she felt the skin come to life.

"Probably not." He wouldn't understand. She didn't want to bring him down with her insecurities.

"Abigail," Sam said, his voice going hard. "Lean forward and press your hands against the mirror. Spread your legs."

Abby looked at him. She wasn't offended by the change, merely curious. "What are you playing at, Sam?"

He stepped back and gave her a dark look. His arms crossed his chest, and his sensual mouth became a flat line. "I'm playing at being your Dom, and if you can't obey me, we won't be in that club tonight. If you can't give me the same respect you give Jack, we might as well change our plans and have dinner in town and find a movie to watch. It isn't safe for you to go in there without protection."

He was right about that. She leaned forward, pressing her hands against the cool glass of the mirror. Her curiosity about The Club grew every time Sam mentioned it. She figured she should be discouraged at Sam's words, but she just found herself more intrigued. She spread her legs wide. She knew what Sam wanted. It was something Jack enjoyed. Or used to, Abby thought, then let it drift out of her mind. She concentrated on finding her balance in the five-inch Jimmy Choos Sam had insisted she wear out of the store.

"That's more like it." Sam's hands stroked along her thighs. "I like this, baby. I love how these shoes make your legs look a million miles long." He gently snapped the back of her thong. "And I love this tiny piece of string between the cheeks of your hot little ass. It looks incredibly sexy on you."

He leaned over and placed a kiss on the small of her back. Because he was Sam, he couldn't leave it there. His tongue came out and traced a line almost to the top of her ass where her cheeks met.

She sighed as she felt the sweet stirrings of arousal. Her pussy was already soft and ripe. This was exactly what she needed. She needed Sam. She moaned and pushed back against his hand when it cupped her pussy. She stirred against him, wanting his fingers in her cunt. A sudden thought split through her growing need.

"Someone will be delivering those packages soon, Sam." They'd gone a little crazy and bought far too much to cart back on the motorcycle. The stores hadn't minded shipping everything to Julian Lodge's building.

He got down on his knees in between her legs. Now she understood why he was so insistent on the shoes. She was petite, but the shoes put her at the perfect height for his mouth to reach her pussy.

"No, they won't." Sam breathed the words, and she could feel the heat of his mouth through the scrap of silk she wore. He ran his tongue over the silk. "I put a sign on the door. Trust me, baby, that sign means something here. No one's going to disturb us." He slid his hands under the sides of the thong. "This is pretty, but it's getting in my way. It's time to take the wrapping off my dessert."

She obediently let him drag the undies off. Sam pressed his nose right into her labia. He breathed in deeply. Abby knew he loved her scent. Sam was an incredibly tactile lover. He used his thumbs to part her folds. She watched him from above. He reveled in the cream he found dripping from her pussy.

49

"I love how wet you get," he muttered before leaning in for his first taste of the day.

She groaned as his incredibly talented tongue swiped across her pussy. Her clit was already begging for his attention. She could feel it pulsing with need.

Sam teased her. His tongue laved gently while his thumb barely penetrated her. He set a steady, maddening rhythm that had her panting but kept her right on the edge. Just a single inch in and then out again with his thumb. His tongue whirled tantalizingly but as soft as a whisper. It felt exquisite, but it wasn't anywhere close to enough.

"Do you want to come, baby?" Sam's deep drawl hummed along her flesh.

"Yes. Oh, please." She moaned as his thumb began to thrust firmly into her channel.

She pushed down against him. It was something Jack would punish her for, but Sam ignored. He got too involved in the sex. He got lost in the feeling and forgot to remain in control of the encounter. Sam's tongue lashed against her clit. Abby pressed against the sensation, riding his tongue. Again, it was something Jack would have spanked her for. By this point, Jack would have her tied down so she couldn't disobey again. Well, that's what the old Jack would have done.

Sam sucked her clit into his mouth while he fucked her with his fingers. She felt her womb clench, and the orgasm rolled over her like a warm wave. Sam pulled his fingers out and his face came up, catching her eyes and connecting them. She knew what he would do next. He slowly, lovingly licked his fingers clean.

"I love the way you taste." Sam's blue eyes were filled with anticipation as he got to his feet. He placed himself between her and the mirror. Big hands cupped her face and his sensual lips covered hers in a lingering kiss. She could taste her orgasm on his tongue. His hands found the front closure on the bra he'd insisted she buy, and suddenly it hit the floor. He cupped her breasts and tugged on her nipples.

"It's my turn, baby," he growled. "Get on your knees."

He was trying, but he didn't have Jack's authority. Still, she obediently got to her knees, the marble cool on her skin. Sam was always impatient. He already had his jeans and boxers around his knees, and his big dick was in his hand. It was a gorgeous cock, large and perfectly shaped, from the bulbous head all the way to his tight balls. She leaned over and swiped it with her tongue, gathering the fluid already seeping from the head and eagerly drinking it down.

"What do you want me to do?" Maybe he needed her to lead him along. He should be barking orders. He should be directing her.

His smile was bright, not dark and dangerous. "Get me hard enough to fuck you, baby."

She sighed. He was already hard enough to pound nails. He was never going to successfully play the Dom. Maybe he could pass, but not if anyone looked closely. Sam was a happy-go-lucky guy. He was light where Jack was dark. Abby ran her tongue from the base of his cock to the head. She might miss Jack's dominance, but she knew she was damn lucky to have Sam for a lover.

"Baby, suck harder, please," he practically begged.

Abby sucked him deep, taking him into the back of her throat. She pulled back, giving up on the teaching portion of this sexual episode. The truth of the matter was she didn't want Sam to be Jack. She loved him the way he was. Her head fell back, taking in Sam in all his glory. "I believe you said something about fucking me."

"I did, indeed," Sam replied with a breathtaking smile. He kicked off his pants and pulled his T-shirt over his head, tossing it to the sink. He hauled her up and into his arms.

She felt delicate and feminine as he carried her through the suite. This was exactly what she needed to feel good. It was hard to worry about age or sagging boobs when a gorgeous hunk of man would do almost anything to fuck you.

He tossed her on the king-sized bed and was on her before she could breathe. He spread her legs wide, making a place for himself. His hard cock was inside her in one powerful thrust.

"Oh, baby, you feel so fucking good." Sam started pounding into her. He kept her legs far apart, leaving her completely open to him. "Next time we go shopping, I'm going to take you into the dressing room and fuck you from behind. I won't give a damn if they hear us, either."

He probably didn't care if the neighbors heard them right now. Any thoughts of neighborly politeness flew out of her head as he hit that perfect spot. He filled her up and made her glow. The headboard of the bed was banging against the wall with the force of his thrusts. She felt everything in her tighten and release as Sam slammed into her, hitting her G-spot with his dick as he dragged his pelvis over her clitoris. Abby moaned, the sound coming from deep inside. A second after she came, Sam followed. His hoarse shout filled the room as his semen poured into her body.

* * * *

Jack tried his wife's cell phone again. It went directly to voice mail. He cursed out loud and slapped at the wall of his hotel room. He'd tried Sam's phone three times already. They were pissed off, and he couldn't blame them. He shouldn't have left a note. He should have explained the situation to them in person. He knew why he hadn't done that. There was no way Abigail and Sam would have let him come here to deal with this alone. He didn't want either of them involved with his biological family. He wanted the Camerons to stay far away from the family he'd made with Abigail and Sam.

With a long sigh, he opened the curtains and looked out over the city. Night was starting to fall, and the city below was lighting up. If Abigail and Sam were here, they would be getting ready for dinner. She would slip into a sexy dress. Sam would hamper her every move. He would try to get his hands on her even while she tried to cover up. Jack would finally have to order Sam to leave their wife alone or they'd miss their reservation time.

He loved watching them play. Jack watched the lights come on, illuminating the street beneath him. He let his forehead touch the glass. He knew he was stuck, but he wasn't sure how to get out of it. When he closed his eyes, he still saw that gun pointing straight at her head. He saw it in slow motion over and over again. He saw Ruby Echols hold that gun up and knew it was about to take Abigail from him. He dreamed about it almost every night, though sometimes it was Sam instead of their wife who was in the line of fire. In his dreams, he failed and they died. He was left alone, and that was the worst nightmare of all. He was such a selfish bastard. He was lucky they put up with him at all.

Jack took a deep breath and tried to banish his dark thoughts. He had a sudden idea. He dialed the number to home.

"Barnes-Fleetwood residence." Benita's voice was brisk and professional.

"Benita, it's Jack," he replied. "Do you know where Abigail and Sam have gotten off to? I've tried for the last several hours, but I can't seem to get either of them to answer their cell phones."

"I only know that they left a note. It seems to be the theme of the day, Mr. Barnes."

He heard the accusation in her voice and winced. Benita had been with them a long time. She considered herself a motherly figure. "What did the note say?"

"Which one?"

Jack couldn't help but laugh a bit. She was also a little saucy. "The one I didn't write, Benita."

"All right. It was from Mrs. Barnes. It says she and Mr. Fleetwood are going to be gone for a while. They seem to have some shopping to do."

That explained it. They had driven into Tyler for the day. It was the closest city of any size to Willow Fork, and it had a shopping mall. They were probably seeing a movie or something. That explained why they didn't answer their phones. It was a bit of revenge on him for walking out the way he had. He didn't begrudge them.

"Thank you, Benita. Just let them know I called." He hung up with his housekeeper and rolled his eyes as the wall of his room started to shake. They were at it again. He swore the people in the suite next door were trying to set a world record for fucking. The man in the room next door might be fooling himself about his dominant nature, but he certainly had stamina.

A knock on the door brought him out of his thoughts. He opened it and was handed a suit on a heavy hanger, wrapped in pristine plastic.

"Mr. Lodge requests that you wear this when you join him in

the private dining room. It's a forty-two long, sir," said the bellhop, who probably also served as a bartender. "It's Hugo Boss."

Jack pulled a twenty out of his wallet to tip him. "Umm, great."

He closed the door. He could have all the money in the world, but he was never going to know suit designers. His obstinate refusal to join the world of the label lovers had always bugged Julian. He didn't need some men's magazine declaring his wardrobe was first rate to enjoy his life. He liked his Levis and cared way more about how a pair of boots fit than the name on the label.

Did Abigail feel the same way? He thought about the outlandish amount of shoes and clothes the woman next door had bought. He hadn't bought his wife anything since he purchased her wedding ring. Women liked gifts. Maybe he should have Julian's sub pick out something pretty and expensive for her. She could pick up something for Sam while she was at it.

He shrugged out of his clothes while he thought about the problems with that scenario. Sally the sub would probably ask all sorts of questions like what size Abigail wore. He doubted that his professional assessment of "she's hot with an amazing rack and an ass I love to fuck" would give Sally a fair starting point. He made a mental note to find out Abigail's size. He would write it on a note and keep it in his wallet.

The mental picture of a small diamond choker around Abby's throat made Jack stop in his tracks. It would sit around her throat, a gleaming collar for his queen, a reminder that she belonged to him.

He walked to the phone.

"Yeah, this is Barnes in 1502. I need a personal shopper. Yes, I'll be up here."

He finished getting dressed. He could tell the shopper exactly what he wanted, a diamond choker for his Abby and a new watch for Sam.

Maybe it would make up for that note.

Chapter Five

"You sure you don't want to go out?" Sam looked down at his wife. She was soft and cuddled up next to him. Her smooth legs slid down his as she snuggled against him. He loved lying in bed with her. The elegant bedroom of their suite at The Club was the perfect place to show Abby how much she meant to him. It was hard to believe it had only been a few hours since they decided to take this little adventure. He'd prefer to stay in bed all weekend, but he wanted to please her, too. "We can go anywhere you want."

She shook her head. "I like it here. It's comfy." Her head was on his chest. He stroked her hair, enjoying the feel of it in his hands. "Do you think Jack's here?"

Sam went still. He knew Jack was here. He'd asked the valet, who confirmed he'd parked Jack's truck sometime after noon. "Yes."

Damn, he didn't want to ruin the moment. It might be the last nice one they had for a while. Once he showed his face downstairs there would be no stopping the gossip. It was possible the few people they had dealt with might not realize who he was and his connection with Jack Barnes. In the bar, there would be no such chance. Someone would ask Jack what Sam was doing here and then the real fireworks would start.

Then he would know where he stood. Then he would know if they were done.

Abby sighed. "Where do you think he's staying? Do you think

he's in one of the other rooms? I wonder if he'll be down in the club. Do you think…?"

He knew where she was going. "No, Abby. I find it difficult to believe that he's going to be down in the dungeon trolling for a date. I don't know why he's here, but it's not for cheap sex. Relax. We'll be in serious trouble soon enough. Now, where do you want to go for dinner? I'm starving. I don't want to face my inevitable execution on an empty stomach."

"I would never let that happen, but I don't want to go out. The motorcycle is fun and all, but I think it would be hard to get dressed up and do my hair only to have it ruined by the helmet. Besides, I already called and ordered room service while you were in the bathroom." Her lips curled up sweetly.

"Damn it, Abby," he complained. He didn't move, though. She felt too good against him. "I do not need another salad. I've been making love to you for hours. I need man food. I need working-man food. You know how many calories I had to burn to perform like that?"

She seemed completely unmoved. She was a sexy little kitten pressed against him. "Well, I can't have you passing out from a lack of man-food. I ordered you a medium-rare hunk of cow flesh, a mountain of mashed potatoes, and steamed broccoli. Feel free to avoid the broccoli, if you must. I also got you some bread pudding."

He gazed down at her suspiciously. "And for yourself?"

She shrugged against him. "I got a salad. I'm not that hungry."

He slapped her ass. "Abigail Barnes. This is ridiculous." He flipped her over and held her down with his weight. She didn't struggle at all. She simply stared up at him with those big hazel eyes. "How many times do I have to fuck you before you realize how much I love your body?"

There was a sharp knock at the door and Sam knew she'd been saved. He slapped her ass again and gave it a soft squeeze. "Don't think this discussion of ours is over. I won't have you turning into some skinny thing. Get dressed, baby. Dinner's here."

He rolled out of bed and slid into his jeans. He fished for a tip as he opened the door to let the room-service waiter in.

"Hello, Samuel," a deep, nearly hypnotic voice said.

"Julian." Sam had to stop himself from looking down. It was an almost conditioned response. He wasn't an alpha male. Years in a youth home had taught him that. He could handle himself in a fight. Hell, he'd started more than he cared to admit. But there was something about those deep, dark voices that Julian and Jack possessed that sent his whole soul into submission. There was no place for that now. Now he had to think about Abby and that meant standing up to his old boss. He stood up, forcing himself to look Julian straight in the eye. He fought to keep his voice even. "Hello, Julian. How have you been doing?"

Julian walked in like he owned the place, which he did. Sam shut the door behind him. There was no way out of this interview of Julian's. He'd hoped to avoid Julian altogether. The small hotel portion of The Club was for longtime members to use. Julian might be the host, but he usually respected his clients' privacy. He should have known Julian wouldn't view him as a client. Julian had only given him a membership because Jack insisted on it. He had to hope Julian hadn't come up to kick them out.

"Is everything to your liking, Samuel?"

Sam stared for a moment at the club owner, arms crossed stubbornly over his chest. Julian Lodge was roughly six foot two. He was taller than Sam. He was as tall as Jack, but he was lean where Jack was broad. His dark brown hair was barely starting to gray at the temples. He was about to turn thirty-nine, but there was a worldliness and wisdom about him that went far beyond years. Julian had an aristocratic face that looked like he could have been in the ads of Abby's magazines. He was polished and smooth in his designer suit. Everything about him screamed money and power, though in a tasteful fashion. Julian always had the best of everything. Julian was everything Sam knew he, himself, was not.

"It's fine," Sam replied shortly. He hated how being in the same room with Julian Lodge always made him feel like he was back tending bar, like he was on the bottom rung of the ladder. Then, of course, Sam couldn't forget the lecture he'd received on the day he and Jack had left. Or the offer Julian had made. "Is there a problem with the bill or something? I can get cash if you prefer."

Julian cocked his head and studied Sam for a moment. "Why so defensive, Samuel? I merely came up to say hello. It's been a while since you came here. I almost thought you wouldn't return."

Sam felt the weight of his perusal. He remembered working for the man. The other employees almost had him believing that Julian could read minds. Sam kept silent, trying to give nothing away, though he felt the heavy weight of Julian's disapproval.

"All right," Julian continued. "How about I ask you a question? I've been wondering why Jackson is here without you and his new bride?"

"I've been wondering why Jackson's here at all," he replied sharply. "You want to explain the situation to me?"

Julian's brow climbed up his forehead. It took everything Sam had to bite back an apology. "I don't like your tone. I've done nothing but show concern for an old friend. As you are not my sub, I'll forego punishment. That's for your Master."

"I don't have a Master." There was no doubting the bitterness in his tone.

"My, Jackson has dug himself a deep hole, has he not?"

Abby chose that moment to enter. She was soft and sexy in her fluffy robe, her hair mussed from hours of lovemaking. "I think I have my appetite back. Oh, you're not room service. I'm so sorry. I'll go get dressed."

She held the corners of her robe together.

Julian smiled slowly as his silvery eyes slid over Abby. Sam wished she'd stayed in the bedroom. Why had he thought this was a good idea?

Julian was every inch the gracious host. He gallantly took Abby's hand in both of his. It was a Dom trick. He'd seen Jack do the same. Hell, Jack used that trick on Abby when they'd first met. It made the sub feel surrounded and safe. "Mrs. Barnes, please don't put yourself out on my account. It's such a pleasure to finally meet you. Felicitations on your marriage to two such wonderful men, my dear. I'm Julian Lodge."

She nodded, and Sam felt a curl of jealousy in his gut as she sounded a bit breathless. He should have been prepared. Women flocked to Julian. "Hello, Mr. Lodge."

Julian let go of her hand, taking a step back.

"Knees, Abigail." There it was. There was that voice that brooked no disobedience.

Abby gracefully fell to her knees, palms open on her thighs. She looked up at Sam. Her hazel eyes registered no small amount of shock.

Anger flashed through Sam's system. "Have club rules changed? I assure you she has a Dom. He would take issue with what you just did. I take issue with it. She's mine. She's not going to kneel for you."

Julian glanced between them. "It was merely a little test."

"Why did I do that?" Abby frowned and looked between the two of them as though trying to figure out what had gone wrong.

He walked over and held out his hand with a sigh. He couldn't blame her. Jack had trained her, and he'd helped. Her hand found his and he pulled her up, his arm curling possessively around her waist. They'd trained her and then given her zero real-world experience.

"You did that because you're a properly trained submissive. At least in this, you are. As for the rest, we'll have to see." Julian sank into one of the upholstered chairs that dotted the living area of the suite, an air of satisfaction surrounding him. "Samuel is not. Oh, he's submissive, but he is not trained, and that is a problem."

"It ain't your problem." He hated the flush that went through his system, the embarrassment that statement brought. Always submissive. Never trained. Never taken care of. Never given all he needed.

"Oh, but it is my problem." Julian's gray eyes were perceptive as he studied the two of them. "Do you or do you not intend to walk into my dungeon this evening without your Dom?"

"I do." Sam heard the will in his own voice. He had as much right to be here as anyone. He'd paid for his membership.

Julian shook his head and sighed. "Can't you see what a bad idea that is? Look at her. For that matter, look in a mirror, Samuel. You'll start a riot. Every Dom and Domme in the building will vie for the lovely, soft new subs. Even I'll admit that most of the submissives who populate my club have a certain used quality to them. It's very rare to find one of your loveliness, much less two."

"We're not trying to cause trouble. I only got introduced to the

59

lifestyle a few months ago. I've never been in a place like this. I only want to see what it's like." Abby slipped her hand into his, and Sam felt her squeeze. "If it's that much trouble, we'll leave. I'm sure there are other places that will be willing to accommodate us."

"And that thought terrifies me even more," Julian said with an elegant shudder. "No, Mrs. Barnes, please feel free to explore. I wanted to warn you that your husband is here. I only mention it because I believe Samuel already knows. As for the two of you being here, I haven't notified Jackson. You're my guests and entitled to privacy. That said, you can't keep your presence here a secret. I doubt you intend to. Jackson will find out, and I don't think he will be pleased when he discovers what the two of you are up to. Are you willing to accept his punishment? I worry it could be severe."

Abby shook her head. "I think you'll find Jack isn't so interested in punishment anymore. If you're worried about a scene, don't be. I think Jack is discovering the whole marriage thing isn't for him. I doubt he even knows we're not at home."

Julian stood and straightened his suit. The creases fell away immediately, and he resumed his masculine perfection. "All right, then. I thought that might be the case." He stopped. "I wasn't referring to Jack being unhappy with either of you, Mrs. Barnes. I was referring to the outrageous scene the two of you are performing. It's guaranteed to make Jackson's blood pressure go straight through the roof and force him to confront whatever has him acting out of sorts. I shouldn't approve. I should go and tell him everything I know. Yet, I find I want to see how this plays out. There's something wrong with Jackson. I don't like it. He seems restless."

There was a short knock on the door. Julian opened it. The young man who pushed in the elegant cart seemed surprised to see his boss.

"Mr. Lodge," the young man said. Sam noted how he deferentially avoided the older man's eyes. Sam thought that if he hadn't been working, the young man would have immediately taken the same position Abigail had mere moments before, on his knees, palms up. He was a sub, no doubt about it. However, the submissive young man did look at Sam and Abby. Sam could see him making some wrong assumptions.

"They are merely my friends, Jeremy," Julian stated firmly. "Don't think I don't know how the gossip mill works. I won't have you causing trouble by telling the staff I have a couple stashed in the Platinum Suite. And don't attempt any of your petty revenges on them. You're almost on your third strike."

The slender young man lowered his head, but Sam noticed how his lips had thinned in anger. "Of course, Sir."

Julian walked over to the waiter. Sam could clearly see the tension. "Eyes up, Jeremy."

Jeremy brought his eyes up quickly. "Yes, Sir?"

Julian smiled slightly, and his hand moved over the sub's chin. Jeremy practically vibrated from his Master's caress. "They really are just friends, pet. Don't get yourself kicked out of your home because you are needlessly jealous. I don't like jealousy. I find it distasteful. And I don't want you upsetting Sally, either. She's been turned down once today."

Jeremy's eyes went wide as though he couldn't quite believe it.

"Yes," Julian acknowledged. "Mr. Barnes was not pleased with Sally's offer of comfort. He rather forcefully turned her down."

"And he lives to see another day," Abby said fiercely.

Sam suppressed a grin. Her face was flushed. He could have warned her that Jack would be offered a whole lot of sex the minute he entered The Club. He'd chosen not to for two reasons. The first was that he didn't want to upset her. The second was his unwavering belief that they could offer all day long, but Jack would keep turning it down.

"You're quite the spitfire, aren't you?" Julian glanced her way, his eyes lit with amusement.

"Continue offering my husband cheap sex and you'll find out, Mr. Lodge," Abby said quietly.

Julian turned a serious face toward her. "Again, not my sub to discipline, but I would expect a firm response from your husband."

"I'll cross that bridge when I come to it."

"As for you," Julian turned back to the man Sam was almost certain was his male sub, "remember what I said, pet. If you pull some of the stunts you have in the past, the outcome might be different. Samuel isn't known for turning the other cheek. He won't give you any warning, either. Cross Samuel and his revenge might be painful."

Sam smiled. "He's referring to the fact that I like to jump people who piss me off. I tend to do it in dark alleys. See, Jack would do a whole bunch of stuff to ruin you financially and make your life a living hell. Me? I'll just beat the shit out of you."

"Sam!" Abby sounded slightly shocked. Her voice got low. "The owner of Delbert's got sent to the hospital a couple of months ago. They said he got mugged. Was that you?"

The owner of Delbert's was an asshole who had treated Abby very poorly. He'd humiliated her in front of half the town. Jack was making sure he went out of business. Sam wasn't satisfied unless there was some severe physical pain involved. He shrugged at his wife. "I don't know what you're talking about, darlin'. The police cleared me on that. I was drinking at The Barn that night, all night long."

Her eyes narrowed, and he was pretty sure they weren't through, but Julian was laughing.

"You see, Jeremy, you should sheathe your claws around that one." Julian turned his attention to the plates covered with shiny domes. He elegantly uncovered the first. "Ah, yes, our chef is excellent with steaks. The mashed potatoes have a lovely truffle oil in them. The beef is Barnes-Fleetwood, of course."

"Then I know it's good." He felt more confident than he had all night. He wasn't a bartender anymore. He was a rancher, and he believed in his product.

Julian uncovered the second meal, frowning at the sight. "Are you a vegetarian, Mrs. Barnes? I can have the chef come up with something more interesting than a salad."

"It's fine." Abby sounded more than a little defensive. "It's exactly what I ordered."

Julian considered her and, for a moment, looked like he would argue further. He sighed and turned his attention to Sam. "If it gets worse, I'm here to help you. I know I was Jackson's mentor, but I was always fond of you. If you and Mrs. Barnes need anything, please let me know. And Samuel, if Jackson calls for public punishment, I will be forced to allow it."

"Then I'll take it," he said firmly.

"Yes, I believe you would." Julian walked out. He snapped his fingers lightly and Jeremy followed. Sam didn't miss the sub's glance back at him. Despite Julian's warning, he was going to keep an eye on that one. He might be trouble.

"I don't know if I like that man." Abby watched the door and then took her seat.

"You might not like him, baby, but he means what he says." Sam sat down across from her. He dug into his perfectly cooked steak. The Club would be open soon. He would need his strength.

* * * *

He waited until it rang three times, then Matthew Slater pressed the *receive call* button on his phone. Slater glanced around his suite before he answered. He would never refuse the senator's call, but it looked good to make him wait a few minutes. He needed to come off as a very busy person. He had found that being too available led to getting more and more work sent his way.

"Yes, Senator?"

"Matthew, have you seen my son yet?" The senator's voice was deep and calm. He rarely yelled and almost never cursed. He would consider it beneath him. Allen Cameron had been raised in a wealthy family, and such language was too common. Still, he knew how to put a hint of malice in almost everything that came out of his mouth.

"No, sir, his flight should be landing soon." He didn't mention that Julian would be sending someone to the airport for him.

"I wasn't talking about Lucas."

Slater attempted to hide his shock. He kept his voice perfectly smooth. "If you're speaking of Jack Barnes, then yes. I had a meeting with him in Lodge's office a couple of hours ago. He seemed concerned with the situation."

Now Slater was concerned, as well. He had thought the senator's threat to expose his prior affair was just that, a toothless threat to force Lucas to back down. He couldn't seriously be considering claiming the rancher as his son. He had enough trouble with Lucas and his headline-making scandals. The last thing the campaign needed was a long-lost love child emerging, no matter how rich and powerful said love child had become.

"Has Jack agreed to meet with Lucas?"

It was time to point out a few truths about his oldest son. Perhaps the senator had blinders on when it came to Jack Barnes. He would try to open his boss's eyes a bit, but with well-trained subtlety. Arguing with Cameron was a bad idea. "He was reluctant. I think if he thought he could get away with it, he would simply beat Lucas into submission."

The man was a Neanderthal and, if the rumors were true, something of a pervert. Slater had seen the report from the very exclusive, very private detective the senator had hired to keep track of his oldest offspring. Jackson Barnes had married roughly six months before, but it was an open secret in the town they lived in that he "shared" his wife with his business partner. Slater shuddered to think about that tidbit hitting the papers. Perhaps the rancher had more in common with his youngest brother than he would like to admit.

There was a chuckle on the Washington end of the line. "I actually envy you, Matthew. There is a large part of me that wishes I could see this first meeting between brothers. I actually think meeting Jack could be good for Lucas. If Jack wants to beat Lucas into submission, well, give it a shot. Rehab certainly hasn't worked. I'm fed up with Lucas's childish demands. He's had everything handed to him, and it's made him a brat."

"Sir, I think I should tell you that I don't believe Lodge or Barnes will give in to this little blackmail scheme of Lucas's." The senator was going to have to start taking this problem seriously. This was no longer a family matter. This had long-ranging consequences.

It had become apparent to him during his meeting with the club owner and the rancher that neither man was the type to pay up and hope that was the end of it. It wouldn't be, of course. There was no end to a good blackmail scheme. Slater would know. He'd run several in his time as a Washington insider. The key was to know your victim. He would never have selected Barnes and Lodge.

"Then maybe it's time we came clean." The senator didn't sound entirely decisive. "I spoke to my wife last night. She's upset, but she knows it could be worse. This Barnes fellow is incredibly successful. Considering the way sports stars and actors have been behaving lately, I'm practically a saint. It was only the one affair, and the boy is perfectly fine."

After years and years of abuse in foster care. Jack Barnes might be "fine" now, but he didn't think those years in foster care would look good in the press. Cameron had abandoned his firstborn son.

"Perhaps we could even spin the story to look like a father-son reunion. They don't need to know anything else," Allen Cameron mused. "I've been doing poorly with the middle class in the polls. Jack is a rancher. He's a man of the people. We could view that five million I gave him as a loan that I chose not to call in. He's my son. I owed it to him, and look what he did with it. That cattle ranch of his, it's organic, right?"

"Yes, I believe it is. It's organic and free-range."

"That will go over so well with the Greenies," the senator said with a chortle. "This could be a huge positive for us. It would be a perfect counterpoint to all the bad publicity Lucas brings in."

Yes, the ménage his oldest son was involved in would more than likely take the spotlight off the youngest son. This was rapidly turning into his worst nightmare. How could he spin this?

"All right, I'm leaving this in your capable hands, Matthew." The senator sounded as though he was shoving off a laundry basket on him rather than a powder keg. "Keep me updated, but do what you have to. Keep Lucas's mouth shut until I'm ready to go public about Jack."

There was a click, and Slater knew he'd been handed his orders. He'd been dismissed. The senator would move on to other more pressing matters, like his barely legal mistress. The way that man fucked around, it was mere chance that Jack was the only illegitimate child the senator had produced.

It took everything Slater had not to throw the cell phone across the room. He knew it wouldn't do him any good, but the impulse was still there. He wanted to destroy something the way Lucas Cameron and Jack Barnes were about to destroy his career.

Slater carefully set the phone down and walked to the mini-bar. He opened the first bottle he found, not caring what it was, so long as it burned a path from his mouth to his nauseous belly.

He was fifty-two years old in a world that was rapidly being given over to the thirty-somethings. The new campaign managers ran on personality and an ability to spin anything. Everyone wanted a young, fresh face for the media. No one cared that he knew more about Washington politics and winning elections than all of the pretty faces put together. He didn't look good on high-definition television, and that was what counted.

He had one shot left and that was making sure that Senator Allen Cameron became President Cameron. If he could pull off that miracle, everything would open to him. He would have his pick of assignments in the White House, or he could become a private consultant to any number of organizations. He could write a book. He could pay off his bookies.

If he could just get through the upcoming campaign, everything would be fine. Once Cameron was in Washington, it wouldn't matter if all of the stuff about Barnes and Lucas came out. There wouldn't be anything anyone could do. Having an illegitimate child wasn't an impeachable offense. If Cameron was actually elected president, the scandal would be big enough that he could make a bundle off of it.

He opened a second bottle. This time he looked at it. It was barely a full swallow of vodka, but he had no doubt it was an expensive swallow.

He could write a tell-all book. Hell, he'd start on it now, so it would be in place when the scandal was fresh in the minds of the public. It would be a best seller.

All he had to do was ensure that the scandal didn't break until after the election.

The vodka started to work, making his stomach calm down and giving him a warm glow. The real trouble lay in Lucas. The Barnes fellow didn't seem to want any publicity. He doubted Jack Barnes would be stumping for his long-lost dad any time soon. He would keep his mouth shut and his head down.

Lucas, on the other hand, was a publicity whore. He'd do just about anything to make the front cover of a magazine. He was sure it had to do with being ignored by his parents, but he couldn't bring that into consideration. After all, he had bills to pay and some of them were with shady characters. They wouldn't care that his future employment was being threatened by some twenty-three-year-old's daddy issues. He had to do something about Lucas Cameron, and that was that.

He was on the third tiny bottle when a sudden thought occurred to him.

A man in mourning was highly sympathetic.

It solved several problems. Death would keep Lucas's mouth shut. It would put the question of Jack Barnes firmly on the shelf. It would also give the senator a platform to talk about drugs and alcohol. Law and order could be his central focus.

It was a gamble, but then again, he was a gambler. He took another drink and then made the call.

Chapter Six

Lucas Cameron briefly wondered if the massive dude who'd been sent to pick him up was also there to assassinate him. He wouldn't put it past his father to do the deed, and naturally when work was rough, his father hired out.

"You coming?" The guy had to be at least six and a half feet of pure muscle, and he was not happy about his assignment. He glanced down at the sign he was holding. "This is you, right?"

Lucas frowned. The sign stated plainly that this man was waiting to pick up one Douchebag Cameron. "That's not my name."

Cool blue eyes looked him up and down. "Hey, buddy, I'm not the one wearing skinny jeans. You want a ride or not because I'm perfectly fine leaving your ass here. I've got better shit to do with my time than favors for Julian Lodge."

The man actually turned and started walking away.

Shit. This was not going the way he'd thought it would. He was supposed to be able to make his threats and get his money and stroll off into the sunset. For good. Forever.

Or until he needed money again. He hadn't counted on an asshole of a driver. He jogged after the man, though that wasn't the easiest of tasks because of the aforementioned skinny jeans. His friends claimed they were all the rage, and he couldn't possibly be caught dead in something unfashionable.

There was only one way to deal with this—brazen through. He strode beside the big driver. "I don't care what you do with your time as long as you get me to Lodge and quickly. I don't want to waste more time than I have to here. I'm needed back in LA."

A total lie, but then *he* was a total lie, wasn't he?

The big guy stopped at a truck. "You really doing this?"

"Going to a meeting with Lodge, yes."

"I meant attempting to blackmail two of the most powerful men in the state of Texas."

Lucas pulled his sunglasses off. "I'm going to have to have a long talk with Lodge about what it means to be discreet. Who the hell are you? You're obviously not his driver."

"For now I'm his errand boy," the man grumbled before taking his keys out of his jeans pocket. "Yeah, that's what happens when you take on investors. They turn into assholes who expect you to work for free. So I'm the guy who will be driving you to Lodge's place. I'm also the one who is currently running a very invasive investigation into all the details of your life, and if you don't choose wisely, I'll be the one who deals with you. I swear, I'm going to find a couple of morons to train properly and give them to Julian so he doesn't call me every time shit goes bad. Now get in the truck and maybe rethink some of your life choices. Starting with that hair."

The lock popped open and Lucas had to decide. Did he get in with the crazy asshole? Or run?

Fuck. He couldn't run. He didn't want to run. He wanted someone in the fucking universe to take him seriously.

He wanted to meet his brother.

Screw that. He wanted what was coming to him, and this big Viking motherfucker wasn't going to stand in his way. He climbed up into the cab.

Cool blue eyes met his as he slid into the seat beside the dude who was probably at one point in time a psychopathic killer.

Damn, but he was hot. Like super hot.

The man's lips curled into a smile that kind of made Lucas's heart rate tick up. Maybe he did have a death wish because he was a little breathless looking at the man.

"I'm flattered, but I don't swing that way, kid," he said, holding out a hand. "Name's Taggart. You can call me Tag. I need to introduce you to Adam. You two have a lot in common. Flippy floppy hair and bad life choices."

He flushed and looked straight ahead. "You're very arrogant, Mr. Taggart. And I wasn't looking at you. Not in that way."

Taggart turned the engine and started out of the parking lot. "Sure you weren't. One of the things I happen to know about you is you're positively fluid when it comes to your sexuality."

"You want to call me bad names, do it. You can't say anything I haven't heard before."

"That's not what I'm saying. I don't care who you fuck as long as they say yes. That's your business. What I *am* saying is if you have a brain in your head, you'll turn this moronic blackmail attempt into a family reunion and you might, just might find a blood relation you don't want to murder."

"You know so much about my family," he grumbled.

"Like I said, the report my firm is writing is super invasive. Your dad is an asshole."

"Tell me about it."

"Barnes isn't an asshole. He resembles one sometimes but he's actually a good man. You are not as sad sack and pathetic as you appear to be. So take my advice and turn this thing around," Taggart said.

"Or you'll do what?"

"Nothing for now," the man replied. "But you can't imagine there won't be fallout. Even if you managed to come up with a way to force a man like Lodge or Barnes to actually cough up the cash, do you think there won't be repercussions?"

"I think there better not be if they want to keep their reputations intact." What was he doing? The guy was making sense, but he couldn't wimp out. After all, this was exactly what his brother had done to their father.

Stop. He had to stop thinking of Jack Barnes as his brother. He had to stop being that dumbass kid looking for someone in the world to give a shit about him. He had to be stronger than that. It was time to stop looking for someone to take care of him and take a tip from his father's bastard. It was time to take care of number one.

"Okay. I get it. This is one of those things you just have to do," the big guy said with a sigh as he stopped at a red light. "But the next time Lodge needs someone to deal with you, I'm sending the crazy Irishman out. He needs to work through some of his shit, if you know what I mean."

Okay, maybe he wasn't so hot. And Lucas probably didn't want to know what the crazy Irish dude would view as therapy. "I don't and I think it's best that you do your job and drive. I don't need advice."

For a moment, Taggart was silent. He glanced over to get another look at the man. Nope, when the man wasn't talking he was hot as hell. Lucas had to wonder if he was a Dom at The Club. A few moments ticked by and he couldn't help himself. "Is it a real kink club?"

"No."

That was disappointing. "Oh, my reports said it was quite notorious."

"It's rich-people kink. It's all pretty and shit, but it's too elegant for my tastes. And who calls their club The Club? What the fuck kind of name is that? Lazy. Or it's a dude who seriously wants to fuck with someone's brain. It's like who's on first."

"I'm sorry, what?"

"Who's on first? The old Abbott and Costello joke. Like 'hey, you going to the club? Which club? The Club? Yeah, which club?'" Taggart huffed a little. "You know once I think about it, it's kind of mean. I like it now."

"What's the difference between rich-people kink and poor-people kink?"

Taggart's hands tightened on the steering wheel, but there was no way to miss the air of satisfaction around the man. He was proud of what he was talking about. "One is in a luxury hotel and the other is in a shithole downtown because that was all I could afford. Businesses are fucking expensive, hence the reason I'm schlepping you around like I'm Lodge's Sherpa. It's going to take a while, but I'll make it something special. And mine has a cool name. Get this—The Retreat."

Finally something the man was one hundred percent wrong about. "That's a stupid name."

Taggart turned to him, his eyes chilly. "No, it's cool and

meaningful."

"It means run away from war." What was the guy thinking? "Unless you have a spa in there. It's a great name for a place where you can get your nails done or run from the enemy."

That seemed to stop the big guy in his tracks, though the truck kept right on moving. "Huh, I hadn't thought of it that way. I guess it kind of is. Not the nails thing. It kind of is a retreat from battle. We're pretty fucked up at this point. I started the place because we have nowhere else to go."

"Lodge won't let you in his club?"

"Too fucking expensive for my blood right now. I put everything I have into McKay-Taggart. Everything Alex had, too. We rock, paper, scissored for whose name goes first. I was surprised. I thought he always picked rock. Luckily none of the others has money or we'd be some weird-ass long lawyer-sounding name. That's the company, but we need someplace we can build that's personal, too. You know how when the shit hits the fan and everything is ashes, you need to start over again? That's how it is with us. We need to build something or we'll burn everything down. You, obviously, are taking the second path."

Was he? Taggart was right about one thing. Everything around him was ashes. "What went to shit for you?"

"Everything. Personal life. Career. All gone. And it happened to my friends, too. So we're building again with Lodge's and Barnes's help. But this time we're doing it together. This time we're not breaking up and expecting shit to work. Because it didn't. Between my best friend and my brother and his old Army buddies, we're a sad sack lot. I can't even tell you what happened to the Irishman. Seriously, I can't. It's classified and shit. So we packed up and moved here. I figure I can either give them a place to be or I can watch them burn out one by one."

Who would care if Lucas burned out? Not his so-called friends. Had he ever had someone who cared about him enough to build a sanctum for him? A place for privacy, a sacred place.

Huh.

"You should call it Sanctum. That's a better name."

"Sanctum?" Taggart started to pull onto the freeway. "I like that. Hold on."

The truck veered and Lucas felt himself smash against the seatbelt.

"Oh, motherfucker," Taggart was saying, but the truck slammed into the side rail and Taggart hit the brakes.

A car flew past them.

What the hell had just happened? Lucas took a deep breath. "I think that car intentionally hit us."

"Or he's an asshat," Taggart replied with a groan. He had his cell phone out. "I've got to call Lodge and tell him he's buying me a new truck. Damn it." Taggart pointed a finger his way. "You use this special time we're spending together to make my life easy. Change your fucking mind about blackmailing my investor."

He hit a button and started talking. If Taggart was any more polite to the man who'd invested millions in his company, Lucas couldn't tell. He was as sarcastic as he'd been the whole trip.

And it didn't matter what he said, because there was no backing out now.

Lucas knew one thing about this world—there was no sanctum for him.

* * * *

Abby felt her eyes widen and her mouth drop as Sam walked out.

"Wow."

She'd seen Sam look yummy before, but this was ridiculous. He was wearing black leather pants with a snowy white dress shirt open at the throat. He'd left several buttons undone, showing off his perfectly cut chest. The leather was tight and looked good against the black motorcycle boots on his feet. His blond hair curled perfectly right below his ears, giving a hint of softness to the square line of his jaw. He was devastatingly masculine, and she wondered why they were bothering to leave the room at all.

Sam turned around, giving her a perfect view of his tight backside. "You like?"

She walked up and cupped those muscled buns. "I love, and you know it."

73

Sam turned and pulled her close, returning the favor by sliding his hands down to her ass. A small smile curved his lips up. "I'm glad you like it, baby. This is pretty much the way the Doms dress down in The Club."

"Is it the way you used to dress when you worked here?" She was curious about Sam's time here. She'd heard a bit about what Jack had done when he'd worked at Julian Lodge's club. Jack had been the resident Dom. He'd played out scenes with submissives and trained clients who wanted to become Doms or Dommes. Jack knew exactly how much pain to give to enhance a sub's pleasure. She knew less about what Sam had done besides his job as a bartender.

"No, I wore way less." Sam smirked a little bit. "I almost never wore a shirt back in those days."

"And pants?"

"Optional on some nights."

Abby wrapped her arms around his waist. "Tell me something, Sam. Who tipped better, men or women?"

He seemed surprised for a minute, and he tensed up briefly. He almost immediately laughed it off. "Men. Men were definitely better tippers."

He leaned over and kissed her. Abby went up on her tiptoes to press her mouth against his.

"They're used to paying for sex." She thought about the way Julian Lodge had practically eaten Sam up with his eyes. "Did Julian tip well?"

Sam stared down at her for a moment. "Julian didn't tip, but he paid well. He was my boss."

She didn't quite buy that. There had been an awful lot of tension between Sam and the club owner.

"Was he your boss, Sam? Nothing more?" She put her hand on his chest to stop him from turning away. "Don't. You don't have to answer me if you don't want to, but don't think I'm judging you. I love you. I'm just curious. And besides, you know how perverted I can be. If you have sex stories about that scary man, I want to hear them."

"Abigail, you dirty girl, I did not have sex with Julian Lodge,"

Sam protested with a prolonged sigh.

"Oh, well, I can fantasize." Abby stared up at him. "He wanted you, though?"

Sam grew still. "When Jack told him we were leaving, Julian called me into his office. I thought it was strange because he didn't pay a lot of attention to me. He was close to Jack, not me. I went, though. I was curious."

Abby could see where this was going. She'd seen the way Julian Lodge stared at Sam. "He asked you to stay with him."

"Yes," Sam agreed quietly. "He saw straight through me. He knew I wanted more from Jack than I was getting. He told me that if I stayed with him, he would make sure I got everything I needed. He promised to take care of me. He promised to be a permanent master for me."

"You said he never kept a submissive for long." Abby was surprised. She'd expected that Julian wanted Sam. She hadn't expected he'd discussed anything permanent.

"He said he was willing to sign a contract. If he wanted out, I would get a good percentage of his wealth. I guess it was kind of like a pre-nup. I don't know what he was thinking, Abby. I knew what I wanted."

"And you didn't want him," Abby surmised.

"No. I tried to tell him I wasn't gay. I didn't care that he was. That's a person's business, but I wasn't. He laughed and told me I was fooling myself." Sam's voice was low. He looked down at the ground. "Abby, I've never slept with a man before."

Abby smiled at him. This was not news to her. "That's because you only want one."

"Yeah, but I want him. What does that make me?"

"Oh, baby, it makes you Sam." She looked deeply into her husband's eyes. She was only five years older than Sam, but in some ways she was worlds wiser. She'd learned to forgive herself for being human a long time ago. "You love Jack. There's nothing wrong with that. If you wanted Julian, there wouldn't be anything wrong with that, either. I don't care who you wanted in the past, Sam, as long as you want me now. As it happens, I want the same thing you do. I want the three of us together in every way."

75

"But he doesn't want that," Sam said sadly. "I think I'm the reason he's pulled away from us. That kiss we had, it threw him off. He hasn't touched me since. We're only in the same bed together because you're in between us. We have to face facts. He's never going to want me the way I want him."

Abby didn't believe that for a second. She remembered the night of that fateful kiss. Jack hadn't held back. He hadn't turned away in disgust. He'd known how turned on Sam was, and it hadn't bothered him.

"Abby, do you think he wants me to leave?"

"No, I don't. You're not going anywhere without me, Sam Fleetwood. And we're not going anywhere without Jack." It was time to move the night forward. They would both be miserable if they just sat up here wondering what Jack was doing. It was time to figure out if they needed to move on. Jack was going to react, or he wouldn't. If he was mildly annoyed and asked them to go home, she would know that it was over. If he called for that public punishment Julian had mentioned, well, she would cross that bridge if she came to it. "Show me The Club, Sam."

"All right."

It was so obvious he was reluctant to follow through with this plan, but he took her hand all the same and led her out of the room. They got on the elevator. It was small and every wall was covered in mirrors. Abby smiled. This was the most decadent place she'd ever been in.

"Hey, hold the—" a masculine voice shouted.

The doors closed, and Sam made no attempt to stop them. He grinned down at her. "He can get the next one, baby. I want you all to myself."

Sam pushed a series of buttons.

"Are we going to all those floors?" Abby wondered exactly what Sam was planning to do.

"No, it's a code to get to the club level of the building," Sam explained. "Everything is done to protect the clients' privacy. If we weren't staying in the hotel portion of the building, we would walk through the lobby properly dressed, get into the elevator, punch in the code and go to the club level. Once there, we would change clothes in the dressing rooms and get checked in for the night. There are all sorts of security measures to help ensure that the public doesn't figure out what goes on in here."

"Why so secretive?"

"Because there are a lot of public figures into this lifestyle. When I worked here, there were politicians and judges and media people. It could hurt them professionally to get caught in a sex scandal. I know you love a good sex scandal, but I bet if feels different from the other side of the magazine cover. Did I mention how hot you look?"

She wrinkled her nose at him. She'd protested the clothes he'd chosen for her, but he wouldn't move on the subject. She was wearing a scarlet red corset over a tight black miniskirt. She studied herself in the mirrors of the elevator. The corset did cinch in her waist, and her boobs looked pretty nice. She was wearing four-and-a-half-inch Valentino peep toes that gave her added height and made her legs look sleek. Her hair curled in soft waves around her face and she'd pinned a pretty white rose behind her right ear. She resisted putting on too much makeup. She wore only mascara and lip-gloss.

Sam reached up, brushing his fingers over the rose. "Where did this come from?"

"I found it on the dresser. I suppose Julian left it. Do you think it was for you or me?" The small white rose's stem had been wrapped in satin and cut so it could be used as a boutonniere or a corsage. Or woven into long hair.

Sam frowned for a moment. "No note or instructions?"

She shook her head. "Nope."

"Then it's definitely for you. You're my beautiful Abby," Sam whispered. He dropped a kiss on her exposed shoulder. "I'm proud to show you off."

She smiled as the doors to the elevator opened. Despite everything she'd said to Sam about not being hungry, she had been watching her weight much more closely. She was married to two men who were five years younger than she was. Jack and Sam were prime specimens. There wasn't an ounce of fat between them. It was hard for her to look in the mirror and truly see what they saw in her.

77

She remembered that moment when Jack had told her not to be so hard on herself. She knew he'd meant well, but it was such a turnaround from the way he'd handled her before. Before he'd come home from the hospital, if she had called herself fat, she would have found herself over his knee for insulting something Jack considered his.

When she thought about it, how much did she honestly know about Jack? She'd only known him for six weeks before she married him. What if this was the real Jack? And if it wasn't, who could she blame for his withdrawal? Certainly not Sam. Jack and Sam had lived together in harmony for roughly seventeen years before they met her. Any way she considered it, she was the one who upset this particular apple cart.

What was she going to do if Jack was tired of her? Could she leave them both behind if Jack didn't want her anymore? The thought of going back to a life without them was more than she wanted to contemplate.

Sam pulled her out of the elevator. "Stop worrying. This is our night. Don't think about anything except relaxing and exploring. We can do anything we want to here and no one will think less of us. They'll just cheer us on."

She squeezed his hand. The freedom The Club offered sounded enticing. "All right."

It would be nice not to think about the future for one night. She glanced around the room she found herself in. Her shoes sank into the thick carpet beneath her. The area was lit by a chandelier, and there was a small desk in the corner. A large man in a business suit sat at the desk with a computer in front of him. He was still. Abby wondered briefly if he played solitaire while he waited for the elevator to open.

"I'm Samuel Fleetwood. My membership ID is 5772356."

The big man's fingers carefully punched in the numbers. "Good evening, Mr. Fleetwood. Welcome to The Club. Do you require anything? I must warn you all the private dining rooms are full."

"No, thank you, we already ate," Sam replied politely.

"Then please enjoy your evening." The host gestured to the door.

She let herself be led toward the inauspicious door. She looked all around, well aware she probably seemed like a tourist. "I guess I expected something a bit raunchier."

"This is the lobby." Sam stopped. "Are you sure you can handle this? This is really hardcore."

She gave him her patented stare. He wasn't buying it for once.

"Baby, just because you watch a whole lot of HBO doesn't mean you're ready for this," Sam said not unkindly.

But there was no way she was turning back now. She wanted to see this place. She'd lied to Julian earlier. If he'd kicked them out, she wouldn't have pressed Sam to find another BDSM club. She was interested in this one for the simple fact that it had such an impact on the two men she loved. They had matured in this place. It had been their home, their first real one. She had to see it for herself.

"You forget, I also read," she said with a confidence she didn't feel. She couldn't help but think about Julian Lodge's words. She would have walked in with Jack and not felt a moment's worry. Sam would defend her to the death, but no one would even question Jack.

"All right, let's go." He took her hand and led her out of the lobby.

Abby walked through the small door and entered a different world.

* * * *

The elevator doors closed, and Jack felt his irritation rise. Was it so difficult to hit the *open door* button or put a hand out to stop it from closing? When he had a talk with the guy in the Platinum Suite, they would also cover a little thing called common courtesy.

Jack pressed the button, and after a few moments, got in the elevator. It was a short trip to the lobby. He tried Abby and Sam's cells one more time. His prior understanding with them was rapidly dissolving into irritation. What were they thinking not answering their damn phones?

"Sam, you call me when you get this. Do you understand? I'm damn tired of talking to your voice mail." He shoved the phone into his pocket.

The elevator opened, and Jack walked into the lobby. Immediately the lobby manager was on his ass.

"Mr. Barnes." The older gentleman was dressed, as were all of Julian's people, impeccably. "Mr. Lodge is running the slightest bit late. Please join Mr. Slater in the waiting room. Can I get you a drink?"

"Scotch, neat." He was not looking forward to his evening. There had always been some curiosity in the back of his mind about his half-siblings. He wasn't sure, but he thought the senator had two sons and a daughter. The curiosity was completely idle and he'd never intended to satisfy it. He didn't need to know them. He had a family. He had Abigail and Sam and his stepdaughter, Lexi. Who knew what the future held? Maybe Abigail would want another child. Maybe he could be a father.

A vision of her with a baby in her arms assaulted him.

He swallowed at the thought. He couldn't handle a baby. He couldn't handle a child. A child was small and fragile. Children died. They got hit by cars, and they fell a lot. And women still died giving birth sometimes.

A sudden overwhelming panic hit him like a freight train. His peripheral vision started to fade.

"Mr. Barnes?"

He shook off the feeling and shoved his hands in his pockets to hide the fact that they were trembling. "I know the way. And make that Scotch a double."

He strode into the elegant waiting room where Slater was waiting. The campaign manager had a glass of red wine before him on the table. Jack didn't like the officious prick, but now he was a nice distraction from the dark thoughts in his brain.

"Good evening, Mr. Barnes." Slater didn't stand, merely inclined his head politely.

Jack nodded and took a seat across from him.

"I wonder what could be keeping Mr. Lodge," Slater murmured. "You don't think he's down in that club of his?"

Jack huffed, completely unsurprised that the unctuous weasel had no idea who Julian Lodge was beyond being a man who ran a sex club. "He's probably dealing with investors. I know they used to keep him on his toes."

"People invest in sex clubs?"

"Yes, actually." He didn't bother to mention that he'd invested in several on Julian's advice. A few weeks before he'd invested in a new security firm run by a bunch of ex-Special Forces members that he firmly believed would turn a nice profit in a couple of years. "They also invest in real estate, stocks, and new businesses. Julian Lodge runs a group of investors that finds small companies with good ideas and gives them a bankroll to become big companies. Have you ever heard of the Masters Fund?"

Slater's eyes grew round. He took a careful sip of his wine and then placed it back down. "Of course I have. So Julian Lodge is one of the investors in the Masters Fund?"

"No, I'm an investor. Julian runs the fund. Masters is simply an inside joke." He called it that because the entire group was made up of rich Doms and Dommes from his club. Jack smiled slightly as he remembered Katherine Johannsen's protests that Mistress should be in there, too. The Domme always brought it up at board meetings, but she hadn't gotten Julian to budge yet.

"That is impressive," Slater noted.

Jack could see him calculating the best way to use the information.

A waiter brought in Jack's double and quietly retreated. He took a thoughtful sip. This was one area in which Julian was right about insisting on the best. The Scotch was rich and flavorful. It was smooth. He made a mental note to ask Julian what brand this was. He decided to change the topic. Julian wouldn't like the senator knowing too much about his business. "Why is Lucas doing this?"

Slater's face flushed slightly. He was a pale man, and every emotion showed on his skin. He bet Slater couldn't play poker to save his life. "I believe Lucas is doing this for attention. He does everything for attention."

"From what I can tell, the boy doesn't need any more attention," he grumbled. "He's on the covers of those magazines my wife reads. You would think he would want a little less attention."

Slater's mouth thinned. "Some people can't get enough. Some people have to push the limits. Lucas won't ever stop." He leaned in, and Jack got the feeling he was trying to look concerned. "Lucas has a terrible addiction problem. He can't stay away from drugs and alcohol. He's been addicted for years. The truth, Mr. Barnes, is I fear for his life. One of these days, he's going to overdose. Or he'll do something foolish while under the influence."

He took another drink of the fine Scotch and wished he hadn't asked the question. The campaign manager's voice was grating. He was starting to wonder why he'd ever thought it necessary to leave Abigail and Sam out of this. If they were here with him, at least he'd have something nice to look at. He could stare at his wife while everyone else was talking. Sam would say something ridiculous to make Jack laugh.

God, he had to figure this out. He had to make a decision and stick with it.

After that terrible day six months before, he'd made the decision to try to be less domineering. He needed to be easier on his partners or he could lose them. Abigail might find the whole submission thing fun for a while, but it would get old fast. He was a demanding man. He'd told Abigail he wouldn't be that way twenty-four seven with her, and then immediately started making decisions for her. When he really thought about it, he'd been twenty-four seven with Sam for nearly twenty years. They simply didn't have sex.

And why didn't they? He asked himself the question as the other guy droned on about all the terrible things Lucas Cameron had done. It wasn't like the idea was repulsive to him. He was a very sexual man. Though, for the most part, he preferred women, he'd had sex with men before. When he was younger, he'd experimented briefly. At some point he realized he preferred females. Except for Sam.

Abby wouldn't mind, he mused as he felt a grin cross his face. He remembered the night he'd given her one request. She'd asked him to kiss Sam. Sam had been shy at first, though Jack knew he was open to the experience. He'd pulled Sam to him and pressed their mouths together. At first, he told himself he was merely indulging his almost wife. After about a minute, he couldn't say that anymore. Sam was an intriguing mixture of soft and hard. His body and that outer armor he wore over his soul were rough and arrogant. The man inside was still looking for someone to take care of him. It brought out every dominant instinct in Jack. He'd taken care of Sam for years, but that one kiss made him wonder if Sam needed more.

If Sam wanted more.

"He's not listening to you anymore, Slater." Julian Lodge's voice was highly amused. "It's a talent of his. He can look as though he's paying attention, but his mind is elsewhere. Believe me, I know. He honed the talent on me."

Jack felt a smile split his face. "I honed it years before you, Julian. You should have seen some of my report cards from grade school. And I heard everything Slater here said. None of it was important to me."

Julian sighed and sank gracefully into the seat beside him. He gave Jack a long-suffering look. "That's because you're not being very self-aware. The universe often puts us in situations that parallel important events in our lives."

"Oh, god, this isn't the karma thing again?" He prepared to go deep if Julian started a lecture on eastern religious practices. He'd just replay the last Longhorns game in his mind. How had it started? Yes, Texas won the toss and elected to receive.

Julian snapped his fingers. "I have often thought you would be an amazing practitioner of meditation, Jackson, if only you could concentrate on something other than sporting events."

"Sometimes I concentrate on sex," he admitted.

Julian shook his head toward the politico. "Never select a cowboy as your spiritual son. I offered him a world of wealth and power. He chose to hang out with cattle."

Jack grinned and propped his boots on the coffee table in front of him. "Cows don't ask my opinions about art or expect me to know which fork to use when I eat them."

Julian threw back his head and laughed. "I missed you, Jackson. You misunderstood me before. I was merely pointing out that it is possible to learn something from the unfortunate Lucas's current predicament."

"Unfortunate?" Slater set down his glass with an outraged rattle. "How can anyone call Lucas unfortunate? He's had every advantage."

Jack pointed to Slater. "Sorry, Julian. I'm with him on this one. That little asshole is blackmailing me. You're not going to get me to feel sorry for him."

"See, now we *are* back to the karma thing. Must I remind you?"

He rolled his eyes. "That was different. You told me Cameron owed me. He was my biological father. I never did anything to this Lucas person."

Julian shook his head. "Lay the concept of karma aside, Jackson. Do you believe Lucas is doing all of this because of his desperate need for people to think the worst of him?"

"No," he replied edgily. He didn't like where Julian was going with this. He did *not* have anything in common with Lucas Cameron. He wasn't Lucas Cameron's brother. He didn't owe the little shit anything simply because they shared a biological father. "He's doing it to get his father's attention. If he can't get good attention, he'll take bad."

"Rather like some subs I recently met," Julian said enigmatically. "You might not understand karma, Jackson, but it certainly understands you." Julian stood and gestured toward the elevator. "I believe our guest has been diverted momentarily. I was told there was some trouble with the car, a minor accident."

Slater's eyes widened. "Is he all right?"

Jack was surprised at how his heart sped up. Not much, but enough to let him know he wasn't as cold as he thought he was about his brother. He remembered the idiot in the Platinum Suite had come on a motorcycle. He would discuss that with him, too. If he wanted to be a Dom, he needed to understand what he owed his sub. First and foremost, he owed her comfort and protection. He couldn't do that if he was dead.

"He's fine," Julian was saying. "The driver I sent to pick him up is quite talented, but there's only so much he can do. I've sent another car out. It appears to be an unfortunate episode of road rage. You know how the streets can be here. It's rush hour on a Friday. Someone took exception to my driver entering the freeway. He was deliberately hit. Luckily he's been well trained. He handled the situation with no injuries. The police are looking into it. It's odd.

Usually people try to kill Taggart because of his mouth, not his driving skills. Shall we start dinner? Lucas will be along shortly."

Jack got up, but Slater sat there with a dumb look on his face.

"We're not going into that club, are we?"

That eyebrow of Julian's made another appearance. "We will be walking through the bar area of the club to get to one of the private dining rooms. How long have you worked in politics, Mr. Slater?"

"Thirty years," Slater replied.

"Then nothing you'll see in my club should shock you."

Jack hid a small grin. Julian was working overtime to keep the condescension out of his voice. It wasn't working. If there was one thing Julian despised, it was hypocrisy.

Slater stood and tried to look blasé. "I'm sure you're right. I don't have Mr. Barnes's experience. I've never married, much less shared my wife with another man."

Julian went still, but Jack laughed. He wasn't ashamed. "Don't knock it till you try it, buddy. My Abigail is far too much woman for one man to handle alone. I need Sam in order to keep her happy."

Jack felt a small satisfaction at the other man's slight blush.

Slater wasn't letting it go. "I'm afraid I couldn't get into bed with a naked man to save my life."

Jack let his whole face go decadent. If that idiot thought he could shame him for not being vanilla, Slater didn't know him at all. "You say that because you've never seen Sam naked. He's a sight. Don't worry. I won't try anything on you, Slater. You're not my type."

Julian laughed as Jack walked toward the doors. Yes, he should have brought Sam and Abigail. Sometimes he forgot that they owed him comfort, too.

Chapter Seven

"It looks like a bar." Abby glanced around, disappointment settling in. She was wearing these god-awful heels for this?

She took it all in. It was a decadent bar, but it was just a bar as far as she could tell. There was a certain Roman orgy scene going on. All the seats were chaise lounges or large ottomans. The room was dominated by a huge chandelier with real candles providing the illumination. The small tables were covered in plates of fruit, cheese, or chocolates. Finger foods. They were all things that were easy to feed to your lover.

Sam shook his head and gestured around the room. "This is the outer room, baby. Consider it a staging area. People mingle here before and after."

"Before and after what?"

"Before and after they play," he said with a wicked smile.

"Sam! Oh, my god, Sam Fleetwood?"

Abby looked over and a statuesque blonde was making her way toward Sam. Like most of the people around them, she wore very little in the way of clothing. The blonde had on leather boy shorts and a black leather bustier. Her long, long legs were covered with fishnet hose and ended in stilettos. Her blonde hair was pulled back in a severe ponytail that accentuated her amazing bone structure. She could be a model.

Sam flashed the woman an open grin that let Abby know he considered her a friend. Abby did not fail to note that the woman had a perfectly toned body.

Stop it. He's here with you. He married you.

Only Jack had married her, too, and he wasn't here.

The blonde threw herself into Sam's arms.

"I can't believe you're here." The blonde was breathless as she hugged Sam. "Julian said there were some special guests coming tonight. I didn't know he meant you."

"I think he probably meant Jack," Sam said with a self-deprecating laugh. He gently pulled himself out of the embrace. "He's here somewhere, more than likely with Julian. Laura, this is my wife, Abigail. Abby, this is an old friend of mine, Laura Michaels."

Laura turned to Abby. The smile on her face seemed genuinely warm and she held out a hand.

Abby shook her hand. "It's nice to meet an old friend of Sam's."

"I couldn't believe when I heard they finally found a woman they wanted to marry." Laura leaned in as though telling a secret. "I figured Sam would, but Jack? He was always so picky. You must be an amazing woman." She turned to Sam. "Is Jack going to be in the dungeon tonight? Did anyone warn the Doms? Jack can be hard on them if he thinks they're not using the proper techniques."

"Who's the in-house now?" Sam asked.

Abby had never heard the term. She glanced between Laura and Sam, hoping someone would give her a definition.

"That used to be Jack's job," Laura explained. "The in-house Dom is the one in residence. He makes sure all the dungeon security is properly trained, and he gives classes for clients. He runs scenes."

"Like spanking and stuff?"

"If that's what the client wants," Laura agreed. "Sometimes it's as simple as a spanking. Sometimes it's more complex, with scripted dialogue and practicing before going public. It can get complicated. Leo Meyer is the Dom in residence."

Sam nodded. "I never met him. Julian trained him, so he must be good."

Laura smiled but noticed someone waving at her. "I better get to work. It's good to see you, Sam."

87

She nodded to Abby and went on her way.

"So…" She watched the blonde retreat.

Sam tried his high-voltage smile on her. When she didn't return it or move to another subject, he gave her his sad-puppy smile. "Yes, I slept with her. It was a long time ago. I slept with everyone. You know that about me."

"I know you had a blonde habit before." There was no real heat behind the accusation. That was all in the past.

Sam ran his hands through her hair. "Now I only like redheads."

"I know," she said, leaning into him. "I'm sorry. I'm being ridiculously jealous."

Sam gestured up and down his body. "Baby, if you weren't, I'd call you crazy. This is a whole lotta man right here."

Abby snorted. "Show me the rest of the club. If this is a staging area, where's the rest?"

Now that she listened carefully, she could hear thumping music coming from somewhere. The music in the staging area was low so people could talk. It was sexy but quiet. She glanced around the bar area. There were several couples sitting and talking. Many of the women reclined at their men's feet. They didn't speak but rested their heads against the men's thighs.

She liked the picture. Jack used to insist on it. It was one of the surefire ways to get him to relax. She would take off her clothes and rest at his feet, her head in his lap. The last time she had tried it was months ago. Jack had pulled her up and told her he didn't want her to get cold. He also didn't want her uncomfortable. He'd gotten her dressed and sat her beside him.

She hadn't tried it since.

Sam was watching her closely. "Do you want to sit down for a minute, baby?"

She shook her head. She knew what Sam would do. He would try to be Jack for her. He would try to fill that role. But she needed them both. "No, I think I'll need the drink more after. Let's go look around."

Sam took her hand and led her toward a short hallway. There were sconces on the wall giving off soft light. There was a big guy at the end of the hall. He was large and bald. The ropy muscles covering his body told Abby he spent a lot of time in the gym. He looked at them and frowned.

"Where's her collar?"

Sam's eyes went straight to her neck. He hesitated and looked to Abby for guidance. "I didn't think about it."

The bouncer shook his head. "For that matter, where's yours, sub? Where's your Dom?"

Abby started to tell the asshole off. Sam stopped her by seeming to grow about a foot.

"She's mine. She doesn't need a fucking collar if I say she doesn't need a collar," Sam said between clenched teeth. "I'm a VIP guest here. Is this the way Julian has his employees treat his guests? If that's so, perhaps I should give him a call. I have his personal number. He can be down here in minutes to clear this up. Do you need me to call him?"

She held her breath as the bouncer actually cast his eyes away from Sam. "No, Sir. I apologize for any misunderstanding. Please enjoy your evening."

Sam pulled her along into the next room.

"Wow. That was impressive." She'd never seen Sam act that way before.

"I watched Jack do that for a long time," Sam admitted. He ran his hand along her throat. "I should have gotten you a collar. I wasn't thinking."

Abby put her hands on his waist. "Just talk like you did to the last guy, and I doubt anyone will give us any trouble." She looked around. This was a huge space. Like the bar before, it was richly decorated, though carpet had given way to hardwood floors. There were various spaces set up with different themes. She recognized some of the settings. "It's a playroom."

Sam nodded. "It's a really big playroom. This is the milder of the two levels. This is for more playful scenes. The dungeon is one floor down. On this level, there's the bar, the playroom, several private dining rooms, and other spaces. Do you see the doors in the back?"

She glanced toward the back of the softly lit room.

"Those are privacy rooms, but you should know there are

mirrors that let people watch. It gives the illusion of privacy. The red door leads to the orgy room. It's nothing more than a big old bed. If you walk in, expect to get fucked and fucked well by whoever happens to be there."

She felt a hitch in her breath. Maybe she wasn't as ready for all this as she thought she was. "I think we should avoid that room."

"Good call." Sam looked like he was enjoying rocking her world a little bit. "How about we watch for a while?"

She nodded and let him lead her. She felt like Alice in a really horny Wonderland. A Domme in full leather regalia led her two male subs around on leashes. They crawled quickly behind her, trying to keep up with their mistress.

"Don't look her in the eye," Sam warned.

She sent her eyes straight to the floor. It would be hard, but she had to remember the rules. Sam had spent a lot of time explaining them to her. She was to keep silent unless he gave her permission to speak. He was in charge of her. She wasn't to look any of the Doms in the eyes. They would view it as a challenge. She was never, never to wander off on her own.

Sam stopped. "This looks like fun."

Abby took in the scene in front of her. It looked like it was just beginning.

"You called for me, Sir?"

There was a young woman in an approximation of a 1960's women's business suit. She carried a small steno pad. There were two men in the scene as well. They both wore suits in keeping with the time period. One sat behind a desk while the other occupied a large leather armchair. They both considered the young secretary.

"Yes, I did, Marilyn," the "boss" said. "We have a very important client here today. He needs to understand why he should sign with our firm rather than one of the other firms."

The scene went on. Abby felt a hand at her side. She turned to see Sally the sub watching, too.

Her eyes were full of mirth. "They watch too much *Mad Men*," she said quietly, so as not to disturb the scene. "Julian is struggling to keep up with the pop culture elements seeping into the lifestyle. It used to be simpler. All a club had to have was a gyno office, a classroom, and a dungeon. Then the geeks took over. You should see the Harry Potter room. Those people are freaks. And I should know."

Vaguely, Abby noticed the secretary was taking off her top. The "boss" had a paddle in his hand. She looked back at Sally. She was dressed similarly to Abby, though she was all in black. Sally was wearing a bra instead of a corset. Abby noticed that two small chains came out of the bottom on the bra and made their way past Sally's navel down into her skirt. She had a pretty good idea where that treasure trail ended.

Sam was watching the scene avidly as Sally continued to whisper. "Seriously, some of these people are geeks of the first order. Julian took me to see *Avatar* and at the end he cried. And not because of the story. He knew. He's invested in blue body paint and a bunch of kitty cat tails. He's opening the room in a month. He hates James Cameron."

Abby wanted to laugh and ask questions, but they had to get a few things straight. Sally the sub had been a naughty girl. "Did you offer my husband a blow job?"

Her eyes went down, and she chewed on her bottom lip. "Julian told me to be nice to him. It was the nicest thing I could think of."

"Do you often blow other women's husbands?"

She shrugged and winced slightly. "Probably more often than I think. Are you going to hit me? Julian would probably let you paddle me. We could go get one right now."

Sam was suddenly interested in what was going on between the two women. "Who's paddling who? Is there going to be any kissing involved in this scene?"

Abby put a hand on both of them and dragged them away from the horny advertising executives' scene. She glanced back briefly. It did seem to be heating up. The secretary was having her bottom paddled by the "boss" while the "client" forced his large penis into her mouth. The girl could really get her jaw open. Maybe she gave out pointers.

She shook her head to get rid of that thought and turned back to Sally, who seemed a bit like an eager puppy now. "I am not paddling you."

"Really? I don't mind. I like it." Her mouth turned down. "I'm sorry about the whole trying-to-blow-your-husband thing. He wasn't interested. Neither was Sam."

Abby looked behind her, and Sam was desperately giving Sally the *silent* command by drawing his hand over his throat. When he realized she was watching, he smiled angelically. "I told her no, too."

Sally was back to chewing that lip. "I'm sorry. It's kind of a bad habit. If it makes you feel any better, I was looking for you tonight to see if you wanted to play. I'm really good at oral sex."

Sam's arm went around Abby's waist. "That's fascinating, Sally. You know, it's a real coincidence because Abby here does enjoy oral sex."

Abby's elbow found Sam's gut. He *oomphed* but took it like a man. She stared at Sally, more amused at this point than angry. At least she was a persistent thing. "Maybe I don't understand the whole master-slave relationship. I thought you were Julian's submissive."

"Oh, yes," Sally agreed. She stood up perfectly straight, pride shining from her eyes. "Julian is my Master. I'm very proud to be his slave."

"But he lets you have sex with his guests?"

Her head shook vigorously. "Never. I was shocked when he told me if I could get any of you in bed, he would allow it." She leaned in. "I'm a terrible sex addict, you see. I've been through rounds and rounds of therapy. Nothing ever worked until Julian became my Master. I now go hours and hours without having sex because Julian demands it. I would never, never do anything to make him angry."

"Because he would beat you?"

"Oh, no," Sally argued. "I mean, he would spank me, for sure, but that's not what scares me. He might not fuck me. He's the best sex I've ever had."

Abby exchanged a glance with Sam. She let her eyebrow drift up in a hopeful question.

"I never slept with him," Sam protested with a laugh. "I did, however, watch some of his public displays. It was quite surprising. There's a reason every sub who meets him begs Julian to take them

92

on. If I'm a horse, baby, Julian must be an elephant."

She felt her eyes widen at the thought. Sally was grinning from ear to ear, but suddenly her face darkened. Abby followed her sight line. A young, thin man in leather pants and a thick collar was staring at them.

"Jeremy," Sally said quietly, looking at him. "I have no idea why Julian took him in. He's all evil and stuff. He's a terrible sub. He plays mean tricks on the rest of us and gets everyone riled up."

"The rest of you? How many does Julian have?" Did the man keep a whole stable of lovely bodies to choose from? Could Jack have the same thing here?

"Jeremy and I are the only ones who live with him, but all the employees call him Master." Sally's voice took on a distinctly academic air. "He takes subs here and there for a night. He never promised us he would be faithful. Julian is up-front and honest about everything. Jeremy gets jealous about all the extras. I just hope I get to join in."

Jeremy shot Abby a calculating glance. She remembered him from earlier. He'd been the one to deliver dinner. She didn't like the gleam in his eyes. There wasn't a whole lot she could do about it, however. What could he really do? Screw up their room service?

She turned away from Jeremy, who was talking to someone else now, a big, bald guy. A scene caught her eye. There was a woman in pigtails and a school girl uniform laid out over the knee of a much older man. Her bare ass was up in the air, and he spanked her vigorously. She howled her outrage.

"That's okay?" She felt a little uncomfortable with the screaming the school girl was doing. She turned back and noted the horny ad guys had their secretary between them now. "Holy crap." She looked up at Sam. "Do we look like that?"

Sam inspected the scene carefully. "Naw, baby, me and Jack are a hundred times better looking than those two."

"And she doesn't have your boobs," Sally said with a critical eye. "As for the woman in the classroom, she specifically requested the full Britney Spears."

"Oh," she mouthed, not sure how to respond to that.

Sam was still watching the office scene. "I think my anal

technique is way better than his." He hissed lightly. "I never pop in and out like that. It should be a smooth glide. We're way prettier, baby. See, you would know this if you let me tape it like I've been begging you to."

She narrowed her eyes. "That is not happening, Samuel Fleetwood. I know that would end up on YouTube." Something Sally had said finally penetrated. "Do you honestly think my boobs are nicer than hers? Hers seem perkier."

"Silicone," Sally and Sam said at the same time.

Abby turned her head to get a good view. Sure enough, they were fake.

Sally leaned over. "Yours are so much prettier than hers. I would like to play with them."

She lightly brushed her lips against Abby's. Abby felt Sam get hard from two feet away.

When Sally pulled back, she looked at Abby as though really seeing her for the first time. Her eyes widened. "You're wearing the rose. Are you sure you want…"

"Since when do subs play openly on the floor?" A large, obviously dominant man was standing over them. He was joined by an equally massive friend. Both topped out well over six four. One had shaved his head along with all his body hair. He was the one Jeremy had been talking to. The other was a strikingly attractive man with long dark hair and bright blue eyes. Though the bald guy was slightly bigger, Abby had no doubt who was really in charge. The dark-haired man reeked authority. He reminded her a little of Jack.

Sally hit the ground, sinking to her knees. It was a feat of grace in that tight miniskirt. Sally's eyes were downcast, her palms open on her thighs.

"What's going on, Sally?" The dark-haired, blue-eyed man stared down at the blonde. His expression conveyed his dismay. "Are you regressing? I'm going to have to tell Julian about this. He'll be so disappointed."

Sam slipped his hand into Abby's. He started to pull her away, but Abby held her ground. She wasn't going to leave Sally to the mercy of men who didn't look like they had any. Even if the blonde had tried to blow both of her husbands.

"She was talking to us." She stared up at the dark-haired man.

"Abby," Sam barked.

Big Baldie's eyes focused on her, and she suddenly knew how a fluffy bunny rabbit felt when a wolf caught sight of it. "No one gave you permission to speak, sub."

She felt Sam pulling at her.

"Where's your collar, little one?" Dark Hair asked.

"She's new," Sam said quickly. "I haven't gotten her one yet."

Baldie laughed long and loud. "Why the hell would you buy her a collar? Did her master send you out and you forgot?"

"She's mine," Sam said firmly.

Dark Hair shook his head, exchanging a weary look with his friend. "Tourists. How did you get in? It would be best if you left. I'm sorry, you're not a Dom. You're far too soft, and no Dom here is going to believe you can hold her. You're going to cause me an enormous amount of trouble if you stay. I need to take this one to her rooms. It will be up to her Master to decide her punishment." He sighed. "Given some of the play we have going on this evening, I don't want to leave the two of you alone. Maybe you should come with me."

"I'll take the redhead, Leo." Baldie gave her a leering glance that left Abby feeling slightly unclean. "She's lovely. I'll show her how a real Dom treats a slave."

"Don't you lay a hand on her." Sam pulled Abby back against him, his arms forming a cage around her. Every muscle in his body seemed tense and ready for action. Abby felt her heart speed up. This could get bad.

Leo reached down and pulled on Sally's collar. She immediately got to her feet. "You should be glad Jeremy told me you were slipping, dear. If you had managed to get these two back to a room, Julian would have thrown you out."

"No, he wouldn't." Abby felt Sam squeeze her arm but continued anyway. She'd never been able to handle injustice. She tried to catch Sally's attention, but the sub had her head down. She didn't protest as Leo pulled on her collar. If Sally couldn't speak up for herself, then Abby would. "Jeremy's a weasel. She totally had permission to try to seduce me. Not that it was going to work. Sally, why don't you tell him?"

Leo turned his now cold blue eyes on her. "She isn't speaking because I haven't given her permission to speak. She knows her place in this club, sub. Something your Dom obviously hasn't taught you."

She had the sudden realization that a good many people were no longer watching the scenes playing out around them. She'd managed to make her own scene.

"Knees, sub," Leo said coldly.

She swallowed and fought the urge to get on her knees. If she did that, it would make Sam look bad. This Leo guy wasn't her husband, and he wasn't her lover. She didn't mean anything to him, and she had no rights concerning this man. In her mind, that meant he had no rights over her, either.

"No." She was pleased with how steady her voice was.

"We're going back to our room." Sam tried to pull her back.

Baldie reached out to grab her. "Too late, sub. No one talks to Master Leo that way and gets away with it."

"Damn it!" Sam exclaimed. "Jack's going to kill me." He shoved Abby back, and with a disgusted sigh, threw the first punch.

She fell on her ass just as all hell broke loose.

Chapter Eight

Jack followed Julian into the bar level of the club. Vaguely Jack noted the slight changes Julian had made. The carpet looked new. He shrugged. He'd never paid much attention to decor. He'd spent his nights prowling the dungeon and the playroom. That had been a long time ago. He wondered if it would be different coming here as a guest. He and Sam had come several times but almost always to find a woman to share for the weekend. Ménage was common among this set. In the past they would hook up with a woman on a Friday night then spend the weekend with her in one of the upstairs suites.

Abby had changed all that.

Still, it might be fun to bring her here. They could take her downstairs and get her hot and bothered watching the scenes. Then, when she couldn't take anymore, he'd get her in the elevator and give her the pounding she deserved. He'd carry her into their suite, and he and Sam would make sure she couldn't walk come Monday morning. She wouldn't have to, he vowed. He'd just carry her around.

What was he thinking? Jack shook his head in disgust. She'd been sick not two days before and he wanted to fuck her until she couldn't walk? He remembered the promise he'd made to himself in the hospital. He'd promised that if he lived, he would try to be a better man. He wouldn't be so demanding. He would have the type of marriage that Abigail deserved and be the friend Sam needed.

He'd done what he promised, so why did he feel like he was losing them?

Julian opened the door to a small private dining room. The room had a distinctly masculine edge to it. All the furniture was comfortable but elegant. There was a fire blazing in the fireplace in the back of the room. It gave the room an intimate glow. Jack knew this was Julian's personal dining room. No one else used it.

"I modeled it after the old White's Club in London." Julian led Slater in. "I did some meticulous research."

Slater relaxed once the door closed. The dining room was elegant, with none of the overt sexuality that hung over The Club. His brown eyes took in the sumptuous furnishings with approval. "Yes, this looks a bit like an old-world gentleman's club. I have to say, I prefer that to the new ones. A gentleman's club used to be a place where men got away from women, not merely found ones with less clothing."

He got the feeling Slater didn't get laid much.

Julian pulled out a wooden box. He flipped open the top. "Cubans." He offered up the rich-smelling cigars. Slater took one. Jack was sorely tempted. Julian only bought the best.

"No," he said regretfully. "My wife would kill me."

He sank down into the chair. His stomach was in knots. They still hadn't called back. He was starting to get worried. He was going to refuse the cigars, and he wouldn't have a second drink. He needed a perfectly clear head. It would take a couple of hours to get home. He knew he should stay the night, but he would never get to sleep without talking to them. He didn't sleep much, anyway, not anymore. If he was going to be miserable, at least he could do it at home where he knew the people he loved were in the next room.

"I don't know if you've noticed, Jackson, but your wife isn't here," Julian said, taking that first puff. The rich aroma filled the air.

"It's easy to see you've never been married." He was going to have to change clothes and take a shower to get rid of the smoky smell. "Abigail's always here."

Slater laughed but shifted uncomfortably in his seat. "This is why I never married. Why would I want some woman dictating my every move? I thought you were into this lifestyle, Mr. Barnes."

"Which lifestyle is that?"

Slater's voice went low. "The bondage thing. The BS thing."

"Yes, Slater, I'm into the bullshit thing." He would have left it at that, but Julian went into teaching mode. Sometimes he thought if Julian hadn't been such a righteous pervert, he would have done well at a university.

"BDSM," Julian corrected. He poured a few fingers of Scotch into a glass. Jack waved him off. Julian shrugged and continued. "It stands for bondage, sadism, and masochism. Alternately it also stands for bondage, Dominance, and submission. I believe Jackson and I are more in line with the latter. We both prefer our lovers to be submissive."

"Speak for yourself," he said. "Abigail isn't very submissive." Except in the bedroom. A vision of her tied to the whipping chair, her body laid out and open to him, assaulted his brain.

"Really?" Julian asked, looking at him seriously. "I'm surprised to hear that. I would have said you could never be happy in a relationship that didn't involve submission on some level. I know you're not a full-time Dom, but I assumed any sexual relationship would be in the lifestyle."

"I can be vanilla. No woman wants to be dominated all the time." He could be demanding. It wasn't fair to ask that of her.

"That has not been my experience." Julian was studying him. Jack was starting to get nervous. The last thing Jack needed was Julian trying to get into his head. "I've found many women enjoy it on some level, even if it is only play. They enjoy the feeling of protection a Dom can give them. A Dom can shelter a woman from everything, even her own insecurities."

"Stay out of my marriage, Julian." He stared at his mentor, trying to get him off the damn subject.

"If only I could," Julian muttered under his breath.

Slater took a long swallow of his Scotch. "Well, I don't understand the appeal of any of it. I wouldn't want a woman to be dependent on me for everything."

"You're not a Dom," Julian said shortly, dismissing the man. He looked like he wanted to pursue the conversation with Jack.

Jack steeled himself to have a lengthy discussion with his old mentor about keeping out of his business. He was saved by the door opening.

He sat up a little straighter as a young man walked in the room. He was pretty sure it was a young man. His hair was strangely shaped. It was black and swept over his face like it was windblown, yet he didn't try to shove it back. It stayed in place, and Jack realized this kid used hair spray. He had bangs. Why the hell did that boy have bangs? He was dressed in a god-awful purple V-neck T-shirt. It was the type of shirt that looked hot on Abigail. It showed off her breasts. The young man in front of him didn't have breasts, so why did he need to show off his milky white chest? Jack's eyes moved down the kid's body, widening in horror. The jeans he was wearing looked like someone had painted them on the man. They were black and fit him like a second skin. He completed the look with a skinny belt that was draped over his hips. It did nothing to keep his pants up. Hell, he didn't need a belt to do that. That man might never get the pants off, but the belt was obviously some form of decoration. Despite the low light of the room, he was wearing a pair of sunglasses.

This was his brother?

The young man swaggered up to the trio. He glanced around the room with a look of cool disdain. "I've seen way better clubs than this. You Lodge?"

Julian nodded. Jack couldn't mistake the small smile on Julian's face. He was extremely amused. Jack was glad someone was having a good time. "Yes, I'm Julian Lodge."

The young man turned to Jack. "Since I know that asshole in the back, that must make you Jack Barnes. I suppose I expected you to show up in a cowboy hat fresh off the range. Did you leave your horse outside?"

He stood up. Though the young man was almost as tall as Jack, he had the slight build of a teen, compared to that of a man. Jack had fifty pounds on him at least. The kid needed some work to put muscle on his frame.

"I left my horse on my ranch," he said. "What the hell is wrong with you, son? Didn't they teach manners in those fancy schools you went to? Take those damn sunglasses off when you're inside."

The sunglasses came off in a flash, and Jack heard Slater's shocked gasp.

"I thought they looked cool." Lucas Cameron sounded far less arrogant now.

"Is the fact that your pants are two sizes too small supposed to be cool, too?"

"Yes." Lucas self-consciously pulled them away from his waist. They didn't budge. He seemed stunned that someone was talking to him the way Jack was. Whoa, without the sunglasses, the face staring at him looked awfully familiar.

"Jackson, it's like looking at you ten years ago." Julian's focus switched between the two. It was obvious Julian was making comparisons. "I've seen him in photographs, but the two of you together, the resemblance is astonishing."

Yes, his half-brother greatly resembled him. There were, of course, a few differences. "Are you wearing makeup, son?"

"It's just a little guy-liner," Lucas mumbled.

"I don't know what that is, but my wife wears something like that. I don't think that's meant for men." He was not able to keep the horror out of his voice.

Lucas suddenly stood up straight, as though surprised at his own actions. "I wouldn't expect a cowboy to know what's fashionable. That monkey suit you're wearing is boring."

He hated it, too. "I find it to be confining. But at least it fits."

"I didn't come here to talk fashion with you, Mr. Barnes," Lucas said, puffing himself up. His dark green eyes narrowed. "I came here to talk business. Sorry, that Neanderthal you sent out to pick me up didn't scare me away, Lodge. Now, what the hell is Slater doing here? Who invited my father's flunky?"

"I came down here to make sure you don't ruin your father's career." Slater's lips thinned with distaste as he looked the young man over.

He suddenly wondered if everyone treated Lucas this way.

For some reason, Lucas reminded him of Sam. He sat back down, choosing, for the moment, to simply observe. Maybe Julian was right and there was more to all of this than simple brattiness and greed. He took in the arrogant set of Lucas's eyes. It didn't match the slump of his shoulders. His feet were close together, while his arms were crossed. He was protecting himself. It was almost as though Lucas wanted to fall into himself. Yet, he was standing here in a group of authoritative men, trying to blackmail them. It was an interesting quandary.

"If he's so concerned about his political future, then he should have paid me off," Lucas said. Jack heard a lot of bravado behind the statement, but a surprising lack of will.

"Your father isn't a fool." Slater nearly spat while he spoke. He got into Lucas's space. "He knows you'll never stop asking him for money. Hasn't he paid enough?"

Lucas's lip curled up, but there was nothing humorous about his expression. "I give him all the free publicity he can handle."

"Yes, the recent articles on your various drug addictions and close calls with the law did wonders for his chances in the primaries," Slater shot back.

"Well, he had my sister to help. Didn't she recently graduate from Harvard?"

"With her Ph.D. in law. She'll have a judgeship in no time. Your brother is already a state senator. They make your mother and father proud. They're assets. What's wrong with you? You've had every advantage, and yet all you seem capable of is doing drugs and having perverse sex. There's a rumor out there that you're gay."

"I'm not gay," Lucas protested with a sneer. "Of course, I'm not straight, either."

Slater rolled his eyes. "I came here because I thought you needed a chaperone. You should never be allowed in this club. It isn't proper for anyone. Places like this shouldn't exist, if you ask me. It could truly hurt your family if you were caught here."

"Should I pull the senator's membership then?" Julian's aristocratic features were blank. Slater was really pissing him off. When Julian's face went blank, that was when Jack got worried.

Of course all that irritation wasn't directed at him so he grinned, somewhat amused. "Did he join before or after we had our little chat with him?"

"Oh, after," Julian assured him. "He was quite intrigued. He stops in every time he's in the area. He quite likes the dungeon. I believe he brought a young brunette with him last time."

Lucas frowned. "That would be Justine. She was my girlfriend for a while."

"The senator is discreet." Julian looked at the boy with some sympathy.

"The senator is an asshole," Lucas muttered. "It doesn't matter. Let's get down to business, gentlemen. Are we having dinner or not? I could use a drink. The whole nearly-getting-run-down-by-a-crazy-person thing has me on edge. And your driver is an asshole, too."

"Well, the being-blackmailed-by-a-spoiled-brat thing has done wonders for my nerves." Julian poured another drink with a perfectly steady hand. "And dear god, please tell me you called Taggart my driver. That alone would be worth the trouble."

"I'm not giving you twenty million dollars," Jack stated flatly.

"Then I'm sure I can make money off a tabloid story about the senator's long-lost son." Lucas's bitterness was apparent in his tone. He took a quick drink and coughed like he hadn't expected what he'd gotten. Jack wasn't so sure about his reputation as a hard drinker. He would bet the drug stories were overblown, too. "You know he holds you up as paragon of virtue, Jack Barnes. You're a self-made man. I could learn a lot from you. You had nothing, but you pulled yourself up. All it took was a bit of blackmail. Hell, he even admires you for that."

"I'm not responsible for your relationship with your father." It was plain the boy was in need of attention, but he wasn't Jack's responsibility.

"Of course, it's all my fault." Lucas held the glass and stared into the fire.

"I didn't say that."

"You didn't have to." Lucas's reply was simple, the answer of a boy who knew the score and knew that he was never going to change anyone's mind. "You're just like the rest of them. I don't know why I thought you might be different." He took a long drink, as though building up his courage. He managed to only wince at that last drink before turning to face the men in the room. "Here's the deal, gentlemen. If I don't get what I want, I'm prepared to sell a story to the tabloids. I intend to out Julian Lodge as James Masters, the head of the Masters Fund. I doubt anyone will want to work with a notorious sex club owner."

"I don't think I'll worry too much about that. Hugh Hefner never hurt for business," Julian said with an elegant sigh. "Besides, I have enough money as it is. If all my investors dry up, I'll take a nice vacation."

That seemed to rattle Lucas. He shook it off and turned to Jack. "Fine, maybe Lodge doesn't think he has anything to lose, but you recently got married. What's your wife going to think about your past in this club? How's she going to feel knowing she married a notorious Dom?"

He noticed Julian hide a smile behind his hand. The boy had no idea how to handle men like them. "I wouldn't call me notorious. I was actually quite good at it. And Abigail knows what I used to do and exactly how I came by the seed money for my business. You can't shock her. Come by the house sometime, and I'll introduce you to her. You can tell her what you know. I think she'll be highly amused."

She wouldn't be amused. She would be pissed off. Abigail could be very protective of her men. Lucas would be forced to deal with one mad cat.

Lucas's face got hard and, for a second, Jack wondered if he looked like that from time to time. It appeared there was some steel in the boy after all. "Fine. Then I'm sure the world would love to know about your ménage. Trust me, cattle ranchers sharing their woman will be a story the world would love to hear. Couple it with the fact that you're Senator Allen Cameron's son, and your sexual activities will be all over the news. I'm sure they'll believe you simply share her. They won't think anything of the fact that you lived with Samuel Fleetwood for years before ever meeting Abby Moore. That business you're in is a macho business. I'm sure a couple of gay cowboys will go over like gangbusters, bro."

"Jackson."

He heard the warning in Julian's voice. He knew exactly what worried the club owner. Julian wouldn't want to have to clean up the blood that he was about to spill. He heard the warning, but it seemed a distant thing. What he could hear plainly was his blood pressure rising. It was a roar in his ears blocking out everything else. He saw what he was going to do like a movie in his mind. He was going to wrap his hands around Lucas Cameron's throat, and then the little shit wouldn't be a problem to anyone anymore.

The door to the dining room flew open.

"Mr. Lodge, we have a code red in the playroom," said a breathless young woman in leather shorts and a bustier. It was obvious she had run in from the bar area. There was a buzzing coming from outside.

"Call Leo." Julian got out of his seat. He took off his jacket and slung it over the chair, as though he knew he would be getting dirty.

"Leo's involved in it. He was on the scene when it started," the woman explained. "They're fighting over two subs. The male started a fight with Patrick, and it's getting bloody. He's smaller than Patrick, but he seems really mean. Sally's in the middle of all of it. I can't find their Dom."

Julian's face hardened. "I know exactly where their Dom is. Jackson, will you forgo killing your brother for the moment? I need your help."

He clenched his fists but got up anyway. He'd promised Julian he would help if the subs in the Platinum Suite got out of hand. It seemed like they had. It was only to be expected. Two subs shouldn't go running around in a club like this. He should have insisted on talking to them earlier, but he'd been thinking of his own problems. He was still thinking of his own problems, but theirs seemed to be intruding. Besides, he couldn't kill Lucas in front of witnesses. That would have to be done quietly and privately. He shook his head as he followed Julian out.

"How bad is it?" Julian glanced back at the blonde woman, but she couldn't keep up in her heels.

Even from the bar, he could hear the fight. It was loud and getting louder by the second. He knew it was bad when Julian broke into a jog.

"Call security." Jack barked the order to the bartender as they ran down the hallway that led to the playroom. Normally a bouncer was standing at the entryway, but the small desk was empty. So he'd likely already jumped into the fray.

There was a mass of people watching the fight. It seemed like all other activities had come to a halt and violence, rather than sex, was the theme of the evening. The sickening thud of flesh hitting flesh hit his ears. He followed Julian as they started shoving their way through the crowd.

"You keep your fucking hands off her!" A familiar voice cut through the mess.

He stopped because he knew that voice. "Sam?"

Through the throng of bodies fighting, he caught a glimpse of his partner. He was throwing a punch at a bald guy while kicking another man. He seemed to be trying to get to someone. Jack had a sudden horrible thought that he knew who Sam was trying to protect.

Julian looked back at him. "Well, would you like to talk to me about karma now, Jackson? Like it or not, it's about to bite you in the ass."

Chapter Nine

Abby scrambled to get up. All around her, people were rushing to get a good place to watch the fight that was going on. The heels and the miniskirt she wore hampered her every movement. She tried to push her way toward Sam, but she kept getting shoved toward the back of the crowd. A big hand clamp down on her arm, hauling her up, and she found herself against a large, masculine body.

Leo, that was what the other man had called him. Leo's blue eyes were blazing with impatience as he towered over her.

"Where is your Dom? Does he know you're wearing that rose?"

She tried to turn away from him, his words not really registering. She didn't have to answer him. Then she saw Sam take a punch to the gut that made her eyes water. She tried to pull away to go help him, but that big hand held her tightly.

"No way, sub." There was a bit of kindness in his voice now. "He's a big boy, and he started this fight. Please tell me your Dom is somewhere in the building."

"He's probably with Julian Lodge." Maybe it was time to bring in Jack. She had wanted to give him a little shock to his system. She'd thought he might be pissed about the shopping. She knew he'd be upset about the motorcycle and the impromptu trip to The Club. She figured he'd blow a gasket over this. It had been such a mistake. What had she been thinking? She'd brought Sam into this.

She clutched at Leo's arm. "Don't get him, please. Look, I'll tell him everything, but if he walks in on this…I don't know what he'll do."

Leo shook his head. "I do. You're going to look lovely on a St. Andrew's Cross, dear. I'll lend him my single tail if he didn't bring his own."

Abby wasn't sure what a single tail was, but it didn't sound good. She knew exactly what a St. Andrew's Cross was and wondered briefly if Jack would really strap her to one for public punishment.

"Stay here," Leo instructed her. He squeezed her arm one last time. It felt like a warning. "I'm going to get your Master. Don't move."

The minute he was gone, she started to force her way through the crowd. She wasn't going to let Sam fight that man alone. He was bigger than Sam. She brushed past bodies and tried not to think about the hands that groped her as she moved through. All she could think about was getting to her man.

She fought her way to the front just in time to see Sam kick the hell out of Baldie. Baldie groaned loudly because Sam was mean. That boot of his caught Baldie firmly in the crotch. It should have been the end of the fight, but Baldie had some friends and Sam refused to go down.

Sam swung out at the two men, obviously security guards, trying to pin him down. He'd more than likely moved past the time when he could make the sane decision to retreat. He was running on pure adrenaline at this point. She needed to get to him so they could make a getaway. Julian Lodge might not care that she wasn't his sub to punish this time around. Then there was the potential that he would bring Jack. Tears sprang to her eyes. Jack might decide she wasn't worth all this trouble.

"Sam!" she yelled over the betting now going on around her. "Sam!"

He wasn't listening to anything but the inner Tyler Durden he'd unleashed. She should never have let him watch *Fight Club*. She was about to walk into the middle of the fight when she felt herself being pulled back.

She turned quickly and looked into dark eyes. The man was tall and dressed in head-to-toe leather. He was slender, and there was a certain cruelty to the set of his mouth.

"No collar, sub," he whispered into her ear. "Someone's got to protect you. And tonight's capture night in the dungeon. All unattached subs are ripe for the picking. Don't worry. I'll take care of you."

Abby pulled away, but that hand was strong and attached to a lean, powerful body. Before she could do anything to stop it, she felt cold metal pressed to her skin. She couldn't hear it over the crowd, but she knew the cuff probably snapped as it closed over her wrist. That asshole had handcuffed her.

Now she was panicking a little. She tried digging her stilettos into the hardwood of the floors. It didn't work. She twisted and fought. Her eyes sought anyone who might help, but everyone around her was focused on the fight.

"Sam!" Abby screamed, not to save him this time, but to get him to save her. There were too many people in the crowd. She couldn't see him anymore.

"You take your fucking hands off her!" she heard Sam shout. She breathed a sigh of relief even though she was still being pulled along. Sam wouldn't let some guy in leather carry her down to the dungeon.

"What the fuck is going on?"

The whole room got still at the loud roar.

Jack! Relief infused her, even as dread rolled through her belly. She'd wanted to shake him up, but not this much. On the bright side, while she could yell all day long and no one paid attention, the minute Jack said a word, the world stopped.

Jack's low growl could be heard easily now. There was a slight parting in the crowd. Abby could see her husbands. Jack's back was to her, but Sam was on full display. "Samuel, would you like to explain why the hell you aren't at home with our wife?"

"Jack." Sam sounded breathless. He stood still. His shirt was torn and there was blood on his face.

Leather Guy decided to ignore the scene playing out behind him. He started to pull Abby along.

"Hey." Abby pulled the other way.

"You stop!" Sally shouted. She was shaking as she stood up to the Dom.

"Get out of my way, little girl," Leather Guy said. "I don't have time to punish you, sub. I have a plaything for the night."

"She doesn't belong to you and she doesn't know what that rose means. She doesn't understand." Sally's voice was tremulous, but she held her ground. She walked back to take Abby's free arm. "I'm taking her back."

Abby found herself being pulled in two directions. Sally tried to force her away from Leather Guy. Leather Guy tugged on the other side of the handcuff he'd attached to her wrist.

"Girl, I'm about to make the time to punish you," Leather Guy swore.

What had she meant about the rose? Abby tried to move closer to Sally. The crowd around her seemed to slow and then she heard a roar.

"What do you mean she's here?" Jack's question came out as an accusation.

"Abby?" Sam yelled.

She saw the small sea of people parting as Sam fought his way to her. He'd taken a couple of rough hits, and she worried his left eye was going to swell.

"Abigail Barnes!" Jack barked.

"I'm here, Jack." She wanted to fling herself against his broad chest and revel in safety. But part of her was terrified that whatever Jack had in mind was going to be so much worse than anything Leather Guy could dream up.

Sam took Sally's place. Sally stepped away quickly, allowing Sam to take the lead. He faced down her would-be kidnapper. "Take your hands off her."

"No collar," Leather Guy insisted. "Face it, sub. You should never have brought her here. If you didn't want to lose her, you should have collared her."

"Perhaps you would like to explain to me why you've cuffed my wife?" Jack's question came out between his clenched, bared teeth. The crowd moved around him, respecting his space.

He was on the edge. She pulled away, trying to get to him. She needed to calm him down. The brow above his right eye was twitching ever so slightly. It was a sure sign that his blood pressure was rising. He would want blood soon. She already had to deal with Sam getting in trouble. She didn't want Jack getting hurt, too.

"I'm fine," she tried to reassure him.

Jack ignored her, choosing to spend his intimidation on Leather Guy. The Dom suddenly didn't look so sure anymore.

"She's not collared," he insisted.

"The wedding ring she's wearing is collar enough," Jack bit out. "I know. I put it on her finger. You can see that fucking diamond from space."

Oh, shit. She hadn't thought about the fact that her wedding ring was upstairs. Unfortunately, it was her left hand that was currently shackled. Leather Guy held up her perfectly ringless finger.

Abby felt the room get extremely cold as Jack stalked up to her. Sam held her hand.

"You're serious. You're not playing. Oh, shit." Leather Guy seemed to deflate as he quickly used his key and uncuffed her. He dropped his hold on her and held his hands up as though surrendering. "Man, I'm sorry. We're playing capture games this evening. The rules of the game include that submissives who agree to play would wear the white rose. I honesty thought she was fair game and that the fighting was part of her kink. I'm so sorry, Master… I don't know your name."

Sam pulled her into his arms. He cursed under his breath. "I didn't know that was going on."

"Really?" Julian's cold voice cut through the now quiet dungeon. "Because the rose would have come with written instructions on what scenes and games would be going on tonight."

Abby shook her head. "It was by itself. I thought it was a gift."

Jack stepped in, gently pulling the rose out of her hair. "I understand why you wouldn't know what that meant. Sam should know that every single thing has meaning in this club. Everything. Now, Abigail, would you like to explain to me why you're half-naked in sex club without your wedding ring on your finger?"

Every single word that came out of Jack's mouth dripped with menace.

Sam pushed her slightly, encouraging her to handle Jack. She knew what he wanted her to do. She thought it was a good idea, too. She sank to her knees at Jack's feet and put her head down. Her hands were trembling as she curved her body into a submissive position.

"I'm sorry," she said quietly. This had been a terrible mistake and she wasn't sure he would ever forgive her for it.

"That is not going to cut it, Abigail." Jack loomed over her. She could practically feel his rage pounding at her. "Answer me now. Where is the ring I put on your finger? I swear to god if you lie to me, I'll strip you down here and now, and you won't be able to walk when I'm through."

A perverse tremor went through her. Jack was using that voice on her. It was the voice that got her wet and ready in seconds. She didn't like to think about the fact that a small part of her wanted to keep pushing him to see what that would feel like. How far would he go? How much could she take? The majority of her, however, went into survival mode.

"It didn't fit under the gloves I had to wear," she explained softly.

Jack's hand came out, lifting her chin up. He forced her to look him in the eyes. "What gloves, Abigail?" She tried to turn to look at Sam. Jack held her in place. "Don't you dare look at him. You look at me. You're answering me. He'll get his chance to answer for what he's done. What gloves? What gloves were so important that you would take off the ring I put on your finger?"

His deep green eyes were practically black in the dim light. It didn't frighten her on a physical level. She trusted him implicitly. Any pain he'd given her before had only enhanced her pleasure. But her heart was a different matter.

"I had to wear gloves or Sam wouldn't let me on the motorcycle," she admitted.

Jack's eyes closed briefly and when he opened them, Abby knew she was in for a bunch of that pleasure and no small amount of pain.

Jack let go of her chin. He nodded as though coming to a decision. He turned and faced Julian. The club owner was a commanding presence in the center of the room. He stood with his hand on Sally's bent head, stroking her as though attempting to give her comfort. His eyes weren't comforting as he looked at Jack.

"Your subs upset my business, Jackson," Julian said evenly.

"I'm sorry." She was starting to think she couldn't say that enough. From the look on Julian Lodge's face, this was more serious than she'd thought.

"Silence," Jack ordered harshly. He stared at her until she closed her mouth. He stood beside her, and his hand went to the back of her neck. His fingers curled around the nape of her neck, and there was no mistaking the warning in them. "I understand, Julian. I apologize for both of them. Their behavior reflects poorly on me. You have the right to require any punishment you think fit. I ask you, as an old friend, please let me administer it."

Julian appeared to think it through. "It will be public. I cannot let this go unpunished or everyone will think such behavior is acceptable. They interrupted scenes that many of my clients practiced weeks for and looked forward to. I wish I could let it pass, but I cannot. Tomorrow night in the dungeon, I want both she and Samuel to feel the lash."

"Damn it, Julian." Jack's hand tightened slightly around her neck. It wasn't at all painful, more a sign of his growing panic. Though she knew he was upset, his voice was steady as a rock. "I've never used anything on her before but my hand and a crop."

"Then you should practice between now and then," Julian replied. "I will allow a single tail, but nothing less. You used to be an artist with it. I have no doubt you can be again, for her sake. If you agree, then they can stay. If not, I have to ask them to leave and I will revoke Samuel's membership. But Jackson, put collars on your subs before they leave their rooms again. Do you understand?"

Jack nodded. The hand on her neck relaxed. "Yes. She won't leave the suite without it. Sam might never leave the suite alive again, so we won't have to worry about him." He glanced over at Sam. "I assume you took out the Platinum Suite."

"Yes."

"Yes?" Jack's voice was sharp.

"Yes, Jack."

"Get down there with her," Jack barked.

She felt Sam kneel beside her. His eyes were down, but his hand found hers and gave her a reassuring squeeze.

"Are we done, Julian? I would like to take my subs upstairs. It's time I had a long talk with them."

She held her breath as Leo stepped forward. "I'm not done." He stood in front of Jack, going toe to toe with him. "I'm the Dom in residence now, Master Jack. I know that used to be your job, but you're a guest now. Had two subs caused the trouble yours did tonight, what would you have requested then?"

Jack's jaw tightened. "I would have immediately requested punishment. Julian would have wanted punishment for disrupting the scenes, but I would have requested punishment for the insult to me."

Leo nodded. "They both will pay for abusing Master Julian's trust. I want her to pay for the insult to me."

The hand on the back of her neck tightened almost painfully, and Abby decided not to argue.

"What insult?" Jack asked.

Leo's eyes skimmed over her. She watched from beneath her lashes. "She started everything. I was attempting to watch over Master Julian's possession. She questioned my authority over Sally in public. She proceeded to ignore direct orders given to her for her own protection. Though the male is the one who fought, I understand and forgive his actions. He was protecting her. He's your partner?"

There was not an ounce of condemnation in the Dom's question. He was merely attempting to outline the relationship.

"We share our wife. But I am the head of the household."

"Well, your wife is topping from the bottom," Leo accused. "I can't let the rest of the subs see her get away with it. Twenty tonight, over my knee, right now."

The hand came off her neck and she heard a sigh. His voice was low, and she couldn't stand the defeated sound of his reply. "We'll be out of here in an hour. Julian, I'm sorry. Consider my membership revoked. Come along, Abigail. Sam, I expect you to pack whatever you need and meet us in the lobby."

"No!" She reached for his hand. Jack did business with the members of this club. It meant something to him. It was the whole reason she wanted to come here. She wanted to see this side of him. It had been the first place he'd called home. Now she would be the reason he lost it. Jack growled at her. She kept her head down, but she couldn't keep quiet. "Please, Jack. Please don't. I couldn't live with it. I'll do whatever he asks. I can handle it. Please don't let this happen."

His hand found her chin again, and his expression was softer now. "Abigail, he could hurt you."

"Nothing will hurt me more than knowing I did this to you." She could feel the tears streaming down her face. "Please?"

He forced her to look him straight in the eyes, his gaze steady. "I will never allow another man to put his hands on you like that. Do you understand me? I don't care what you've done or what their rules are. I only trust Sam. This relationship is between the three of us. I won't let anyone else in, not even for a moment, no matter what it costs me. All right?"

Though it hurt her heart, she knew he wouldn't move. She nodded.

"Leo, I wonder if you would indulge me." Julian's voice cut through her misery. "If Jackson administers the punishment, will you be satisfied? He's serious. He will leave and not come back rather than allow you to touch her. It will more than likely cost me a friendship I would prefer not to lose."

The slight incline of the dungeon master's head indicated his assent. "But I expect him to take this seriously. It's obvious to me he has no control over his subs. He needs to reestablish control or allow them their freedom so they can find more appropriate Masters."

"How about you let me worry about my wife and my partner and you keep your hands off of her." Jack took a threatening step toward the other man. "Don't think I don't see the way you look at her. You don't want to punish her. You want to get your hands on her. It's not going to happen while I'm still breathing. Get me a chair."

Jack hauled her up and she let him. If this was what it took, she could handle it. Hell, a part of her was already soft and wet. Deep down it was what she had hoped for. She glanced around at the crowd of people watching while Jack was brought a chair. They were going to watch him spank her. She hadn't really hoped for this part. She felt her skin flush as they watched her.

Julian and Leo seemed particularly interested, but Sally's head was up, too. There was a strangely familiar face in the back. He had black, fashionably tousled hair and wore trendy clothes. He was young, but he watched the scene before him with a fascination that was hard to miss. An older man in a suit, however, stood right behind the young man, and his disdain shone on his pinched face. It took her back to a time when she saw that look on a lot of people's faces. She felt seventeen again, with the contempt of her hometown all around her. She'd been young and pregnant, and they'd called her a whore.

"Abigail." Jack's voice brought her back to reality. He sat on one of the office chairs from the horny ad execs scene. "Come here."

She turned away from the man with the disgusted expression. The rest of the room didn't seem shocked at what was about to happen. They were excited. A thrill went through her. Screw the guy in the back. She wasn't going to let people like that affect her anymore. She walked to Jack and let him pull her over his lap.

Her pussy throbbed in anticipation. Her mouth went dry as Jack's big hands stroked up her legs and began to push her skirt up. She was suddenly glad she'd fought Sam on her choice of underwear. He'd pushed for a thong, but she was eager to wear the cute silk bikinis that matched her corset. Now it would give her a bit of modesty.

"What the fuck?" Jack fingered the underwear. "Since when do I allow you to wear panties? Get me a knife."

So much for modesty. She felt a touch of metal as Jack cut the super-expensive underwear off her body. She watched them fall to the side.

"You're just running wild aren't you, baby?"

His erection poked at her belly. How long had it been since she'd felt that? She would do anything to get to that hard cock. God, she'd missed him so much. Abby felt her eyes fill with tears. He'd been right there and yet so far away for the last couple of months.

116

This was the first time she'd felt close to him in forever, and it pierced her heart.

"Twenty," she heard Leo say.

That was a mighty big number, but before she could protest, Jack's hand came down on her ass and she struggled to breathe. It had been a long time since she'd been spanked. She'd forgotten how much it hurt at first.

Just as the pain was starting to bloom into something more, he struck again. He counted it out. She was grateful he wasn't making her do it. Her brain was whirling, emotions far too high to do anything as logical as count. Her ass was on fire as he brought his hand down. He struck her right cheek and then her left. He moved down, striking her thighs, and then back up to the soft place where her cheeks met.

Unable to hold it in any longer, she cried out. She cried, and it wasn't merely about the pain. She'd held it in for so long. She'd been strong. God, she'd almost lost him to that bullet. It had been a close thing. She could still feel his blood on her hands as she worked to save him.

For so long she'd been strong, holding it all in because he was the one who'd taken the pain. She hadn't processed what had happened, had kept a wall up between them as surely as he had erected one.

She could still lose him. The count hit seventeen. She didn't care who was watching. She cried because she couldn't not cry anymore.

"Twenty." Jack was breathing heavily as he finished. He immediately flipped her over. He was careful with her tender ass, placing her on his lap and pulling her close. "Don't cry, baby. I'm so sorry. I won't do it again. We don't have to do this. Damn it, I knew I was too hard on you."

She put her face close to his. He didn't understand her at all. She pressed her lips against his. "I love you, Jack. I love you so much. I'm not crying because you hurt me. I'm crying because I've missed you. I've missed this. This is part of us. Please don't pull away again. We need you."

Jack leaned back slightly, as though trying to read her face. His

117

deep green eyes studied her carefully. Whatever he saw there convinced him. His hands tangled in her hair. "I wasn't trying to pull away, baby. I love you."

He tugged her close and his lips sealed over hers. His tongue plunged into her mouth, devastating her with his dominance. He turned her in his arms, and she found herself straddling his lap, her wet pussy on display.

"Who does this belong to?" Jack's arm wound tightly around her waist, holding her up. The other hand slid in her juices, parting her labia.

Everyone was watching and yet arousal screamed through her. She felt Sam's eyes on her. They were hot, and she could see the erection tenting his jeans. He smiled slightly at her, letting her know he was there with her always.

"You," she breathed. "It belongs to you. You and Sam."

"Damn fucking straight it does." Jack thrust two fingers straight up her pussy. He stretched her, adding a third finger. It still wasn't as big as his cock, but it was enough to make her feel tight and almost painfully full. Her head fell back against his shoulder as she gave over to him. This was what she'd missed, knowing that she could give him everything, and he would take care of her. "You come for me, Abigail Barnes. You come for me now."

His knees spread her legs wide. She was completely on display as he fucked her with his fingers. The hand on her waist tightened around her as he picked up the pace.

His fingers curled up and scissored inside her. He brushed his thumb firmly against her clitoris, and she came apart. She rubbed herself against him, desperate to prolong the soaring feeling. It rushed across her every nerve ending and left her shaking. As she came down from the high, he kissed her again and then stood with her in his arms. His lips curled up softly as he looked at her.

"Are you all right, baby?"

Perfect. That was what she was. Perfect and languid and sexy. She'd come in front of a crowd, and damned if she wasn't willing to do it again. She nodded.

"I've been selfish." He softly kissed her hair. "I was foolish. I won't be again."

"Is the boss back?"

"The boss is back, baby," he replied surely. "You're in for a rough night." He turned his attention to Master Leo, who stood silently watching them. Jack's face became gloriously arrogant again. "Are you satisfied, Master Leo?"

"Not even close," Leo muttered. "She's beautiful, Master Jack. You're a lucky man. I believe that scene makes up for the ones we lost."

Jack turned to Sam, who was still on his knees. "Samuel, take our wife. I have something I need to deal with before we retire for the evening."

Sam stood, and she was passed to him. His blue eyes gleamed as he looked down at her. Jack stared across the room, his face taking on a distinctly predatory expression. Abby followed his line of sight and noticed he was staring down the young man who seemed so familiar.

"Oh, my god." Sam gawked at the man, slack jawed.

"What?"

"That's gotta be Jack's brother," Sam said. "His biological father had three legitimate kids and that has to be one of them. It's like looking at Jack ten years ago. Well, if he'd dressed like a metro douchebag, that is."

Lucas Cameron. Now she knew where she'd seen him. He was on some of the worst tabloids she bought at the supermarket for the kitsch value. She had a thing for ridiculous headlines. It was a guilty pleasure.

Jack didn't look like he was pleased to see his baby brother. He stalked toward the young man, the crowd parting and giving him a wide berth. Lucas's eyes went big, and he took a couple of steps back. It brought him in contact with the wall. She had the feeling Lucas would have run if he could, but Jack was quick. He wrapped a single hand around his brother's throat and suddenly Lucas was dangling a good foot off the ground.

"Listen here, you little shit," Jack ground out. "I'm not paying you a dime. You will keep your mouth shut. Do you want to know how I know you'll keep your mouth shut? Because if you don't, I will kill you. I will beat you to death, and then I'll take your body apart with a chainsaw. I own a whole lot of land, boy. I'll be burying your body parts all across it. They won't ever find you, Lucas. You'll disappear, and no one will know what happened except you and me. Do you understand me?"

"Yes," Lucas managed.

She sincerely hoped he didn't pee himself.

"Good, now get back home and don't bother me or mine again." Jack let his quarry fall to the ground. "Samuel!" He barked the order and then walked out without looking back, certain his command would be followed.

Sam trotted after him, carrying her all the way. She stared back at Lucas, who looked a bit lost. He didn't seem scared. He seemed almost sad as he watched his brother walk away. He was shaking his head as though he should have known that would happen.

Abby watched his face fall as they left the playroom.

Chapter Ten

Jack's hands shook slightly as he strode into the elevator that would take them back to their rooms. He wasn't sure if anger or raging desire was going to win out. The truth of the matter was both felt good. He'd been in a daze for so long, holding himself apart from everything, that the war of emotion flooding his body felt awesome.

He felt alive for the first time in six damn months.

He felt Sam follow him into the elevator and wondered exactly how he should handle his partner. Abigail looked soft and sweet in Sam's arms. She'd been thoroughly satisfied by the experience in the playroom. Jack had to wonder why he'd stopped playing with his wife. He'd pulled back because he was terrified of losing her. Though he'd played a little and shared her with Sam, he was afraid that if she saw the real Dom side of him, she would turn away in shock.

"Nothing shocks you, does it, baby?" His voice was low as he remembered just how wet she got when he spanked her. What had he been thinking? He'd been viewing her as something fragile since that day she'd been attacked. Their wife was far from fragile. She was a rock.

"I don't know about that." She seemed a bit drunk on the experience. Jack was worried he might have created a monster. It was a good thing they hadn't gotten kicked out of the club since it seemed like she would want to come back. "I was pretty shocked when Sally kissed me."

Jack felt his eyebrows rise. He looked at Sam, who was smiling. "Sally kissed her?"

"Apparently she decided since she couldn't get to me or you, she'd enjoy Abby instead," Sam explained.

Jack focused on Sam, letting his wife's brief foray into lesbianism go for a moment. He might have to have another talk with Sally. Male or female, he didn't care. No one touched his subs without his permission. "You understand what Julian wants for tomorrow night?"

Sam's face went blank. Jack couldn't read it. It bothered him. Sam was almost always an open book. "I know."

"Are you all right with that?"

The elevator door opened and Sam plowed through. He set Abby on her feet, and there was concern in their wife's hazel eyes. She tried to reach up and touch Sam, but he turned away, preferring to get the door to the suite open. Jack followed, wondering exactly where Sam was going. The tension he'd felt in Sam for some time seemed to be ready to burst over.

Everything changed tonight.

He took a deep breath. Everything was going to change and he had to make the decision as to which direction they went in. It was time to put aside his sad-ass fears and be the Dom they needed him to be.

"Samuel, I would like an answer." He made sure his voice was deep and even.

It was his Dom voice, but it felt right now. He rarely used it on Sam. Now seemed like the time to. He needed to get his house back in order. There was only one way to do that. He needed to smash through any barriers they put up to get at the heart of the problem.

Sam turned, and Jack nearly stepped back at the rage he saw in his partner's eyes. "You want answers? Fine, Jack, I'll give you an answer. I'm leaving. I'm sure as hell not letting you take a bull whip to my ass in front of a hundred people when every damn one of them knows I don't belong to you. I don't belong to anyone. I never have. Fuck this. I'm done following you. I'm done waiting for you to see what I need. You're never…"

He stopped suddenly, as though he couldn't quite believe what he was saying. His face went slack and his cheeks stained with embarrassment. Then he shut down, his face going blank.

This was a conversation that was long overdue.

"Go on, Sam." Jack held out a hand to stop Abby from interrupting.

She would want to kiss Sam and make him feel better, but Sam needed this. Sam needed to make his stand. It was a long time coming. Jack could see that now. He carefully made his face a polite blank. He didn't want to give away what he was feeling. It might stop Sam.

Sam's hands clenched into fists at his sides. His face was still slightly bloody from the earlier fight. "You can't just walk in here after months of ignoring us and snap your fingers and expect us to fall in line like nothing ever happened."

"Watch me." He stood still, studying his partner.

Sam swallowed as though he suddenly realized he was being stalked. That was good. Sam needed to realize he wasn't about to let him go. Now that he was standing here, facing his oldest friend in the world, a few things occurred to Jack. His selfishness had hurt more than Abigail. He should have given Sam what he needed a long time ago. He should have seen it. He probably had seen it, but it had been easier to keep the relationship friendly. Love was messy, and Sam was far too important to lose. Now he could see how cowardly that had been.

Jack was steady and kept his eyes on Sam. "I'm sorry, Sam. I've neglected you for a long time. I've neglected Abigail, as well. But I'm back and I'm not going anywhere. I've been stuck in a bad place. All I can say is I won't do it again."

Sam's jaw clenched. He glanced at Abby. There was a dullness in his normally clear eyes that ate at Jack. It killed him that he'd been the one to put that look there.

"Good, I'm glad," Sam said. "You need to be there for Abby. You brought her into this lifestyle and then stopped taking care of her. It wasn't fair."

Abigail sat silent on the big chaise that dominated the richly decorated room. Her hazel eyes looked worried as they flitted from man to man. Damn it, he'd created this chaos and it was up to him to fix it.

"I haven't been sleeping well, Sam." He owed them an explanation. "I keep seeing that woman try to kill Abby over and over again. Every time I shut my eyes, I see it. I can hear the crack of the pistol."

"Damn, Jack," Sam breathed. "I didn't know. I knew you weren't sleeping well, but I didn't know it was that bad."

"I didn't tell you. I didn't tell either one of you. It was easier to pull away from you than to admit I felt lost. This evening was the first time in six months I've felt like myself."

"I knew something was wrong when you stopped spanking me," Abigail said with a reassuring smile.

He returned it. "Spanking you is the best part of my day, darlin'. I won't let it go again. I thought I was too pushy. I worried I would push you right out of my life."

"You can't do that," she replied before turning to Sam. "And I can't let you go, either."

Sam shook his head. Weariness drew his mouth down, made his eyes dull. It hurt Jack's heart to see him that way. "I'm glad that you and Jack are all right now, but you have to see that I can't stay, Abigail. You know me. You know what I want, and I can't fool myself anymore. I'll be fine. I'm going to stay here. Julian will give me a place to live for a while."

Blood started to pound through Jack's system again. His vision started to bleed a slight shade of red. Instinct. Sam was fucking his. He was not going to ignore his instinct ever again. "If you think for one minute I'm going to let Julian get his hands on you after all these years, you're insane, Sam."

Sam's eyes were suddenly latched on him again. "What are you talking about?"

Jack let his jealousy out. It felt good. It felt like something had been dammed up for a long time and only now was allowed to flow naturally. "I am talking about Julian wanting you, Sam. I am talking about Julian trying to take you away from me. Why do you think I left this place?"

Sam's blue eyes were round. "You knew about that?"

"Of course I knew. I'm not an idiot." Jack moved closer. He

wondered if Sam even realized he was inching in, ready to pounce. It was a move he'd perfected on Abigail, but it was time to bring his other sub into the fold. Jack felt his cock harden. He took a deep breath and let the arousal flow over him. He turned and looked at Abigail, who was watching with deep concern. He winked at her. He turned back to Sam. "Did you think I'd let you fuck Julian, Sam?"

Sam was dumbstruck for a moment. "I guess not. I guess it would make you think less of me."

Jack rolled his eyes and prayed for patience. "When, in all of our years together, did I give you that idea?"

Sam was silent.

"Sam, you know I've slept with men before, right?"

"What?"

Jack chuckled. "Sam, I've fucked just about everything I could at some point or another. Even when we were here at The Club, I had nights with both men and women that I didn't talk to you about. I've had a lot of sex, but I've only loved two people in my life." He was standing in Sam's space. It was easy to reach out and draw him in. He didn't fight. "I've loved Abigail, and, Samuel, I've loved you. I prefer women, but I can certainly enjoy a man. I am your Dom, Sam Fleetwood. I have been since we were fifteen years old, long before either of us even understood what the word meant. It's past time for me to ask the question a Dom always asks his sub. What do you need from me?"

Jack shoved his fingers into Sam's thick gold hair. It was dense but soft. His skin was tan from working in the sun. Sam shivered the instant he touched him. It wasn't with distaste. He could feel the desire pouring off his friend. All that jealousy disappeared. Sam was his. He merely had to take him. He chuckled lightly and discovered he was really looking forward to the next few minutes. It felt good and right to be this close. He brought his lips against Sam's ear. "I asked you a question, Sam. I expect an answer. Don't be a pussy. Ask for what you want."

Sam's jaw clenched, He let out a deep breath and stared Jack straight in the eyes. "I want you."

Jack smiled, a deliciously decadent desire flowing through him. He let his eyes go slightly hard. "Knees, Sam."

Sam fell to his knees, not gracefully the way Abigail did, but with a small crash. It was something they would work on. He gently twisted his hands in Sam's hair, pulling his face up. "Who do you belong to, Sam?"

"You, Jack." He breathed the words like a benediction. "I belong to you and Abigail."

"That's right." He stared down into Sam's clear blue eyes and saw relief in them. He cocked an eyebrow, waiting.

"What?" Sam asked, obviously confused.

Jack looked to Abigail, whose eyes were hot as she watched the scene playing out before her. He hadn't worried about Abby being jealous. Now he could see she had been pushing for this. He shook his head. She really did try to top from the bottom. He mentally added it to her future spankings. "Abigail, you're going to have to instruct Sam. Please join us."

She was off the couch in an instant. He pointedly studied her from head to toe then frowned. Sam wasn't the only one who needed some instruction.

"Sorry." She was breathless as she hurried to get out of her clothes. She knew the rules. It was time Sam learned. Jack wasn't a full-time Dom and never would be, but in an intimate situation, there would be no question that he was in control. When Abigail was naked, all he had to do was lower his right hand and she dropped to her knees beside Sam. He placed a hand on her head to show he was grateful for the submission. Having a hand on both of them gave him a deep feeling of satisfaction.

"Abigail, could you explain to our lover why I requested he get on his knees in front of me?"

Abby's lips curled up, reminding him of a naughty kitten. "He wants a blow job, Sam."

Sam turned quickly to her, his mouth open in a good approximation of what he wanted. "Really?"

She nodded. "I'm happy about it, too. You're completely orally fixated, Sam. It gives you something else to suck on. My nipples get chafed."

Jack snapped his fingers. If he let them, they would seriously discuss Abigail's nipple chafing while his dick languished in anticipatory hell. "Focus."

"He wants you to undress him," Abby explained. "Jack doesn't undress himself. Be careful though. His cock is huge, and it's incredibly hard right now. He'll spank your ass if you get it caught in the zipper."

Sam nodded and stared at the erection for a moment before his hands went to the button on Jack's slacks. Jack nodded to Abigail, who had been waiting for the command. At least one of his subs was well trained. She was up, pulling the jacket of his suit off and working on his tie and dress shirt while Sam was still stuck on the zipper. She quickly folded the clothes and was back in her place when Sam managed to get Jack's cock free.

He sighed as it sprang out of its cage. Sam stared at the monster with undisguised fascination. There would be time for him to look later. An unfamiliar impatience was on him. Now that they were here, he realized how long he'd been waiting. He wanted to feel Sam's mouth. He stroked his hard cock and lined it up with Sam's lips. "Open."

Sam's mouth came open, and Jack firmly took hold of his hair. He planted his feet and eased his dick into Sam's mouth. If he worried that he'd have to direct Sam's every move, that anxiety was immediately shoved away. Sam's mouth closed over Jack's cock and his tongue ran over it, licking him from base to head and back again.

Jack had to work to stay on his feet. Sam's mouth felt completely different from Abigail's. Her tongue was small and he struggled to force his dick into her small mouth. There was no such trouble with Sam. Sam swallowed him down easily. His lips closed over Jack's erection and he sucked in long passes. His head worked up and down. Jack found himself fucking hard into Sam's mouth, trying to find that soft place at the back of his throat. Sam might not have given a blow job before, but he was a fucking natural. Jack felt himself rushing toward orgasm.

"Stop." Jack pulled out of Sam's mouth. He looked down at the man he'd been with since they were both teens. It felt good and right to be with him this way. He wanted this first time to last. "Your mouth is like a furnace, Sam. I don't want to come, yet. Abigail?"

He turned slightly and his wife's tongue ran across his dick. He hissed between clenched teeth. If Sam was a Hoover, Abigail was a butterfly running across his cock. He loved the differences between them.

They were his. They were finally both his.

"Lick my balls," he demanded. "Play for a minute, then I'm going to shoot everything I have straight down Sam's throat."

She ran her small hand around his balls exactly the way he liked it. She gently cupped them, rolling the sac up as she sucked the fluid weeping from the slit of his cock. After a moment, she bent down and licked the line separating his balls. She sucked one and then the other into her mouth. His balls drew up, ready to shoot off. She felt so good.

Jack pulled her off gently. She sat back as he turned to Sam. "Suck my cock, Sam." He tangled his fingers in Sam's hair as he fed him his cock. Sam's tongue immediately started rolling over him, and he knew he wouldn't last long. "Relax. I'm going to fuck your mouth. Just concentrate on breathing and following my directions."

Sam relaxed slightly. His tongue still teased the underside of Jack's cock, but he gave up control of the movement. Jack took over. He gave in to his instincts. Sam could take a hell of a lot more than Abigail could. He could be a little brutal, and it would merely get Sam hot. Jack ruthlessly fucked his partner's mouth, hitting the back of Sam's throat and pressing down before pulling back almost to his lips. Those lips sucked, desperately trying to keep him in. Jack could have explained he wasn't going anywhere, but he was concentrating on the way his balls hit Sam's chin when he shoved his way in.

"I'm going to come," he said, the words harsh to his own ears. His eyes found Abigail's hot, hazel ones. He was certain her pussy was dripping by now. "Tell him what I want."

He wanted to hear her sweet feminine voice tell their lover exactly what he required.

She moved close to Sam, putting her hands on him. "He wants you to suck him dry. Oh, baby, he tastes so good. Swallow him down. Don't miss a drop."

Her hands ran up Sam's sides, and her tongue traced Sam's ear.

Jack allowed it because Sam didn't miss a beat. His mouth sucked hard at his cock, daring him to come. Jack's balls drew up painfully. He groaned as he hit the back of Sam's throat. Sam swallowed, and Jack felt himself shooting off jets of steaming cum. Sam worked furiously, milking him for every drop.

"Lick it all off." Abigail was whispering in Sam's ear. Jack knew she was going to start rubbing herself soon. She wouldn't be able to help it. "Let me help," she practically begged, and then Jack was treated to two tongues running along his softening cock.

He watched the lovely sight of his gorgeous subs licking him clean. Their tongues played along his dick, running against each other lovingly. He let his hands find their heads and stroked them both. He chuckled. His dick was already starting to get hard again. Fucking both Sam and Abigail would be hard work.

"Enough," he ordered softly. Sam would be going out of his mind at this point. Jack could see his hands were shaking with need. His partner was incredibly impatient. It was a problem he intended to work on, but not tonight.

"Jack?" Sam was breathing heavily. His mouth was red and swollen. Jack leaned over and brushed his lips across Sam's, tasting himself there.

"Go on, Sam," he said softly.

Sam was on his feet, lifting Abigail in his arms before Jack could step out of his slacks. "Samuel, the bedroom please."

Sam cursed and turned. Jack knew what he'd been planning. Sam would have found the nearest flat surface and shoved his dick into Abigail the minute he got her legs spread. As Jack intended to join them, he preferred the bed. They disappeared into the bedroom. He heard Sam grunt and knew it hadn't taken him long to start fucking their wife. He probably still had his clothes on. Jack shook his head and stripped out of the rest of his clothes, folding them neatly. He walked into the big bedroom and was greeted with the sight he'd expected.

Sam had her on the edge of the king-sized bed with her fuck-me shoes wrapped around his neck. He stood driving his dick into her pussy with a single-minded strength. He'd gotten his shirt off, but his pants had simply been shoved down far enough to set his cock free. It was a lovely sight. Sam had a damn near perfect body, and Abigail was so feminine it made him sigh to think of her. He watched them for a moment. Sam was dragging in oxygen as he pounded into her. If the tense set of his muscles was any indication, Sam was getting close.

"Sam, you are not allowed to come yet," Jack said with his arms across his chest.

Sam turned his head to look at him, his handsome face wearing a startled expression. He didn't stop fucking Abby, but he did slow down. "What do you mean? I gotta come. I'm dying here."

"You should have thought about that before you pulled that shit tonight." He strode over to the dresser and opened the bottom drawer. It was where Julian kept the toys. It was his version of a mini-bar. He selected a tube of lubricant, though he noted a few other items they would need very soon.

"I don't think I'm going to be able to stop from coming, Jack," Sam said a little desperately.

Abigail didn't seem to be paying a bit of attention to them. She bucked her hips up, trying to force Sam to fuck her harder. Jack swatted her hand as she tried to toy with her clit.

"Mine, Abigail." He was amused at the way she pouted and gave him her sad-puppy eyes. It wasn't going to work. "Did you think I would let you get away with all the shit you've pulled? Do I even know all of it?"

"No." Sam pulled out of her.

She whimpered at the loss.

"Hands and knees, Abigail," Jack ordered. "Sam, underneath her. You take her pussy."

Sam sighed. "Thank god." He threw himself under her and was pulling her down onto his cock before Jack could get the lube open. Sam gritted his teeth as he thrust up into her. "You feel so fucking good, baby. I'm going to fill you up tonight."

"Not until I say so," Jack warned.

Abigail was riding Sam, grinding against his pelvis when Jack gently pushed her forward. He loved the feel of her soft skin against his hands. She was the reason they were all here. If she hadn't come around, he and Sam would have gone on the way they had before.

Loving Abigail had made being physical with Sam possible. Before her, both he and Sam had been too afraid to upset the status quo. Her complete open acceptance of everything she was had shown him the way. "Hold still, sweetheart."

She leaned forward onto Sam, presenting Jack with the lovely sight of her little ass waiting for him. He felt his cock lengthen as he spread the lube into the rosebud. He covered his cock in the slippery stuff and worked the lube into her ass with his thumb. He loved the feeling of her clenching around his thumb. It would be even tighter around his cock. He pulled his hand away and got his dick ready. Though he'd come only minutes before, he was ready to shoot off again. He spread her cheeks and pressed in.

"Oh, god." She moaned as she thrust back against him.

He sighed in pure pleasure, pushing forward past the tight ring and fully seating himself in her ass. He held himself there for a moment, enjoying the heat and the feel of Sam's cock against his, only a thin bit of their wife's body keeping them apart. Jack looked over her shoulder into the eyes of his partner. "Tomorrow night, you're in the middle, Sam."

Sam hissed, the sound a little like pain. "Please, Jack."

Jack pulled out and slowly tunneled in. "All right. Let's fuck our wife."

She groaned and pushed back against him. He held onto her hips, his hands brushing Sam's as they pulled her back and forth between them. He enjoyed the slow slide of Sam's cock against his as he thrust forward and Sam retreated. Abigail moaned between them. It couldn't last. There was too much. There was too much of everything riding the three of them tonight, too much lust, too much love. It would be over far too soon. He could feel Sam swelling, getting ready to go off. The intimacy of his cock brushing Sam's had him on the edge, too. He reached around and toyed with Abigail's clit. Her head fell back, and she went off with a scream.

"Fuck," Sam cursed as his face contorted. He shook with the force of his orgasm.

Jack held Abigail's hips and slammed into her. The lube made it easy to slide in, but it couldn't mask her tight heat, and Jack let go. He pressed deep and flooded her ass with his cum. It seemed to go on forever, pleasure flowing through him. She sighed and fell forward, slumping onto Sam's chest. She didn't protest as he pulled out and rolled to the side.

"Up, you two." Jack pulled the sheets and comforter back. Now she grumbled, but Sam had her under the covers wrapped in his arms. His partner was relaxed and peaceful as their wife snuggled against him. The tension that had been riding Sam for months seemed to have disappeared.

"Come to bed," Sam requested with a soft smile on his face. "We don't care if you wake us up because you're restless. We just want you with us."

Jack climbed in and slid his body alongside Abigail's. Her head fell back against his chest, the weight comforting. His hands cupped her soft breasts. No matter what happened between him and Sam sexually, she would always be the one they cuddled afterward. He let his head rest against hers. It was time for some honesty with his lovers. "It's more than restlessness. I have terrible dreams. I wake up in a panic sometimes. Hell, sometimes I don't have to be asleep. Sometimes it comes over me when I'm awake."

"PTSD." Abigail reached for his hand and gave it a squeeze.

"Is that something you're going to make me see a doctor for?" He'd been trying to avoid that. He knew Abby would make him do something.

Her eyes were sleepy but sympathetic. "Not a medical doctor. A shrink."

He groaned. "That's worse."

"Man up, cowboy, because you're going, and I don't care if you spank me and tell me I'm…what did that awful man say I was doing?"

"Topping from the bottom, baby," Sam supplied helpfully. "You do it all the time."

She shrugged. "Yeah, well I just like the sex part. And Jack is going to see someone about his post-traumatic stress disorder. I'll go with him."

"I don't see what the problem is." Sam snuggled closer to Abigail. The bed was huge, but they weren't taking up much of it. They were pressed together as though none of them wanted any space. Sam stared at him over her head. "I don't think about that day the crazy lady tried to shoot Abby but got you instead. It was an awful day. When it does cross my mind, I turn it around and think about something nice, like Abby's pussy. I take a deep breath and picture it in my mind. It's my happy place."

"Don't you ever tell a psychiatrist that, Sam," she said, laughing "She'll have you in sex addict rehab."

Sam shuddered at the thought. "I don't want to be rehabbed. I'm only addicted to having sex with you and Jack. And Abby needs the Dom thing for more than sex. You told her she shouldn't be so hard on herself when she thought she was fat and now she won't eat."

Abigail pushed at Sam. "Tattletale."

Jack flipped her over. That was one thing they would have out here and now. "If I ever hear you talking that way again, Abigail Barnes, you will be lashed to a whipping chair so fast it will make your head spin. I'm sorry I've been neglectful but I won't have you talk bad about something I love. And you will eat every bite I order for you tomorrow, is that understood?"

She nodded. Her eyes were soft and submissive. "Why is your brother here?"

He sighed inwardly. Her big doe eyes pulled him in every time. Leo was totally right about her, and he knew there wasn't a thing he would do about it. He was crazy about her exactly the way she was. And he owed them both an honest explanation. "He's here to blackmail me."

Sam was half asleep. "Seriously? What's he got on us?"

Jack stared at his lazy partner. He really should be more upset. "He's promising to out me as his father's love child, and then he intends to expose our ménage lifestyle."

"That's nice," Sam said.

But Abigail sat straight up in bed. Her mouth was a perfect *O*. Jack felt his whole soul sink. She'd had to deal with a lot of contempt in her lifetime. He hated the fact that he might be the reason for more.

"Baby, I'm so sorry." He would take care of this. He would make sure she wasn't hurt.

"I'm going to be on television." She nodded and her smile lit up the room. "I'm going to have to find something to wear."

"What?"

Sam snorted, but his eyes stayed closed. "Neither one of us cares, Jack. Let him tell the world. We don't give a shit."

Abigail slapped him playfully. "I do. I'm totally going to be on all the talk shows as the woman in the middle of two cattlemen. Do you have any idea how big this story could be? Ménage is very hot right now. Everyone will want to interview me."

Jack shook his head and reluctantly rolled out of bed. He wanted to stay with them, cuddle, and sleep. "Now I can't let him tell our story because I don't want to lose our wife to the talk show circuit." He leaned over and kissed her shoulder. "I'll come back to bed, but I have something to do."

She frowned at him. "It better have something to do with practicing, Jackson Barnes. You are not touching me with that whip until you're comfortable with it again."

He grinned. "I promise to practice, darlin'. You never know, you might like it. We might end up coming back here because you like coming in public. God, Sam, she was so freaking wet."

Sam winked up at him. "She's a pervert. That's why we married her."

Jack stared down at them, completely heedless of his own nudity. The sight of them cuddled up in bed together warmed him. He wanted nothing more than to sleep close to them, but he needed to get some practice in. He had no intention of hurting either one of them. A thought suddenly leapt to mind. He needed to do some other prep work, too. He thought Abigail might like to help him on that piece of work.

"Sam—" Jack made his voice deep. Sam immediately responded. His eyes opened and he sat up, giving Jack his full attention. "You understand what's going to happen tomorrow night?"

He nodded. "I've seen you work with a whip before. I'm not worried."

"I was talking about the fact that I intend to fuck you tomorrow night."

Sam's face flushed, and Jack was pretty sure he'd just gone

hard again. He concealed a smile. Getting Sam hot was as fun as watching Abigail writhe. Sam took a deep breath. "Okay."

"You need to be ready."

Sam's slow smile did something to his insides. Maybe Sam wasn't the only one getting hot. "I'm ready."

Jack shook his head. "No, you're not. You know I don't ever take a lover anally without careful preparation."

Abigail was the first to realize what he was saying. Her lovely face went blank, and then an expression that could only be described as great joy swept over her. She clapped her hands. "Do you have any idea how long I've waited for this day? Can I pick it out? I think I should be the one to do it."

Sam's face was a mask of horror. "Jack, you can't be serious. Come on, I can take it. I don't need to walk around for hours with a plug up my ass."

He shook his head as he walked out the door. He needed to get dressed. "You will. I won't treat you any differently than I treated our wife. I love you, Sam. I won't have you hurt. Abigail, you're in charge of that. I've got to go practice."

Jack got dressed, laughing as his lovers argued over whether Sam's plug would be pink.

Chapter Eleven

Lucas Cameron looked out over the bar area and wondered where the hell he'd gone so wrong. Maybe that Taggart guy hadn't been such an asshole. Maybe he should have turned the whole thing into a family reunion, although he kind of thought Jack Barnes still wouldn't have been happy to see him.

All around him people in very little clothing partied on, but he couldn't work up the will to care. He found a quiet corner with a couple of seats and a large table. He slumped down into one of the overstuffed chairs and sighed.

He'd gone wrong by being born.

He'd never been able to do anything right, certainly not in the eyes of his father. By the time he was in kindergarten, he'd been compared to his smarter siblings and disregarded as a nuisance. Over the course of his twenty-three years, he'd managed to get himself kicked out of ten boarding schools and three colleges. Each time his father had sent one of his lackeys to make sure he made it to the next school on the list. He'd simply pack up and move without ever going home. It had become a bit of a game to Lucas. Could he come up with something so awful his father would have to bring him back to DC to handle it?

It wasn't until he'd threatened to out his father's love child that Senator Allen Cameron had given him a personal call. Lucas had become a little desperate. After finally making it through a complete four-year degree, he was burning through his trust fund at an alarming rate. He hadn't meant to. It just happened. He'd come into it at twenty-one. He'd thought ten million would last a lot longer than it had. Getting involved with the Hollywood crowd had gotten him a lot of publicity, but it had come at a cost. He was going to lose that amazing house in the Hollywood Hills if he didn't come up with some money and soon.

He'd really thought Jack Barnes would cave. From everything he knew, Barnes was a private man. He'd blackmailed their father, but the money he'd made after that was his own. Barnes was filthy rich. He had money to spare. Why would he want to out himself as a complete pervert?

And there was no doubt that his big brother was a perv. He'd spanked his wife and then finger fucked her in public. What kind of a man did that? Lucas was almost sure that the hot, blond guy who'd been kneeling was doing big brother, too. Those two were amazing. The redhead was curvy and soft. Lucas liked her tits and the creamy glow of her skin. The guy was sex on a stick.

He was terribly jealous of Jackson Barnes. He should hate the fucker after that extra scene he'd played out. His throat still hurt from the way Barnes had lifted him up like he'd weighed nothing at all.

And yet, he would like to sit down and talk to him. The big cowboy didn't seem to struggle with the fact that he liked both men and women. Lucas had been struggling with it his whole life. He'd get in a relationship with a female, and after a while he'd need a man. It was wrong to want both, his father had told him. He'd slapped the shit out of him the first time Lucas had been caught in bed with the gardener's son. It had been the last time he got to come home for the summer. Lucas had been seventeen, and he could still remember the way that felt.

He shook his head and groaned. His hair was in his eyes again. He shoved it back. Why was he such an idiot? He did look like a douchebag. He needed to be honest with himself. Why had he come here? He'd come because he wanted to meet his brother. He'd come because he wanted to see if one person in his family line might find anything to like in him. How had he gone about it? He'd attempted to blackmail the man.

He thought of how satisfied his brother had seemed when he'd walked through the bar thirty minutes before. He'd been dressed in the same slacks and shirt from earlier, but he'd ditched the tie and jacket. The shirt was slightly wrinkled, likely because it had hit the floor at some point in time. Jack had looked more relaxed and happier than he had before, as though something had fallen blissfully into place. Of course, he'd paid no attention to Lucas, who watched him walk into the other part of the club.

Now Lucas had found someone who he might have been able to talk to, but instead of talking, Barnes threatened him with horrible murder. Barnes would do it, too. How could he tell the man he never would have gone through with his blackmail threats? Did he admit how pathetic he was in his quest for any sort of father figure?

"Hello," a soft voice said.

He glanced up into brown eyes. The young man was slender, but there was a pleasing strength in his frame. "Hi."

The young man was dressed in leather pants. There was a small leather collar around his throat. Lucas wasn't sure what that meant, though he'd heard Julian talking about it with his brother. His brother wasn't allowed to bring his subs back in without collars. Lucas had touched his throat and wondered what it would feel like to wear one.

"I'm Jeremy." The young man with dark hair and sultry eyes sank down across from Lucas, gracefully placing two drinks on the table. He slid one across to rest in front of Lucas. "Rum and coke. It's my favorite. You looked like you could use it."

He picked up the glass. He wasn't going to mention to the man that he rarely touched the stuff, despite what the tabloids said. He had a reputation to uphold. He'd done a lot to cultivate and maintain his reputation as a pure hedonist. He took a sip. It wasn't bad. It was way better than the crap his brother drank.

Lucas smiled at the hot guy sitting across from him. Maybe the night wasn't a total loss. It would be nice to sleep with someone. He hated to sleep alone. He didn't like to think about all the stuff he'd done just so he could feel warm skin next to his. Drinking with a guy was an easy thing to do if it meant he spent the night in someone's arms.

Jeremy smiled as Lucas took a deep drink. That was a sexy smile. Yes, not a total loss at all.

* * * *

Jack flicked his wrist and the whip cracked, the sound splitting the air around him. Suddenly everyone in the dungeon was watching the man with the four-foot whip. The balloon he'd been aiming at popped, leaving the rest clustered around it completely untouched.

"You always were a master with that thing," Julian said approvingly.

He stared back at his mentor and shook his head. He reset the whip on the ground behind him and prepared for an overhand throw. There was no need to worry about the speed of his throw. He concentrated on making sure his form was flawless. Everything flowed perfectly when the form was right. "I didn't intend to use it again."

Julian shrugged. "Talk to your naughty subs. You could refuse. You haven't been back to The Club in a long while. You haven't been down here in the dungeon in years."

"I visit. Sam and I spend time here." Jack turned to his target practice. The rhythm was coming back to him. He'd done this a thousand times. It was an easy rhythm to fall into. He let his arm flow, the whip an extension of his body. There was a comfort to letting his instincts lead him, but then hadn't that been the theme of the whole night?

"You went to the bar to pick up a female," Julian pointed out. "You rarely went into the playroom, and you never came down to the dungeon after you left my employ. I wondered why that was."

He turned to his mentor. A mellow happiness flowed through his system. He was even looking forward to tomorrow. He had plans for his lovers. They were going to understand the limits of his indulgence tomorrow morning. It brought a curl to his lips and honesty to his mouth. "I was afraid I would lose Sam. He's a sub and has a little streak of masochism in him."

"A little?"

He couldn't lie to Julian. Julian had seen the same things in

Sam that Jack had. "Fine, a lot of masochism in him. I wasn't ready to be responsible for that. I was afraid he would find someone else. It was selfish, but it's the truth."

"And now?"

"I'll take care of Sam, Julian." He needed to ensure that his mentor truly understood. Julian truly cared about Sam. "You don't have to worry about him anymore. He'll get what he needs."

Julian's dark eyes were a bit sad as he crossed his arms. Sally sat quietly at his feet. Julian's hand came out and gently tangled in her hair. "I'm glad for him. I'm glad for you as well, Jackson. You'll be happier this way. Is your wife fine with the new arrangement?"

Jack snorted and cracked the whip again. Another pop cracked through the dungeon. "My wife has been pushing me and Sam to get it on since the first night she spent in our playroom. I tanned her hide and as part of her aftercare, I gave her one request."

"Yes, I like to do that as well," Julian conceded. "What was Abigail's request?"

"She wanted me to kiss Sam."

A brilliant smile broke over Julian's face. It was a rare sight. "I like your Abigail. She isn't a very good sub, but she seems like a perfect wife for the two of you."

He felt a funny twitch in his heart. "She is. She's everything I ever wanted. She's smart and kind and ridiculously funny." Jack took a deep breath. "You know, Julian, you've given me a lot of advice over the years. Do you mind if I give you a piece?"

Julian paused and took a deep breath before coming to his decision. "I would love to hear it."

"Don't become such a slave to your own rules that you let something special pass you by. You have some hard and fast rules that cut you off from people."

"Rules are there to protect us. You should know that."

"Rules protect us, but when we no longer need them, rules are made to be broken." He switched to a six-footer. He wasn't going to use that on Abby or Sam, but he was curious. He used to be accurate with it.

Julian took a cautious step back, pulling Sally with him. "Did you break a rule tonight, Jackson?"

He aimed for the balloon on the far left. He decided to try a reverse snap. The whip snapped over his head and cracked. His shot went wild. Nope. He wouldn't be touching his lovers with that one. He put the six-footer down and turned to Julian. "I did. It was a rule we didn't need any more. I got the best blow job of my life from breaking that rule."

Julian made a small motion with his hand. Sally got to her feet. He nodded at her and she began to take off her top, then her skirt. "Go on, dear. He needs a warmer target."

Jack started to protest but then realized he really did. It was selfish, but he'd rather practice on Sally than Abby or Sam. He looked at the sub. "Are you all right with this?"

She smiled brilliantly. "Oh, yes. I'm a bit of a pain slut. I make no apologies for it. Some people like puppies and kittens. I like spankings and bondage. Do your worst. Master Julian will take care of me after."

"I will, pet," Julian promised. "It's all right. She's under my care. Have you ever known me to place a slave in danger?"

No, Julian took excellent care of the people who gave him their trust. He might not keep them for long, but he looked after them. Sally walked to the St. Andrew's Cross and took her position. Julian quickly had her bound. She glanced back at Jack.

"Your wife is a good kisser." Sally turned her head, staring back at him with a grin on her face. "She tastes sweet. Does she taste sweet all over?"

Jack groaned at the sudden vision of his wife and Sally tongue kissing. He couldn't help it. He was male, and two women kissing did it for him. He would never allow Sally into their bed, and he would call for punishment if she touched his wife again. He was possessive, but the image still lingered. "I wouldn't try to find out, subbie. She's mine and I won't give anyone permission to touch her."

"Cheeky sub," Julian barked. Sally smiled at him. "Blame me. I told her to be accommodating when it came to the three of you. Right now she's trying to get you upset so you'll be a bit rougher on her. Don't fall for it. That one is a bit manipulative, too. Rather like your wife."

141

"They know who's really in charge," Jack murmured.

Sally was in place, and there was a crowd eagerly watching. He made sure no one was in his range and then cracked the whip. Sally didn't even move when a delicate line of red appeared across her back. He was satisfied it wouldn't scar or bleed. He saw Sally relax and knew she would soon be in that place where submissives went. They called it subspace, and they welcomed the pain when they were in that place.

Jack quickly laid three more lashes across her back, buttocks, and thighs. She shuddered, but it was a pleasurable thing.

"Tell me something, Jackson." Julian watched the scene. His shoulders were relaxed and his stance a bit lazy. Sally was getting something she needed and that satisfied Julian. "Do you remember a very long time ago when I asked you how such a possessive man could stand to share his toys with someone like Samuel?"

He cracked the whip again, forming a pretty pattern across the sub's skin. "Yes, I do. I remember I told you it was all right to share with Sam. He was my friend."

"You were lying to yourself. Do you have a different answer for me today?"

Sally sighed as the whip cracked over her left thigh.

"Yes, Julian," Jack admitted.

"Why do you share with Samuel?"

He turned to his mentor. "I don't. I don't share with anyone. They're both mine."

"Very good. It's important to understand and accept our own natures. I believe I'll take my sub up to our rooms. She'll need someone to take care of her now." Julian strode to the stage, released Sally's bonds, and scooped up his slightly high sub. She had a beatific expression on her pretty face. Her arms floated up around Julian's neck. "Thank the nice man, Sally."

Sally smiled at Jack. "Thank you, nice man."

"Go to bed." Julian tossed the order over his shoulder. "You'll be fine tomorrow evening."

He laid the whip down and began to make his way up the stairs and out of the dungeon. Sam would flourish in here. After all, Sam was a pain slut, too. He'd have to teach Abigail how to handle Sam.

She'd never hold a whip, but she could paddle him from time to time. Jack remembered their playful fight from the other day. They had argued about whether they were a triangle or a straight line. Sam was right about that line, but he was wrong about the order. Abigail was definitely in the middle of that straight line.

He walked through the playroom thinking about climbing into bed. He had high hopes that he would sleep through the night. He wasn't even contemplating sleeping in the room he'd taken out. Sam was right. If he woke up in a cold sweat, Abigail and Sam would hold him until he came down. It was selfish to hold back his fears and problems from them. His troubles were theirs. They were a family.

As he made his way into the bar, he saw Matthew Slater pulling Lucas Cameron out of his chair. Lucas's eyes were slightly dazed. His body was slack and Slater seemed to be having trouble with him. A brown-haired sub in a collar pulled on the other side of Lucas, and together they managed to get the young man up.

"He's heavier than he looks," the sub said.

"We just need to get him out to the car I have waiting. I'll take him back to my hotel," Slater promised.

Shit. He stopped, watching the trio. He didn't like Slater period and didn't buy the idea of him helping Lucas out. There was something there beyond a desire to get his boss's son home safely. Jack sighed. Stupid karma. This was what Julian had been talking about. Not the fact that he'd blackmailed his father, and it was karma that Lucas blackmailed Jack. Julian, the sneaky bastard, was referring to how he had mentored Jack at a time when he was lost. Jack had never met a person more lost than Lucas Cameron.

His brother.

"How much did that boy drink?" Jack heard himself ask.

Slater almost lost his footing when he started at the sound of Jack's voice. The sub immediately averted his eyes. Slater stumbled, and Lucas slumped back down into his chair.

"He's a terrible drunk." Slater struggled to keep Lucas upright. "I was going to get him back to my hotel where I can look after him."

Slater didn't seem like the paternal type. Lucas likely wouldn't get any sympathy from the campaign manager. Maybe he didn't deserve any, but then there were times when Jack hadn't deserved what he had been blessed with.

Perhaps it was time to take his brother in hand.

He walked over to Lucas and looked down. His brother's eyes were glassy, but there seemed to be a plea there. Jack reached down and hauled Lucas up and over his shoulder without breaking a sweat. The boy needed to put some muscle on. He didn't weigh a thing. "Don't worry about him. I've got an extra room. He can sleep it off there. I'd like to have a talk with him in the morning anyway."

"Wait!" Slater practically shouted. He pulled at Lucas's shirt as though trying to force Jack to put him down. Jack took a step back, placing a small but needed distance between them. "I don't think he should be alone with you. I'm standing in for his father, Mr. Barnes. I doubt his father would want some stranger taking off with his son."

He snorted at the thought that his father would act like a father. "Face facts, Slater. Dear old Dad wouldn't give a shit. And I'm not a stranger. I'm his brother. He's going to know what that means in the morning. Buck up, man. Once he realizes what I have in store for him, he might hightail it back to DC with you. Good night."

He started toward the elevators, ignoring the further protests of Matthew Slater. He strode into the elevator and pushed the button to take him to the seventeenth floor. Lucas pounded slightly on his back.

"Go to sleep, Lucas," he commanded. "You'll be fine in the morning."

His brother grunted. "Thank you," he slurred.

Jack sighed. He wondered if his brother would be thanking him in the morning.

Chapter Twelve

Lucas came out of his daze to the sound of two people talking. It was all hazy at first, but they seemed to be arguing about something. The whole world seemed thick and heavy, but their voices were light and filled with warmth.

"What's wrong, Sam?" the feminine voice asked. "You seem to be struggling with something."

Lucas felt the bed shift as though someone was wiggling.

"I don't know what you're talking about, Abigail." Sam's voice was deep. "I love it. It's very comfortable."

"Is it? I'm glad to hear that." There was a wealth of amused satisfaction in the female's voice.

"It's the best day of my life," Sam said with a bite in his tone. "I don't know why you complained about it all this time. You must be a wimp."

Abby giggled. "Or maybe I'm just better at insertion than you are."

Sam snorted. Lucas tried to open his eyes. If there was something being inserted somewhere between those two, he wanted to see it.

"I'm a master at insertion, baby. Please tell me one thing. Why pink?"

Her laughter seemed slightly maniacal to Lucas. "You love pink. Turnabout is fair play. Remember all those times you told me how cute I looked with a little pink plug?"

"You could have picked something more masculine, baby," Sam complained.

"Next time I'll see if NASCAR has a line of licensed butt plugs."

Lucas forced his eyes open. He definitely wanted in on this conversation.

"Oh, look, he's awake." The lovely redhead peered down at him. Her hazel eyes were full of mirth, and she was wearing pajama bottoms and a tank top that showed off her breasts. Even with a massive hangover, Lucas could appreciate them. "Hello, Jack's brother."

"Hello, Jack's wife," he managed to mumble. Sam helped him sit up. The sheet slipped. Someone had stripped him down to his boxers. The room started to spin and he held his head. "What happened?"

"Apparently you can't hold your liquor." Sam pressed a cup of something warm into his hands. "Coffee. It should help."

Lucas brought it to his lips. He didn't really like coffee, but he didn't want to disappoint Sam. He was surprised to find it smooth and rich. It wasn't horribly sweet like the lattes he'd had before. He took another sip. Maybe it would clear his head.

"Where am I?" The last thing he remembered was talking to the guy named Jeremy. He'd been planning on spending the night with him. How had he ended up in the middle of his brother's ménage?

"Jack brought you up." Sam shifted as though he was slightly uncomfortable. "He said you passed out in the bar downstairs. You're in a room in the hotel over the club. We're in the suite next to you. Abby wanted to come in and stare at you while you slept."

She slapped at Sam, looking horrified. "I did not. I wanted to come in and take care of him. Besides, Jack won't let us leave until he comes back from whatever it is he's doing. Now, I ordered breakfast. I hope you like bacon and eggs."

He nodded. He did like them. He hadn't had them in months since he'd been playing the vegan for his Hollywood friends. His stomach rumbled. The night before was a blank space after he'd started talking to Jeremy. How much had he had to drink?

Abby put a tray in front of him, and the heavenly aroma hit his nose. He was suddenly starving. He shook slightly as he held the fork.

"So, you're going to blackmail Jack?" Sam asked.

Just like that, his appetite took a nosedive. He stared at the two people sitting on his bed. His eyes slid down, unable to meet the faces of the people he'd inadvertently threatened. They would have been hurt, too. Now that he thought about it, he'd threatened them every bit as much as he had Jack. "Sorry about that. You're safe. I'm not going to say anything."

"Really?" Abby sounded upset. Lucas looked at the redhead. She was pouting slightly. It was sexy on her. "That's disappointing, Lucas."

"You want me to blackmail Jack?"

"No." Sam rolled his blue eyes. "She thinks if you sell our story to the tabloids, she'll get to be on all kinds of talk shows. She wants to be on *Ellen*."

"Don't forget the *Today Show*," Abby added.

Lucas shook his head. "Aren't you worried about the public finding out?"

Abby winked Sam's way before answering. "Am I worried that the public will find out that, at the age of thirty-seven, I managed to get not one, but two superhot multimillionaire cowboys to marry me?"

Lucas couldn't help the laugh that shot out of him. Put like that, it didn't seem so bad. He felt the need to point out some facts to her, however. Someone had to be realistic. Lucas was surprised it was him. He wasn't known for his practicality. Something about Abby Barnes brought out his protective side. His brother's wife was a sweetheart. He used some of the intelligence he'd dug up on her. "What about your family? Your mother is still alive. Won't she be upset?"

Sam waved that question off. "She lives in our guest house. She knows some weird shit goes on and she's fine with it. We love her daughter."

"Often," Abby agreed. "And usually with toys involved. Besides, I got kicked out of my hometown at the age of seventeen. I was pregnant and had a flaming affair with a boy from the other side of the tracks. She's used to me causing gossip. And don't think it will upset my baby girl, either. I have it on the highest authority that she's dating a musician. Her bohemian friends think it's cool she has two stepdads."

"Yeah, a musician," Sam said with a shake of his head. "We're thrilled about that. Is there a reason she hasn't brought him out to the ranch?"

Abby wrinkled her nose. "Well, I think she doesn't want her stepdads to scare him off. She seems crazy about him. His name is Aidan. Don't worry. She's bringing him to Sunday dinner in a few weeks. I'm sure Jack will threaten to horribly murder the boy if he so much as touches a hair on Lexi's head."

She shook her head at Lucas in a manner that made him think she knew that more than Lexi's head had likely been touched already.

She wasn't getting it. Lucas tried a different approach. "Okay. How about the business? Have you thought about how a scandal could affect Barnes-Fleetwood? Who wants to buy beef from pervert cowboys?"

Abby laughed long and loud. "They're organic cattle ranchers. Have you walked through a Whole Foods lately?"

"Well," Lucas said, defeated, "it's just as well I decided to not go through with it, then." There was a moment of silence as they regarded him expectantly. "I'm sorry. I really…I don't know. I'm just sorry. I'll be out of your way as soon as I can get a shower."

Sam exchanged glances with Abby before turning back to Lucas. "Where are you going to go?"

Lucas shrugged. That was the question he needed to answer. Where did you go when you didn't have a home? "Back to California, I guess."

He needed to sell everything he owned so he could pay off his debt. After that, he had no idea what he would do. He couldn't crawl back to his father.

"Are you going to do more crazy drugs and wild sex stuff?" Abby asked. "I loved that cover of you, by the way. It was the one where you were covered in cocaine and the headline read *Is he killing his father*? I thought that one was really funny."

Lucas felt himself flush. "It was baby powder. A friend of mine took it. I've never actually tried it. Cocaine, that is. I don't do drugs. I don't drink that much either. I'm kind of boring."

Her mouth turned down in a disappointed frown. "See, I knew those things were fake. It's like pro wrestling, except with famous people."

"Abigail, pro wrestling is real," Sam insisted, but Lucas didn't miss the twinkle in his eye. "And I don't think Jack is going to let you hightail it back to California."

"What do you mean?" Lucas sat up straight and wondered if his brother had decided to kill him anyway.

"He means I've decided to take you in hand, Lucas," Jack said, walking into the bedroom.

His brother was a huge presence in the room. He was tall and broad, and everything about him screamed authority, though strangely not in the way their father did. Lucas had always seen his father as a suffocating presence, even when he was ignoring him. Jack was the kind of man you knew would take care of things. Now his brother was rolling a luggage cart containing a strange cube of metal. It was about the size of an ottoman. He rolled it up to Sam.

"There you go, buddy." Jack was cheerful as he patted the cube.

"What?" Sam glanced down at the gift.

"Damn it, Jack Barnes," Abby cursed. "You have got to stop doing that."

Sam's face fell. "You cubed my motorcycle."

His hands went out to pat the cube. He stroked it sadly.

"Yep," Jack agreed. "The good news is now it's safe for our wife to sit on. And you've both got a cube." He shot Lucas a look. "I cubed Abigail's car about six months ago. I've found that crushing an unsafe vehicle into a tiny square makes it less offensive to me." He took his wife's hand. "Now that I've dealt with Sam, will you follow me, please? You've had a delivery I'd like to discuss with you, Abigail."

He started to pull his wife along, Abby hustling to keep up. "Now, Jack, let's talk about this."

Sam was grinning as he got up. He winced as he straightened his spine. "Come on, Lucas. This is going to be good."

149

He tossed Lucas a pair of jeans and sighed at his cube. He patted it fondly before he walked out.

Lucas pulled on the jeans and wished they were a little looser. He struggled to get the jeans on and then hurried to follow Sam into the suite next door. What the hell? There was a crazy amount of boxes in the living area, each one stamped with the Neiman Marcus label.

"How much, Abigail?" Jack was asking.

She chewed on her bottom lip. "I was upset, Jack. I guess I was trying to get your attention. I can take it all back. Well, everything except the stuff I already wore."

"Consider my attention completely focused on you, sweetheart. How much?"

Her face bunched up sweetly. "Twenty."

Lucas was pretty sure she wasn't talking about twenty dollars. His brother's face flushed, and Lucas prepared for a screaming session to start. He hoped Jack didn't get rough with her. Lucas would have to do something about that. She seemed like a sweet lady. Instead, Jack took a deep breath and let it out slowly.

"All right," he managed evenly. "I can handle it. You haven't exactly been extravagant since we got married. We have plenty of money. Let me make another rule. Purchases of over ten thousand dollars need to get cleared by me. I think that's reasonable."

Abby nodded eagerly. "Absolutely."

Jack's eyes narrowed. "I can let the money go, but there is one thing I won't stand for. You know the rules."

He picked up a handful of delicately colored fabric. Lucas stared at it for a moment before he realized it was a big mass of panties.

"Jack, what are you doing with my brand-new undies?" Abby asked the question, but it sounded to Lucas like she knew what was about to happen.

Sam snorted and elbowed Lucas. "He's going to do something crazy now."

Jack opened the door to the big balcony.

"Jackson Barnes, don't you dare!" Abby shouted.

Jack walked straight to the railing and opened his hands.

Designer panties rained down from seventeen floors up.

Abby stomped her bare foot. "Damn it, Jack! Those were La Perla."

"I don't give a damn whose they were," Jack replied with a smirk. "You're not allowed to wear underwear."

"They matched my new bras."

Jack shrugged. "Do you know what matches every bra you own? Your lovely, naked pussy. It better because that's all you get." He pulled a long box out of his pocket. "Maybe this will make up for the loss of your precious panties, darlin'."

Abby took the box, a stubborn expression on her face. She looked like she would reject anything he gave her. That look slid off as she opened the box. She gasped as she stared down at the diamond necklace. Even from his place, Lucas could tell it was stunning.

"Oh, Jack." There were tears in her eyes as she held it up. "Put it on."

Lucas felt so jealous as he watched his brother fasten the diamond choker around his wife's throat. Jack belonged somewhere. Jack had people who loved him enough to fight with him.

Abby touched the diamonds that marked her as Jack's. "I love it. It's the best collar ever. I promise to be fairly submissive when I wear it."

"Good to know," Jack said sarcastically as he leaned down and kissed his wife. It was a simple, sweet kiss that made Lucas wish he had someone to buy jewelry for.

"As for you," Jack started, turning to Sam.

Sam crossed his arms over his chest defensively. "I already got my dream bike made into a footrest, and the other thing. It's pink, Jack. She picked the pink one. Isn't that enough punishment?"

Jack laughed and kissed the blond man swiftly. It was just as sweet as the one he gave his wife. "No punishment, Sam. You need a collar. You'll lose anything I give you, so I've arranged for something else. There's a car waiting. You do everything they tell you to do."

Sam nodded, his face slightly flushed. "All right, Jack." Sam gave Abby a quick kiss. "I'll be back."

Sam walked out the door to wherever Jack was sending him. Sam didn't ask questions. He didn't argue. He simply did what Jack requested. The trust he placed in his lover was awesome. Lucas had never trusted anyone the way Sam trusted Jack.

Jack was watching him. "Don't look at me like that. I'm sending him to a tattoo parlor. Trust me, he'll be thrilled."

"He's wanted one forever," Abby said with a grin. "What's it of?"

"It's a very tasteful tattoo. Julian knows a skilled artist. She drew it up for me this morning. It has our initials wound together with barbed wire and a little rose for you," Jack explained. "I'm going to get one, too, though not on the back of my neck. I think my chest is the perfect place for it."

Abby went up on her toes. "I am so glad the boss is back."

"Love you, baby," Jack whispered before kissing her. He turned back to Lucas and eyed him suspiciously. "So, you think you can handle this? I have no intention of hiding the way I live my life, son. If the fact that I sleep with both Abigail and Sam is going to bother you, then maybe you should head home."

Lucas tried to follow the conversation. "I thought I didn't have a choice in that." He shoved the stupid hair out of his face again. He should never have let that hot celebutante talk him into this ridiculous haircut. "You were going to kill me if I didn't leave and promise to never open my mouth."

Jack's hand was around his wife's waist as he stared at Lucas. Lucas felt like squirming but managed to hold his ground. "I changed my mind, Lucas. I don't have much family. You're my brother, but you're also an asshole. I think we can change that."

"Really?" Lucas hated that the question came out as an expectant squeak.

Jack's face took a paternally amused air. "Yes, really. A friend recently pointed out to me that sometimes we get a chance to pay the universe back for the good things it brings us."

"It's karma." Abby cuddled close to Jack. "You're Jack's karma. Julian took him in when he was a young man, and now he's going to do the same for you."

It took everything Lucas had not to break down. He held

himself still for a moment. They could be playing with him. Sometimes people liked to do that.

"I know about your money trouble, Lucas," Jack was saying. "Here's the deal I'll make with you. I'll pay off your debt, and you come and live with us for a year. You'll work on the ranch. Think about this, son. This is hard work. This is physical labor. You'll live in the dorm I have for the unmarried ranch hands. There's only three of them, and I think you'll get along. You'll eat with us, though. You'll be my brother. You'll be part of our family. At the end of the year, you can stay on or I'll pay for whatever training you need to get a good job. I'd love it if you worked for me. I could use a lawyer or an MBA. It's your choice."

"Why?" Lucas heard himself ask. He fought hard not to cry. No one ever offered him anything like this before. No one offered him something in return for simply working hard and being himself.

"Because it looks like you could use the help," Jack stated plainly. "But, son, that hair is going to have to go."

"Thank god," Lucas breathed. "Can I do that today? This hair is awful. I hate hairspray and it's constantly in my eyes. And I promise to get some jeans that fit, and I won't ever wear guy-liner again. I get to work with cows, huh?"

"Yes, Lucas. You'll get to work with them and be kicked by them and probably step in more of their crap than you ever dreamed possible. It's not easy."

"I can do it." He felt himself get a little defensive. He heard his father's voice insisting Lucas couldn't be trusted with anything.

"I know." Jack's voice was strong and encouraging. "You can do anything you set your mind to, Lucas Cameron. Do you have anything you need to get before we leave tomorrow? Let me warn you, Willow Fork is a small town. There's no Best Buy out there."

Lucas shook his head. He didn't own anything he gave a damn about. He had that house in California, but it would be easy to sell it. The thought of a whole new life without the encumbrances of his old one sounded heavenly. He was ready to let it all go. "I'm ready whenever you are."

"You're going to love living on the ranch, Lucas," Abby promised him.

He wasn't so sure, but he was more than willing to give it a go. Not a go. He would make it work. He would give his brother a year of hard work and then decide what to really do with his life. Jack would help. Jack would give him advice, and he would probably lecture him on all sorts of things. Jack would ride his ass, and there would be times when Lucas would wish his brother would keep his nose out of his business. Lucas smiled. It sounded great. "I know I will."

Jack's green eyes narrowed. "What kind of car do you drive, son?"

"Whatever kind you tell me to, sir," Lucas replied quickly, remembering the little metal cube that still sported a visible Ducati symbol. He wasn't going to mention the two-seater roadster he kept in LA. He had a feeling it would be cubed and added to Jack's growing collection of offensive vehicles.

Jack nodded. "Good."

Abby sighed. "Well, at least you'll fit in."

Jack gave Lucas a look that told him he should probably do whatever Jack said next. "Go on and get ready. We're leaving in the morning. You should enjoy your last night in civilization. Don't drink too much."

"Okay," he promised as he opened the door.

"And Lucas," Jack called out. "Stay away from that Slater fellow. I don't like him."

"You got it, Jack." That was the easiest promise Lucas had ever made.

Chapter Thirteen

Abby looked up at her husband as the door closed behind Lucas. Jack was so big and handsome, and what he was doing for his brother was beyond kind. He was everything she could have wanted in a mate. "It's a good thing you're doing for Lucas."

Jack's green eyes gleamed in the early morning light. His eyes went straight to the diamonds at her throat. She could see the possessive satisfaction he took in the sight. "It might be the dumbest thing I've ever done. That boy is going to be a handful. The other hands will eat him alive if he shows up in that makeup he wore yesterday."

He was a bit behind the times. "It's called metrosexual. It's very trendy."

"Not in Willow Fork it isn't, and certainly not at the ranch." Jack was standing perfectly still, but Abby realized he had something on his mind. She thought she knew what it was. Her body heated up just thinking about it.

"I have a feeling we can get him looking a little more masculine," Abby allowed. "After all, he looks so much like you. Once we get his hair cut and put him in a pair of jeans and a T-shirt, he'll look the part."

"He looks like me?" Jack didn't sound so sure. He obviously didn't study himself the way she studied him. There was no doubt Lucas was a close relation.

"On the surface. He looks like a boyish version of you." She pointedly ogled her husband. "You're the man version, baby."

"I'm the Dom version, Abigail." His expression changed, and he seemed to grow even larger. He stood straighter. Abby instinctively dropped to her knees. "Very good," Jack praised her in deep, silky tones. "When you're wearing that collar and we're in private or downstairs in the club, you will behave properly. Is that understood?"

"Yes, Jack." She concentrated on keeping her breathing even. It was hard work since every cell in her body was humming in anticipation. It had been far too long since she'd been dominated by this man, and she'd missed it sorely.

She kept her head lowered submissively in an attempt to prove she could behave that way when it was necessary. She heard him move toward her. His boots came into view.

His hand tangled gently in her hair. "I am an indulgent man, my love. I get the feeling you're going to want to come back here to play from time to time. When we are in this club, you will remember at all times who your Master is. I don't use that term in our everyday life, but I will use it here. Do you understand?"

"Yes, Jack."

He nudged her head up to look him in the eyes. "I am never to find you in the club again without me. That rule is not negotiable." He didn't wait for a reply. It wasn't needed. She knew an inescapable dictate when it was handed to her. "Abby, we're alone and you're wearing my collar. What is wrong with this picture?"

As quickly as she could, she tossed off the tank top and pajama bottoms she was wearing. Yesterday she would have worried about sagging boobs and those five pounds that never seemed to come off. Today, all that mattered was obeying Jack. She sighed as she shimmied out of her cute boy-short panties. It would be the last time she would see them. She handed them to Jack, who shook his head as he held them.

"Such a naughty girl," he commented. "Give me your hands, Abigail, wrists together."

She held her hands out, pushing her wrists together as he asked. He quickly twisted the panties around and about her wrists until she was tightly bound by her own undies. He hauled her up. She was barely on her feet before Jack led her to the center of the room. She looked up and saw a hook extending from the ceiling. Julian's rooms came fully equipped for bondage play. Jack pulled it down, adjusting it to her height, and then hooked her wrists over it. She could still touch the ground but just barely. It kept her slightly off balance and completely at his mercy.

"That's nice," Jack commented as he walked around her bound body. His hands traced her waist and buttocks. "You look pretty like that. You're going to look like this tonight."

She opened her mouth to speak.

He gave her butt a squeeze. "No, darlin'. We're practicing. When we're in the dungeon, you don't speak unless I give you explicit permission. If you don't like the rules, then we can leave this afternoon. I really am all right with that."

The whole not-talking thing was going to be frustrating. Jack grinned as she struggled to stay silent. She would do it, though. She would do it because she'd embarrassed Jack. She'd made him look bad in a place he enjoyed. She would also do it because she was so curious about that dungeon she thought she would burst. After a moment, she calmed down and made sure her face was serene.

"Much better. If you have a problem being naked in the dungeon, then we'll leave. No? I didn't think so." He ran his hand down her spine, making her shiver with anticipation. "This is my plaything. I want to show it off."

He chuckled as he began to strip out of his clothes. She watched with avid eyes as his big, hard body was exposed. He folded every piece, and she forced herself to stay quiet. She wanted to tell him to hurry the hell up. She was getting wet merely watching him. He was broader than Sam, his shoulders and arms corded with heavy muscles. His big chest tapered into a lean waist. When he stood in front of her completely naked, she had to admit she loved the indention where his hips met his powerful legs. She loved to run her hands over the little valley where muscle flowed into muscle.

He was one gorgeous slab of cowboy.

"You do wonders for my ego, darlin'. You look like you could eat me up. What's this Sam told me about you not appreciating this incredible body?" He ran his large hands along the curve of her waist and up to her breasts. "Who does this body belong to?"

"You, Jack," she replied. His direct question gave her permission to speak.

"Why do I love this body?" She could feel the warmth of his mouth over her right nipple.

"Because it's beautiful." She sighed as he flicked his tongue over her turgid nipple. She knew the answer he wanted. When he played with her like this, she felt beautiful.

"Because it is so fuckable I can't help but shove my dick in it," he swore before sucking the tip of her breast into his mouth. He wrapped his arms around her waist, lifting her up slightly so he could suckle with ease. His tongue whirled around the nipple. She reveled in the warmth of his mouth. He pulled strongly at one and then the other breast, giving her the bare edge of his teeth. "If you didn't have some punishment coming this evening, I'd put you in clamps. I bought some clamps with pretty emeralds on them. I like dressing up my plaything."

Bondage Barbie. That was her.

He toyed with her nipples, pinching them lightly and making her moan. "I'll put the clamps on you, and then I'll shove a vibrator up that hot pussy of yours. I'll tie you up while Sam and I watch a football game. The vibe is on a remote, of course. We'll make you come so many times you'll forget what it was like not to. You'll beg me to let you go, but I'll keep it up. You better hope the game doesn't go into overtime, baby. That's what's waiting for you the next time you decide to insult something I love. Am I clear, Abigail?"

She nodded. "Yes, Jack."

It came out as a breathy moan because he was doing a damn fine job of torturing her now. His hand slid down her body and teased her clit. He rubbed in and around the desperate nub, but managed to avoid brushing across it. One stroke and she was pretty sure she'd come, but Jack knew how to make her crazy.

His green eyes were sleepy with desire as he started to gently push a single finger in and out of her pussy. It wasn't anywhere close to enough. It was just enough to tantalize, to make her want to scream for more.

"Was there something you wanted, my pretty sub?" Jack asked.

"Please make me come."

His eyebrow shot up.

"Jack," she quickly corrected. He didn't like Master or Sir. He wanted to hear his name on her lips. "Please make me come, Jack."

"Well, since you asked so sweetly." Jack sank to his knees.

He pulled her legs around his shoulders. She was completely at his mercy. The bonds overhead held her up, but all of her grounding came from the man she was wrapped around. Her feet dangled behind his back. His breath was warm on her pussy.

"Please, Jack," she begged, because he was taking his time.

There was a sharp slap to her ass. "I didn't ask you a question."

She closed her mouth. She had a bad feeling that if she fought him, he might stop what he was doing. She'd pushed him hard over the last twenty-four hours. She'd spent twenty-thousand dollars on clothes, shoes, and lingerie, a good portion of which was currently sitting on the streets of downtown Dallas. She decided not to argue with him.

"Good girl," he said after a moment of compliance.

He let his tongue slide through the juices flowing out of her pussy. She bit back a moan, not entirely sure how silent he wanted her. His hands caressed the spot he'd smacked, and he held her in place while his tongue plundered in and out. She let her head fall back as he fucked her with his tongue. The slow build started low in her pussy, radiating outward. She wanted so badly to push against him, to force him to flick at her clitoris. It was right there. She was right on the cusp of coming. Then his hand came forward, and his thumb swiped firmly across her pulsing clit. The orgasm bloomed outward, exploding through her. There was no holding back her scream as she fell over the precipice.

Before she could come down from the orgasm, Jack was lifting her up and off the hook. He did nothing to unbind her hands. He merely arranged her over the arm of the sofa.

"Spread your legs," he ordered. His voice was rough and gravelly. He was on the edge, and she was thrilled to be the one who put him there.

She complied, breathing heavily into the cushions of the sofa.

Her whole body was pulsing and languid. She felt like she was flowing rather than moving. Jack moved in behind her, spreading her legs further.

He held her as he thrust in. She buried her face in the pillows to mask her groan. He was so big from this angle. He felt so good filling her roughly with his cock. She heard him grunting as he pounded into her.

"Never again, Abigail," he swore as he shoved his way into her pussy. "I will never again find you in a place like that without me. You will never get on the back of a damn motorcycle, and you will wear your fucking wedding ring."

"Yes, Jack," she managed as the pleasure built again.

He'd positioned her so that every thrust of his cock brought her clit in contact with the side of the couch. It was almost too much. She couldn't control it. She cried out into the pillows as she felt her body explode with sensation.

"Oh, yeah, baby. Oh, fuck that's beautiful." He pulled at her hips. She felt him grind against her, giving her every ounce he had. He held himself tightly against her as though he was unwilling to give up the connection, but after a moment, he pulled his cock out. He hauled her up and into his arms and made his way back to the bedroom.

A laugh welled from deep inside her as he tossed her on the bed. He was back on top of her in an instant. This was what she needed. This was the man she'd missed so damn much. She got the feeling she wouldn't be sight-seeing today. She held her bound hands up questioningly.

Jack gently pushed her hands over her head and into the hook at the top of the headboard.

"I like you like this," he said, trailing a hand down her torso. "I might keep you like this today." He fingered the material that kept her hands bound for his pleasure. "And maybe I should relent a little on the underwear. They make awfully good bindings."

Her whole body softened as he covered her again, skin sliding over skin. She was in for a rough day and looked forward to the experience.

* * * *

Slater turned the volume on the television down and picked up his phone.

"He hasn't left the club." Jeremy's voice was hushed, as though he was afraid someone might be listening in.

At least he had that much. He sat down on the edge of the bed housekeeping had made up not an hour before as he considered what was happening in the hotel across town. "Have you seen him this morning?"

He wasn't exactly sure how the drugs he'd had Jeremy put in Lucas's drink last night worked. He was pretty sure they wouldn't kill him, but he could always hope. No one would question an overdose.

"I took room service up to the room he's staying in. I didn't see him, but I heard Barnes's submissives talking about him. They didn't seem terribly concerned. Apparently he was sleeping it off," Jeremy explained. His voice was so quiet. Slater had to listen intently.

He turned off the television in his room. He'd been watching C-Span, but this was far more important to Slater's future than anything Congress was doing.

He'd come across Jeremy Walker last night after watching the disgusting display Barnes had put on with his wife in the club. Slater had been shocked, but he couldn't turn away. He'd noticed Lucas's reaction. The pervert had been fascinated by the scene before him. Lucas had eyed the blond man first and then the female. He'd practically drooled over his brother's wife as she was displayed in that vulgar fashion. The look on Lucas's face had hardened Slater's resolve. Lucas was going to ruin everything. It was merely a matter of time. Cameron was running on family values. How could he do that with not one, but two perverted bisexual sons?

Barnes could be counted on to keep his mouth shut, but Lucas? No way. No how.

Jeremy Walker had stood out in the crowd. He'd been just as disgusted, though Slater believed it was for different reasons. Young Jeremy hadn't actually watched the cowboy spank his wife and put her on display. Slater noticed the slender man staring at Julian Lodge and the odd woman who sat at his feet. The blonde had clung to Lodge, and he'd shown her great affection. It hadn't gone over well with Jeremy. There was jealousy in his eyes. Slater had known immediately he could use the boy to his own purposes. Slater had worked long enough in politics to know a stooge when he saw one.

Jeremy had supplied the "roofie," as he called it. He'd explained that it would make Lucas very malleable. Lucas would be vulnerable under the influence of the drug. Slater might have misled Jeremy into thinking that he was of the same persuasion as he and Lucas. He might have inferred to Jeremy that he wanted Lucas sexually. It was distasteful but necessary. He'd slipped Jeremy enough money to play his part. He was supposed to get Lucas to drink the drugged rum and coke and then talk him up a bit. It had worked brilliantly. It hadn't taken long before Lucas was heavily under the influence of the drug. Jeremy agreed to get Lucas downstairs and into Slater's car. The young man had no idea Slater had been taking pictures with his cell phone. It clearly established Jeremy as the villain of the piece. When Lucas's body was found, it would go one of two ways. Either they would assume the troubled young man had simply come to the bad end he so richly deserved or they would find the drugs in his system. At that point, Slater would come forward with his photos. He would admit he had been worried about his boss's son and followed him. He'd tried to convince him not to go with the stranger, but Lucas never listened to sound advice.

Jeremy Walker was the perfect patsy. If only that fucker Barnes hadn't shown up.

In the back of his mind, he'd rather hoped Barnes had decided to follow through on his threat from the previous night. Apparently, he had no such luck.

"Do you have any idea what Barnes intends to do with Lucas?" Slater asked.

"A little, sir," Jeremy replied politely. Slater had found that Jeremy was polite, but the look in his eyes gave him away. "I overheard my Master speaking with Master Barnes earlier this morning. He's been busy. He said something about taking Lucas with him to the ranch he owns. My Master sounded pleased with this. I do not believe Master Barnes intends to harm his brother. I know that they are staying at The Club tonight. Master Barnes will publically punish his slaves. They deserve it."

Slater was glad they were speaking over the phone so he didn't have to hide his distaste. The way these people behaved disgusted him. It could never get out that the senator had a membership. It would ruin his wholesome image. Naturally Lucas knew about that now, too. "So I'll get another chance with Lucas?"

Jeremy sounded eager. "Oh, yes. I'll help you if you help me. I'll make sure it works this time. Master Barnes will be involved in his scene. No one will notice you slipping away with your treat."

Jeremy had turned out to be a young man of flexible morality. He didn't seem to think anything of drugging a potentially difficult lover. He did, however, want reciprocity. Slater had promised to dig up dirt on one Sally Hanover. He had no intention of wasting time doing it, but he had to string the young man along. Jeremy wanted Julian Lodge all to himself, it seemed.

"Yes," Slater promised in smooth tones. "I have a private investigator working on it even as we speak. If he can't come up with something, I'm sure we can make something up."

"Good. I hate that bitch. The sooner she's gone, the happier my Master will be with me."

Slater wasn't sure. The "master" seemed pretty pleased with the blonde the night before. It didn't matter. All that mattered was the accident Lucas was going to have this evening. After tonight, Slater could put this mess behind him and concentrate on the upcoming campaign.

A candidate in mourning was a sympathetic man. After he hung up with Jeremy, Slater began writing a powerful eulogy for one Lucas Cameron.

Chapter Fourteen

All around him, The Club's bar buzzed with excitement over the evening's entertainment, but Sam found himself strangely calm. No worries. No anxiety. There was simply a level of calm satisfaction like nothing he'd ever felt before.

He belonged here now. He belonged in a way he never had before because he had a Master. He had Jack.

"Does it hurt?" Lucas examined the elaborate tattoo that now covered the back of Sam's neck.

"Nah." He was lying. It had. It hurt like hell. He'd liked every minute of it, too. He was seriously considering another one. Of course, he'd have to convince Jack, but he thought putting the Barnes-Fleetwood brand on his right bicep was a cool idea.

Lucas carefully put the bandage back on and took the seat across from Sam. "It looks good."

Sam sat back in his seat in a particularly comfortable section of the bar. He couldn't remember a time when he felt so relaxed. Even knowing what was coming, he was quiet deep down. He wasn't worried or afraid. He was excited, but he could wait. Jack would take care of it.

He stared at Lucas. He looked like a completely different man. No one who had seen him here last night would even suspect it was the same sad-sack boy Jack had threatened to kill violently. His hair was short, and he had on jeans that fit and a plain black T-shirt. Getting that hair out of his face made him look more like Jack than before. It showed off his square jawline and made him look harder, sharper. He would never have Jack's authority. Lucas just wasn't that guy, but boy, he resembled his brother.

"New boots?" Sam asked.

Lucas held out his foot, admiring the snakeskin boots Jack had claimed were the most comfortable, durable boots he'd ever worn. "Yeah. Apparently Mr. Lodge has a bunch of people who do nothing but shop for the guests."

He smiled at the thought. What Julian had was a bunch of submissives willing to do anything to get the Master's attention. It was weird to think how close he'd come to being one of those slaves. He glanced around the bar. It was a richly decorated room, but it wasn't a home. Julian's penthouse was spectacular, but in Sam's mind it was more of a museum than a real home. A real home was the ranch house with its big fireplace where he cuddled up with Abby.

He would never admit it to Jack, but he'd thought about Julian's proposal. He'd thought about becoming his slave. It had seemed like a safe thing to be. Sam had followed his heart and he was glad he did. If he'd stayed with Julian, he would have been one of many, and Julian didn't share. He would have been Julian's plaything. He was Jack's partner and Abby's husband. It was a good place to be.

"Hey, does anyone know where I can find Julian Lodge?"

Sam looked up and two men were frowning down at him. The odd thing was they were both wearing street clothes. Even in the bar, fet wear was required. One had on slacks and a button down. He looked like he'd walked in from one of the offices that surrounded the building. The other one was a big-ass dude who looked like would he spit nails when he talked.

That big dude was a total Dom. No question in Sam's mind. But still, there were rules. "I haven't seen Master Julian, but you should know he requires fet wear in this part of the building. I'm sorry, Sir, but you'll have to change and so will your submissive."

The biggest smile cracked the Dom's face and damn, but when that man smiled, he lit up a room. Sam would bet he didn't smile often.

The sub frowned, holding his file folder like it was some kind of weapon. "Wait. What?"

The Dom held out a hand. "Name's Jacob Dean. This is my…" He bit back a laugh. "…Adam. Adam Miles. Our company works for Mr. Lodge. We're not here to play."

"And if we were we sure as hell wouldn't be playing…that way," the one named Adam said with a huff. "Seriously, what is with people? A man takes care with his appearance and he's suddenly the bottom? I'll have you know these slacks are very manly and I like them because I can fit any number of weapons in them and no one knows."

Sam stood up. "Weapons are not allowed in The Club."

"They are when you're security," Jake assured him. "We're with McKay-Taggart. We train your security team and we have a report the big boss is going to want to see. He marked it *urgent* and then Big Tag got on our asses and now we're here."

"And I'm not the sub. Not the sub." The one named Adam claimed. "We're partners and I'm the smart one."

Sam wasn't so sure about that, but who was he to argue? "I haven't seen Julian. Have you, Lucas?"

Lucas shook his head. "Nope."

Jake's brows rose over dark eyes. "Lucas Cameron? Wow. You are not what I expected."

"I told you Big Tag thinks everyone's a douchebag. You can't listen to the man. He said Lucas Cameron was a metro idiot and he's obviously just another dude who can't dress himself with any amount of style," Adam said with a shake of his head.

Lucas frowned. "I thought I looked good."

Jake gave him a thumbs-up. "Don't listen to Adam. He's my best friend but he's totally a metro douchebag. Big Tag's right about him. And nice boots. Those are my favorites."

Adam sighed, rolling his eyes like this was what he got twenty-four seven. "Call Lodge again. I need to get out of here. It reminds me of how super sad our club is."

Jake nodded Sam's way. "Nice to meet you. If you do see Mr. Lodge, please let him know we're waiting in the lobby with his intel."

Adam walked off grumbling, but Jake had a grin on his face. He put a hand on Adam's shoulder. "One day, buddy. One day, we'll have a club that's even cooler than this. You'll see."

Lucas watched as the two men walked away. "What do you think he meant by intel?"

He shrugged. "I don't know. Julian is always up to something."

"I think it's about me," Lucas said, his face flushed.

Sam leaned over. "Even if it is, it doesn't matter. If that's a report on you, Jack'll burn it. He won't care about your past. He'll care about the man you are from this moment forward."

Lucas took a deep breath and sat back, his eyes still on the door.

Jack strode into the bar, followed closely by Abby. Sam did not miss the fact that Jake and Adam held the door open and then as though the two men were one, both heads swung around and watched Abby as she walked by.

He didn't blame them. She was spectacular, but damn Jack was sexy, too.

He wore tight black jeans and a black Western-style shirt he hadn't bothered to button. It showed off his cut chest and that six-pack that always made Sam drool. It had been hell seeing that body for years and years and not being able to touch it. Even now he looked away for fear that his desire would be on display.

"Sam." Jack sat down next to him. Hell, he didn't simply sit. Jack occupied whatever space he happened to be in. "Are you ready for tonight? We start in thirty minutes. I'm going down to get set up. You two give me a couple of minutes and meet me there. Julian and Lucas will escort you to the dungeon."

"I'm ready." His dick got hard at the thought of Jack wielding a whip. The damn thing was so hard he had to shift in his seat to relieve the pressure. This was really happening. He'd seen it so many times before, but he'd never been the one to feel the lash in public.

Jack's arm went around his shoulder. It was a friendly gesture, but now there was intimacy in it as well. Sam relaxed against him. Abby was suddenly on the other side, her hand a welcome presence on his knee.

"Sam, I want to talk to you about something," Jack said quietly. "It's a decision I want us to make together. You know Julian has decreed thirty lashes as a punishment."

He knew what the punishment was, but now a thought struck him. "That's not for each of us. That's all together. That's fifteen each, but I can handle way more than Abby can."

"Sam," she began.

"Hush," Jack interrupted. "Sam knows exactly what I was thinking. He can handle more than you, darlin'. It's been a long time since I did anything like this. I practiced last night, and I'm confident it will be fine. If I wasn't, both of you would be in my truck right now, whether you wanted to or not. Now I say Sam takes twenty and Abigail takes ten."

"Why can't I take them all?" It made sense to Sam. Abby didn't mind a spanking, but if Jack got the whip even the slightest bit wrong, it could really hurt. He wouldn't mind the experience, but he hated the thought of Abby being in pain. She wasn't wired the way he was. "That way Abby stays out of it. She got spanked last night, after all."

Abby's pretty mouth formed a stubborn line. "I don't think that would satisfy Julian. I can take ten. How much worse is it than a spanking?"

"Well, it's a flipping whip," Lucas pointed out. "I don't think it's supposed to feel good."

"It can be horrible." Jack ran his hand along Abby's arm gently. She shivered at the sensation. "Or it can be like a whisper across your skin."

"Screw that." Damn, Sam wished he hadn't said it out loud.

"I'll be sure to note your preferences," Jack stated with a sarcastic smile on his face. "Sam likes a pretty big bite of pain, Abby. You like a small one. If you like the whip and want to play with it at home, then we can talk about it. But I'm not putting you through that here. I'll give you ten light ones and then move on to Sam. What I'm going to do to him should satisfy the crowd. While I handle Sam, Lucas is going to take care of you, Abby."

Lucas sat up and leaned forward, his face serious. "I've been fully instructed. I'm to hold you if you cry and rub some salve into your butt so it doesn't sting anymore. I am not to play with your boobs."

Jack sent his brother a stern look.

"Or anything else," Lucas concluded with a gulp. "I can pat your back and try hard not to get an erection."

"That won't happen." Jack stood up and affectionately ran a hand through Sam's hair. "She'll be naked. Every man in the room will have an erection."

"Sally would, too," Sam interjected. "If she had a penis."

"Lucas, Julian will come for them in twenty minutes. You walk down with them," Jack instructed. "I'm trusting you with this, son."

Lucas sat up straighter, and his voice was deeper as he answered. "Yes, sir. They'll be there safely."

After Jack left for the dungeon, Lucas stood and walked across the room. He stopped at the bar. When he came back, he had a beer in one hand and a small glass of pink stuff in the other. "You're allowed two. Beer for Sam, vodka with cranberry juice for Abby."

They could hear the table next to them discussing the day's events, including the miraculous rainstorm of fine lingerie.

Sam laughed and downed his beer. He cuddled Abby as she bemoaned the loss of her undies. It didn't take long before Lucas was watching for Julian's entrance. He took Abby's hand, threading their fingers together. A magnificent sense of anticipation threatened to overwhelm him, but he could feel her trembling.

He wrapped his arms around her. She was perfectly placed in his lap. "Baby, it's going to be fine. Jack is great with a whip. I promise you'll barely feel it. He's going to go so easy on you."

Her eyes were wide as she peered up at him. "What about you?"

"He's going to tear me up, and I'll love it. I like the pain. Did I ever tell you what Jack caught me doing when we were still in the foster home?" She shook her head and he told her something he'd never told another person. "He caught me cutting. I used to run a knife along my thighs and my calves."

"You told me those were old rodeo wounds."

"Nah, I did those myself," he admitted. "It made me feel better. Jack caught me and made me stop. That was about the time I started getting into a whole lot of fights. It was harder back then. I'd recently lost my parents and my brother in a car wreck. I was the only one who survived. I liked the pain because it made me feel closer to them. That went away, but I still like pain, Abby."

She pulled him close and murmured something about understanding. He sincerely doubted that she did or ever really would. The important thing was she would accept it. She would accept him and try to give him what he needed. Her love had no conditions. It made it so much easier to accept himself.

"Good evening," Julian said as he walked up. He was dressed for the dungeon. Unlike Jack, he'd left off the shirt. Jack would eventually ditch the shirt, too. Julian's pants were leather and rode low on his hips. Julian's long, dark hair was down for the occasion, released from its normal sleek ponytail.

He hoped Julian wasn't planning on derailing things between Jack and Lucas. "Did those two security guys find you?"

Julian smiled, but it was a little like the smile of a cobra right before it struck. "Yes, Mr. Dean and Mr. Miles did find me. Despite their boss's unsavory need for sarcasm, I believe that investment is going to go quite nicely. They're training a couple of former Navy SEALs right now to work as our in-house investigators. Their work is impeccable, but nothing for you to worry about now."

"If this is about…" he began.

Julian put a hand up. "It's nothing for you to worry about. Any of you."

And that was all Sam could do unless he wanted to get into even more trouble.

"It's good to see Jackson followed at least one of my dictates. You look lovely in your collar, dear." He nodded to indicate the three strands of diamonds around Abby's throat. "Normally it's all leather and metal down in the dungeon. I believe your husband wants you to stand out."

"Her husbands think she deserves diamonds," Sam corrected. "She's our jewel."

Abby's face softened and she kissed his cheek. He held his hand out, indicating it was time to go, and she took his hand and rose from the sofa. She wore only a silk robe and her heels. Abby nervously straightened the thin, fine fabric around her body.

"I don't see your collar, Samuel." Julian's irritation was plainly written across his face. "Have you decided to forgo your punishment?"

There might not be anything he was prouder of than that damn collar. He pulled his T-shirt off. He wouldn't need it. "If you don't see my collar, Julian, it's because you're not looking close enough."

He got rid of the bandage. He wouldn't need that, either. Abby would redo it later.

"I wondered about that request from your Master." Julian inspected the tattoo. "It looks good on you."

Sam nodded and took Abby's hand firmly in his. Up ahead, he noticed that the man from last night was in the bar. He'd taken note of the man the night before because he stood out like a sore thumb. He'd been wearing a suit and not enjoying the scene Jack and Abby had unwittingly performed. He looked like the type of man Sam usually tried to avoid.

Julian noticed him, too. He didn't seem particularly happy to see the man, either. "Mr. Slater, I would have assumed you would be back in Washington this evening."

The man with the bland face and graying hair crossed his arms over his chest. There was no small amount of belligerence in the gesture. "My business is not finished here, Mr. Lodge. Lucas still threatens everyone in this club and his father."

"No, I don't," Lucas protested.

"You don't have to worry about Lucas anymore." Abby squared her shoulders and straightened her spine. She was as dignified as a totally hot woman in a short robe with pretty pink toenails could be. She frowned at the newcomer. "He's coming home with us. He's completely out of the blackmail business. He's going to be a cowboy."

"Probably not forever," Lucas interjected. He'd noticed Lucas seemed much more confident than he had this morning. Something had given Lucas a sense of self, and he doubted it was the haircut. Lucas stood up to the man named Slater. "I'll probably go back to school. Jack said he could use a lawyer. I think I could be good at that."

Slater snorted derisively. "You never were before. Your sister is the lawyer. Don't even try to compete with her."

"He isn't trying to compete with anyone." Abby practically

growled at Slater. Sam hid a smile. Abby's mama bear was coming out. Slater should step carefully. His wife had some nasty claws when someone threatened her loved ones. "He doesn't have to. He only has to be Lucas. You get on a plane and head back to wherever you came from. Don't you give Lucas another thought. He's not going to give you one." She slipped her arm through a surprised Lucas's. She patted his hand comfortingly. "Good-bye, Mr. Slater."

She turned and started to lead Lucas off. She seemed to remember that she was supposed to follow someone. Her red hair shook as she impatiently waited on Julian.

"I wouldn't mess with that one, Mr. Slater," Julian said smoothly, taking his place at the head of the group. "She seems to have taken your charge under her wing. It's a delicate wing, but I believe you'll find it has claws."

"Damn straight it does," Abby shot back.

Julian frowned. "Language, Abigail."

She shrugged. "Sorry."

"No, you're not." Julian sighed, and his head gave a shake of despair. He looked the campaign manager over. "Are you still going to try to talk to Lucas? He doesn't seem interested in talking to you."

Slater followed doggedly behind. "Yes. The contract I signed gave me club access through tonight. The senator wants his son to come home."

Sam doubted that. The senator wanted his son to shut up. Julian stopped and stared at Slater for a moment, his mouth flat and his eyes flinty. Sam knew that look. It was the one Jack always sported when he was plotting some terrible revenge. Sam wondered what the hell the older guy had done to put that expression on Julian's face. Or what was in the report in that file folder.

Maybe it wasn't something he needed to worry about.

"Fine, Mr. Slater," Julian finally allowed. "I'll honor our contract. You will honor your end. I believe the rules of the dungeon were fully outlined. Have a good evening, Mr. Slater. Abigail, Samuel, please follow me."

Julian turned and started to walk again. Sam walked beside his wife, slipping his hand through her open arm. He smiled as Lucas leaned over.

"Abby, are you going to insist on acting all motherly toward me?" Lucas sounded disappointed.

"I can't help it, Lucas. I am a very motherly person."

Sam caught Lucas staring at the gap in her robe. It showed off her perfectly creamy skin and the round beginnings of the breasts Sam loved so much.

"All right, but you gotta know, I already have an Oedipus complex about you," Lucas shot back.

Julian and Abby laughed. Sam wasn't sure what that was, but he doubted Lucas could ever look at Abby like a real mama.

"It's good to know his education wasn't a complete waste," Julian tossed over his shoulder as he led them into the playroom. "Lucas at least paid attention in English class."

He walked into the playroom and stared at the stairs in the back that led to the dungeon. He'd been there a hundred times, but it felt like the first time.

Sam took a deep breath and strode toward his new life.

* * * *

The dungeon was awfully dungeon-like. Abby took a deep breath as Lucas helped her off the last step. Sam's hand was on the small of her back as she took in the space. The lighting here was soft and lent the entire place a bit of a gloomy atmosphere. The walls were black and the floor a dark wood. The fixtures were all a heavy wrought iron, giving the place a medieval feel. She preferred the playroom. If she had the choice, she greatly preferred the playroom at their ranch. It was more intimate. It didn't have the amount of toys Julian's large playroom did, but it was theirs.

It seemed as though everyone had gotten the word. The dungeon was full. Club members milled around, quietly discussing the evening to come, and they tended to look up when they caught sight of her. The white silk robe she wore made her stand out in this crowd. Jack had orchestrated this carefully. The night before, Sam had tried to make her blend in by wearing the leather miniskirt and bustier.

Blending in wasn't on Jack's to-do list. The white silk she wore was different from the leather and black fetish wear everyone else had on. Her hair was soft and flowed down her back. The only makeup he'd allowed her was a bit of lip-gloss. As she walked through the severely dressed club members, she realized Jack had done it on purpose. She looked like a virginal sacrifice. Of course, the robe wouldn't matter in a little while. Jack would take it off, and she had nothing at all on underneath. Abby's breath caught on a scene in front of her.

"What's that?" Abby nudged Sam.

There was a young man intricately tied up and hanging from a hook over his head. Jack liked to bind her hands together, but it was nothing like this. Rope wound around every part of the sub in an elaborate pattern. The thin rope wrapped carefully around his waist and the *V* of his thighs. His penis was on full display, caught in the bindings.

"It's called Shibari," Julian explained as he led them through the dungeon. "It's a Japanese bondage art. Master Leo teaches a class."

"I do, indeed." Master Leo joined them. He appeared to be roughly thirty, though the perpetual air of authority around the Dom made him seem a bit older. He gestured to the man in the ropes. Despite the tight bindings, his eyes were closed, and he seemed peaceful. "I taught his Domme how to bind him. I believe this sub finds it soothing. I would be more than willing to show you, Mrs. Barnes."

"You're going to get your ass kicked if you don't leave my brother's wife alone," Lucas said before Sam could.

Abby was grateful Lucas was taking charge. Sam was an acknowledged submissive. This Master Leo person didn't like it when subs offered up a potential ass kicking. Lucas was acting as her guardian. It seemed perfectly acceptable that he make all manner of threats.

There was a slight smile on Julian's face. Abby got the feeling Julian rarely smiled brightly. Even when he looked amused, there wasn't a sense of joy about him. He was always in control. "I wouldn't push Jackson tonight, Leo. It's a special night for him. He won't have you disrupt it with your obvious admiration for his wife."

Master Leo inclined his head toward her. "She's a lovely submissive. I can't help but admire her. I think training her would be a challenge."

"I'm as trained as I'm going to get," she muttered under her breath.

Lucas clutched her arm and stared at the Dom. "We're supposed to be finding my brother, not taking a tour."

Julian held out a hand. "I believe Jackson has found a loyal friend in you, Lucas." He turned to Leo, who was following the group now. "Did you get the report from McKay-Taggart?"

"I did indeed," Leo replied.

"And is all in readiness for our final scene of the night?"

Leo inclined his head slightly. "Of course, Master Julian. Taggart is en route. He's dropping off our friends as we speak. He promises we have several eager participants."

"Participants?" Abby wasn't sure she liked the sound of that. And weren't they supposed to be the final scene of the night? Not that she minded. She intended to go straight to their suite and play out a hot scene of her own with her men.

"Not for you, dear," Julian assured her. "I have another matter to take care of this evening. Don't worry about it. It no longer concerns you."

She would have asked about when it had concerned her, but she suddenly saw Jack standing on a large raised stage. He looked dark and dangerous and entirely yummy. He held a long whip in his hand.

"You're sure it's not going to hurt?" Abby squeezed Sam's hand.

She moved closer to Sam. His gaze didn't move from the sight of Jack with that whip. His clear blue eyes had taken on that sleepy look she equated with desire in Sam. "It'll hurt a little, but then it's going to feel good."

Julian flicked his wrist. The crowd parted quickly at his command. She wondered if everyone obeyed Julian. If everyone did his bidding, who was he friends with? Who did he argue with and discuss things with if everyone was submissive toward him? She felt a bit sorry for the Dom.

Then Jack was holding his hand out and she wasn't thinking about Julian any more. Lucas gave her a hand up. She was enfolded in Jack's arms.

"You are the most beautiful woman I've ever seen, my Abigail," he whispered in her ear. "Show them."

She took a deep breath and shrugged out of her robe. She was naked in front of a crowd of people, but there were only two who mattered. A slight shiver went through her despite the warmth of the room. Jack ran his hands down her shoulders. "Just follow my lead and Lucas will be taking care of you in no time at all, sweetheart. I love you."

She kept silent because he hadn't asked her a direct question. She nodded, letting her love for him shine. He put his hand out, and she sank into her submissive position. She tried not to think about the St. Andrew's Cross that dominated the stage. It was a large wooden X, and she'd taken note of the fastenings she was sure would be used on her wrists and ankles. Once she was bound, there would be no getting out until Jack deemed it time.

Jack sounded very formal as he began. "Master Julian, this woman belongs to me. She wears my collar and my ring. She shares my name and my home. She has offended you and seeks to make reparation. Will you accept?"

"I will," Julian replied.

Jack turned to her. She could only see the tips of his boots. "Abigail Barnes, who is your husband and Master?"

"You are, Jack."

He used the tip of the whip's handle to bring her chin up so she looked at him. "Do you submit to me?"

"Yes." There was no hesitation. She trusted him with her body and soul. She breathed out all of her anxiety and let Jack take control.

"Then prepare to serve me." Jack motioned for her to get up then led her to the cross. Gently he bound her face-first to the apparatus. The straps were leather but cushioned with something soft. Jack made certain they wouldn't cut off her circulation. He made her wiggle her fingers and toes. When he was satisfied, she felt him pressed against her back.

"Your safe word is *pink*," he whispered. "I expect you to use it if this gets to be too much to handle. I'll stop immediately and get you out of here. Julian said nothing at all about silence, so scream all you like."

He stepped back, and she knew she wouldn't. She would do anything to avoid it. It would bother Jack. He liked the sounds she made when he spanked her, but she didn't think he could handle it if she was in real pain. She gritted her teeth and prepared to survive this experience.

She closed her eyes. There wasn't anything to see except a black velvet curtain. The crowd got quiet and in her mind she could see Jack unfurling the whip. He would stand for a moment, getting used to the feel of the weight of it in his hand. She tried to think about every fantasy she'd ever had about Indiana Jones.

"You will count, Abigail," Jack demanded. "Count of ten."

CRACK!

She tensed when she heard that terrible sound. Every muscle in her body did exactly what she didn't want it to do. When the lash struck the fleshy part of her ass, she was rigid. All the breath left her body as the burn sizzled. It wasn't exactly pain, but it wasn't comfortable, either. Her breath stuck in her chest.

"I need a count, Abigail," Jack said patiently.

"One," she managed with a shaky voice as she wondered how she could get through that nine more times.

It happened quickly the second time. She felt the burn across her thighs and gasped.

"Two," she nearly shouted.

Her mouth had gone dry and her breath came in pants. She was grateful for the bindings. Her fingers curled around the leather that held her in place.

Again. The third blast came across her buttocks. Fire seemed to splash across her skin. It sizzled and cracked and retreated, leaving something else in its wake.

"Three," she managed.

Jack worked fast. He didn't give her time to think or prepare for the next lash. The minute he heard her count, he struck again. By the time she made it to ten she was crying, but the burn was sinking into her skin. It seemed to course through her veins and it hurt, but it also made her feel awfully alive. A strange sense of pride washed through her. She'd made it through and hadn't screamed, hadn't begged him to stop. By the time the lash had bitten her the last time, she'd felt an odd kinship with the whip. It was taking her someplace. The cessation of that horrible burn was a pleasure in and of itself. She sagged against her bindings, so tired she didn't think she could walk. She wished Jack didn't have to deal with Sam. This was the time she craved, when the pain was over and her body hummed, when Jack took such sweet care of her.

"You were wonderful, sweetheart," he murmured as he efficiently pulled her out. Lucas was at his side. Jack worked on her hands while Lucas pulled her feet out. "I'm so proud of you."

His hands lightly traced the skin where the whip had landed. He gently checked each mark to make sure he hadn't done any real damage. After a moment, she felt him relax and knew he was satisfied. It was easy to tell the episode had done something for him. He was aroused as he pulled her into his arms and kissed her soundly before passing her off to Lucas. Lucas helped her into her robe as Jack turned to Julian.

"Are you satisfied with my wife?" Jack asked.

Julian nodded briefly. "She did well for a novice. I take it Samuel has chosen to take the majority of the punishment. Or did you force that on him?"

She watched Sam practically bound onto the stage. He was grinning as he shrugged out of his clothes.

"Yes, I was terrible to him, Julian." Jack watched as Sam approached. Sam tossed his clothes to the side. "I had to force him."

Sam got into position, head down, palms up, as Lucas helped her off the stage. Jack was going through the ritual he'd performed with her for Sam. Lucas found a chaise lounge set aside for the occasion. There was a small table with another vodka and cranberry juice waiting.

"Here you go." Lucas pressed the glass in her hand and steadied her. "Are you all right?"

She nodded as she took a gulp. It was okay. She was okay. The entire episode had been enlightening. It wasn't the last time she'd feel the bite of that whip. She'd been close to going someplace else. What started as punishment had opened a door for them as a couple.

"Does it hurt?"

"Yes, Lucas, getting your ass whipped hurts," she replied sarcastically, but she gave him a wink and a smile. "It hurts at first. It's a little like jumping into near-freezing water. Have you ever done that? There's a creek in Willow Fork. I don't know why, but it's always cold. Like crazy cold, even in the middle of the summer. So, of course we all jumped in it. There's this moment when you hit the water that all the breath leaves your body and you're sure you can't take it. So you jump out as fast as you can. And then the sun hits your skin, and every pore is open and the world seems like a different place. That's what it was like."

"I think I might like to try that," Lucas said quietly. He cleared his throat and held up a bottle. "I'm supposed to wipe this across your ass."

She shook her head. There was no way she was letting Lucas rub her naked bottom. He was her brother-in-law. "It can wait for Jack."

Lucas let out a sigh. "He said you would probably refuse, but he wanted it here just in case. Do you want me to take you back to the room?"

"No." She wasn't going to leave while Sam and Jack were still on stage. She gingerly sat down and Lucas followed, sitting next to her. The pain was already gone, and she was surprised she wasn't very sore.

There was a mighty crack and Sam shouted out, "One."

There was an almost jubilant satisfaction in his voice. Lucas hissed.

"Wow," Lucas said. "That is not what he did to you."

A line of red appeared on Sam's backside. It looked angry and painful, but Sam counted through it. The whip cracked through the air. It was a harsh sound and made her jump. Somehow it hadn't sounded that way when she was tied to the St. Andrew's Cross. The sound had been gentler even when the whip stung along her skin.

Sam tensed the first few times. The muscles of his back bunched up and he groaned. After the first few, he seemed to relax. She stood and watched as the whip danced. It seemed almost like an extension of Jack himself. The man and the whip moved in perfect harmony, the action sensual in its fluidity. She found herself holding her breath as the whip flew back and Jack began again.

She wished she could see Sam's face. It would give her a sense of what he was feeling. She could see Julian's. He watched with rapt attention. While others switched their attention between the two men working the scene, Julian Lodge watched only Sam. After a moment, his serious gray eyes found hers. She looked away but not before she saw that Julian, for everything he had, was a lonely man at heart.

She let her attention get back to her husbands. Sam's back was red and swollen. Abby watched as he let his head sag when the count reached ten. His voice got languid and heavy.

"That must be that subspace thing Jack told me about." Lucas gazed at the scene playing out before him. His eyes were clearly focused on Sam's back. She began to wonder just how much he was like his brother.

"Mr. Cameron?"

She looked up at the same time Lucas did. A man in leather held out a drink. She wasn't pleased to see Julian's male sub. There was something about the young man that she didn't trust.

Lucas took a moment studying the other man's face before he came up with a name. "Jeremy?"

Jeremy smiled down at Lucas. He completely ignored her. Suspicion played around in her brain. She couldn't forget how this weasel had gotten them all in trouble the night before by misrepresenting Sally's actions to Master Leo.

"I missed spending time with you last night," Jeremy was saying. "Your brother seems a bit overprotective. Here. You said you liked rum and coke."

Abby's attention was pulled away as Sam grunted and managed to say, "Twenty."

He slumped against the apparatus, his head hanging forward. She wanted to go to him but Lucas held her hand.

"No. Jack said to keep you here." Lucas's eyes softened as though he understood her worry. "He'll come for you, Abby. Sam is fine."

"Let her go," Jeremy cajoled. He sat down on the sofa across from them. It was not a submissive move in Abby's mind. Julian's slave pushed the drink forward. "Come on. Let the girl go and we can have a drink and talk. We got along really well last night. We could have a lot of fun, you and me."

Julian proclaimed his satisfaction with Sam. All around the dungeon, the crowd was buzzing. The scene had everyone talking.

"I don't think that's such a great idea."

Abby heard Lucas talking, but her eyes were on Sam. Julian handed up a robe to Sam. There was a slightly dippy look on his face. He grinned as he stumbled a little. Jack's shoulder went under Sam's arm to give him balance. Sam didn't fight him. He let his head lean against Jack's broad shoulder. They were so beautiful together. Abby felt her heart speed up.

"Seriously, I don't think I can see you tonight," Lucas was saying. "I have to be up early in the morning. I don't know exactly what happened last night. I didn't drink anything except that one glass of Scotch and the drink you gave me. I guess I got sick. Maybe I'm allergic or something. It was weird."

Jack helped Sam toward a chair and a small table. It was a recovery station, Jack had explained earlier. Sam would need immediate aftercare. He wouldn't be given the option of waiting until later, as she had.

"Come on, Lucas," Jeremy cajoled. "If this is your last night, then you should party."

Something was off. There was a problem with this scenario. Abby quickly estimated Lucas's weight with the trained eye of a nurse. "How did you pass out from two drinks? Jack said you blacked out. You wouldn't do that from two drinks."

Even if Lucas had never had a drink in his life, he wouldn't have blacked out from a single Scotch and a rum and coke. Unless he had some help. She glared down at the glass in Jeremy's hand. Several things fell neatly into place. Matthew Slater walked up behind Jeremy. He glanced around as though to make sure no one was looking.

"Lucas, I need to speak with you," he said urgently.

"I don't have anything to say to you. You're wasting your time. Tell my father not to worry about me. My days as a blackmailer are done." Lucas looked through Slater. He was kinder when he turned back to Jeremy, but just as sure. "And I'm not hooking up tonight. I'm going back to my room. I have to leave early. I promised Jack I would take care of Abby and then turn in."

She took the glass out of Jeremy's hand. Though she knew if her suspicions were right she wouldn't smell anything, she sniffed it anyway. "Lucas, I think this has drugs in it. Surely Julian has some of those test strips."

Women had started carrying them into clubs to make sure no one slipped something in their drinks. Her daughter, Lexi, had shown her some. She never went into a club without them.

Lucas's face bunched up in confusion. "Why would he drug me? I was perfectly willing to sleep with him last night."

"I have no idea, but he isn't going to do it in my club," Julian said smoothly.

He was behind her. Jack had Sam over a chair, smoothing salve into his back and buttocks. Jack nodded over at her. Sam was draped over the chair, his eyes slightly hooded. She could see the pleasure on his face as Jack's hands slid across his skin.

Master Leo slipped up behind Slater. Slater was too busy to notice. His eyes were on Julian. Jeremy had gone completely white. He tried to toss the drink, but Julian's hand came out.

Julian pulled the glass from Jeremy's hand. "It doesn't matter, Jeremy. Do you think I don't know everything that goes on in this club? I see everything. There are video cameras in places you can't imagine, sub. I saw you spike his drink last night. I merely wanted to see if you would try again. And I suspect you were also behind Mrs. Barnes receiving that white rose without any information about what it would mean. This isn't mischief. This is malice, Jeremy."

Jeremy fell to his knees. "Master, I can explain."

"I am no longer your Master." Julian nodded and the bald guy from the night before pulled Jeremy up by the neck. "Please escort Jeremy off the grounds. He is no longer welcome in The Club."

"Master!" Jeremy's face flushed and his mouth opened to protest, but before he could say another word, he was being hauled bodily out of the dungeon.

Slater turned to walk away. Master Leo didn't move to let him by. He smiled. It was an intimidating thing. "You're not going anywhere."

Julian stepped forward. "I also saw what you did last night, Mr. Slater. You were the one who talked my slave into betraying his home. I do not allow drugs of any kind on the premises. You should have noted that in the contract you signed."

Slater's eyes darted around the room, looking for a way out. He was surrounded. One minute he appeared defeated, and the next he was grabbing Abby, pulling her into his clutches. She winced as she felt something cold and metallic against her ribs. It was a gun.

Again.

She really wished people would stop trying to kill her.

Chapter Fifteen

Lucas took a step toward her.

"Don't." Slater pressed the gun into her belly as he addressed Lucas. "Don't you come any closer, and the guy behind me better move, too."

She went perfectly still, looking over at the stage where Jack was fully into his aftercare, talking Sam down, soothing him. His big hands ran over Sam's skin. He wasn't paying any attention to the fact that his wife had a gun shoved in her belly. Julian was, though. The club owner's face had lost its color, but other than that, he appeared outwardly calm. Like this wasn't his first rodeo.

"We can talk about this, Slater," Julian said in that authoritative voice of his.

Lucas was trying to get Jack's attention, but there was an awful lot of noise now that the punishment was over. People were milling about, some starting scenes of their own.

Leo moved to stand beside his boss, but his eyes were on her. There was an air of competence about him as though he was merely waiting for the opportunity to present itself. If she had to guess, she would definitely say Master Leo was ex-military.

His voice was steady as he stared at Slater. "Where do you think you're going, Slater? Do you honestly believe you can get out of here with Mrs. Barnes?"

Slater's hands tightened around her upper arm painfully and she bit back a cry. She'd just had a whip applied to her ass, but this hurt far worse. Her mind was racing. Jack was going to flip out. He didn't need this. In her panic, she knew exactly who to blame. She felt her face get stubborn. It was the only way to stem the tide of panic. "Maybe you should install some metal detectors, Julian."

Julian's eyebrow shot up. He glanced around. "Have you seen my clients, dear? No one would make it through."

Leo shook his head ruefully. "That little sub still needs a spanking."

They were being awfully calm about her kidnapping. Julian actually checked his watch. Lucas was the only one who appeared concerned.

"Look, Matthew," Lucas started, his hands shaking. "I'm the one you want. I'll go with you. Let Abby go. She doesn't have anything to do with this. I'll go talk to my dad. We'll work everything out. All you have to do is let her go and take me instead."

"I think she'll be easier to deal with than you, Lucas. I'm leaving, and I doubt Lodge there is going to call the cops on me." Slater was trying to be tough, but there was a distinct tremor in his voice. "I'm sure he doesn't want the police to know what goes on in this place."

Julian shot Leo an acerbic glance. "I thought I saw the police chief in the playroom."

Leo nodded. "Yes, I spoke with him earlier. He was with the district attorney. They brought their 'nieces.'"

"And I am not going to be easier to deal with than Lucas," she proclaimed.

Jack was staring over at the group, a worried look dawning on his face. She tried smiling at him to keep him calm. The last thing this unplanned scene of hers needed was her bull of a husband rushing in to save her. He'd been shot once in defense of her. It was someone else's turn.

"You are going to be quiet, Mrs. Barnes, or I'm going to shoot you," Slater promised.

"I doubt that." This time Julian's voice was all smooth satisfaction. "Look, Leo, our guests have arrived."

Slater turned. It was just the opportunity she needed. The gun dropped slightly from her side and she brought the heel of her four-and-a-half-inch purple peep-toe Christian Louboutin down on her captor's toes. He howled, the gun dropping from his hand. Lucas reached forward and pulled her away, covering her body with his.

"What the hell is going on?" Jack's shout resonated through the dungeon.

Leo calmly picked up the gun and tucked it into his pants. He was far too comfortable with the revolver. Sam's arms were suddenly tugging her back, and she found herself watching the rest of the action from behind Sam and Lucas.

"Don't worry yourself, Jackson." Julian nodded to the three men in pinstriped suits currently helping Slater stand up. "I believe Mr. Conti is going to take care of our friend." He turned his attention to the new group in the room. "You spoke with my security manager? I was informed that you have some business to handle with Mr. Slater."

"Indeed we do, Mr. Lodge. And I thank you and Mr. Taggart for reaching out and giving me this chance." The man talking was the smallest of the three men, but there was no doubt that he was in charge.

She stared at him from behind Sam's back. When she tried to get a better view, Lucas held her back. Damn protective men always kept her out of the good stuff. The three newcomers looked out of place in the dungeon. They did not, however, act uncomfortable. The largest of the three had a hold of Slater's neck from the back. He held the campaign manager like he would hold an unruly puppy.

Slater's face flushed. His eyes had a distinct sheen of moisture coating them. His gaze was fully concentrated on the leader of the pinstriped suits. "I've got the money. I really do. I just need a little time."

Mr. Conti smiled, though there was nothing humorous about it. It was the smile a shark gave his next meal. "Your time was up three days ago."

If Abby had to guess, she would say Mr. Conti was straight out of Jersey.

Slater puffed up. "I am well known. You can't harm me. Do you know who I work for?"

The three dark-haired men laughed. Mr. Conti smoothed down his tie. "I talked to your boss not an hour ago. The senator understands business. I believe you will find yourself out of a job."

"The senator might be annoyed with his son," Julian interjected, "but he would never allow you to harm him."

"He saves that for himself," Lucas said, nodding.

"Did that man pull a gun on my wife?" Jack's question was ground out of his mouth.

Julian put a hand on his shoulder. "There's nothing you can do, Jackson, which will compare to what Mr. Conti has in mind. His organization has a long history of handling people like Mr. Slater."

Conti nodded at his compatriots, and Slater was hauled off before Jack could decide to go after him. "As always, Mr. Lodge, it is good to do business with you. As for Mr. Slater assaulting the lovely lady, I will make sure to add it to his tab. Good night."

Mr. Conti nodded and followed his men. No one seemed to think a thing about the crying, pleading man being carried bodily out of the building.

Sam finally relented, and Abby hurried to get to Jack.

All in all, it had been a hell of a night and she wanted to talk about everything that had happened. "That man was from the mafia, Jack."

Jack didn't seem to share her enthusiasm. "You think?"

She ignored him. Jack sometimes didn't see how exciting life could be. "I do. I think Slater was planning on doing something terrible to Lucas so he could save the senator's political career. But Julian's a paranoid pervert and has cameras all over the building and caught him helping Jeremy when he tried to drug Lucas last night. I think they were trying to hurt him. That's when Julian laid his trap. He had his investigative people find out that Slater owes money to the mafia and called them in." Abby glared at an amused Julian. "Your timing might have been better." She sighed. "I was the woman in the middle of it all. I bravely faced down a killer and was rescued by the mob."

"Damn it, Abby, this is not going on some crazy talk show," Sam said. "Julian isn't going to expose his ties to the mafia. Jack, did you know he had ties to the mafia?"

Julian brushed off the implication. "I do not have ties to the mafia. I merely know a few people. And I'm sorry, Abigail. If I had thought for a moment that Slater would bring a gun into my

establishment, I would never have permitted him to enter. In this
case, I was more trying to catch my slave in the act than Slater."
When Julian turned to look at Lucas, he seemed very satisfied.
"Don't worry about him, young Lucas. He won't be a problem
anymore. He has much more to worry about now than your father's
potential presidency."

"Why did Slater try to have someone drug me?" Lucas sounded
slightly horrified, like he knew the answer but didn't want to admit
it. "Do you think he had something to do with that guy who tried to
run me down the other day?"

"It doesn't matter now, though I am thankful Taggart is a good
driver. Don't think about it again. Jackson Barnes is my family. You
are his family. That means my door is always open to you," Julian
pronounced.

Jack hugged her to his side. "Are you all right?"

"Beyond the fact that my career in the tabloids is over before it
even began, I'm fine." She gave him a reassuring hug.

Sam ran his hand through her hair, smoothing it back. "It might
not make the front of a magazine, but I promise to do some truly
scandalous things to you tonight."

"Let's go," Jack said, and she could tell he was still thinking
about what had just happened. There was a tightness around his eyes
that told her this wasn't over.

Julian smiled. "Have a nice evening, Jackson. Invite me to this
ranch of yours sometime. It would be nice to get out of the city."

Julian nodded and walked out of the dungeon, Leo following
behind him.

"So, Slater tried to roofie me. He was going to kill me. He
would have killed me if Jack hadn't come along. Maybe I shouldn't
drink?" Lucas asked.

Abby managed to not laugh. "Yes, Lucas. You should abstain
for a while."

* * * *

Sam didn't think about the ache in his back as the door to the suite
closed behind him, and he was finally alone with Abby and Jack.

The ache was a delicious distraction, but the main thought in his brain was getting that look off Jack's face. It was haunted.

Abby had tried to reach him. She'd already gotten his Scotch and sat in his lap. Jack was saying all the right things, but that look wouldn't leave his eyes.

Sam hoped that asshole Slater was being tortured because he'd ruined one of the best nights of Sam's life. He would never forget the moment Jack strapped him to the St. Andrew's Cross. He'd loved the feeling of leather around his wrists and ankles. He'd pulled at the bindings, but they held him tight. They wouldn't let him fall. He loved the crack of the whip, and he was starting to think there was absolutely nothing better that the burn of the lash. He could still feel it sizzle across his flesh. It stung, but every nerve in his body was awake in those moments. He was so alive in that place. His back was sore, but it was a good thing. Somewhere between lashes five and seven, he'd found that peaceful place. It had been perfect, better than any drug.

He'd even liked the aftercare stuff. He didn't want Jack to cuddle him or anything, but the massage was nice. The stroking of Jack's hands soothing the burn from his flesh made him feel wanted and loved. Next time it would be better because Abby could do the cuddling. He'd like to rest his head against her soft breasts while she told him how much she loved him. Sam wondered if he could get Abby to whip him, too. He would like that.

Jack stared off into space. Abby gave up. There were tears in her eyes as she walked past Sam and into the bedroom. He started to follow her, his hand on the door that would lead them back to the bedroom portion of the suite. He would take her into his arms, and they could comfort each other.

It wouldn't solve the problem. Sam had been to heaven now, and there was no way he was going back.

"What the fuck is wrong with you?"

It took Sam a moment to realize the words had come out of his mouth.

Jack's head came up. He was almost irritated for a moment, then a familiar blank expression came over his face. It was the same look Sam had seen on Jack's face almost every day for the past six months. Yesterday and today had been different, but now it was as though none of those breakthroughs had happened.

"I'm fine, Sam." Jack's hand tightened on the Scotch. "I'm a little tired. I had a rough night."

He shook his head, unable to believe what he was hearing. "You had a rough night?"

"Yes," Jack replied through clenched teeth. He gave Sam a look that normally would send him into complete submissive mode. "I did. If you don't mind, I'd like to be left alone for a while. Go to bed with Abigail. She needs someone with her."

Sam's first impulse was to do exactly what he said. He should walk into the bedroom and comfort Abby. But he'd been with Jack for almost twenty years. Obeying Jack was second nature. For the most part it was a good thing to do. Jack loved him. Sam knew that. Jack had Sam's best interests in mind almost always. Tonight, Jack needed for Sam to think of Jack's best interests, and walking out on him wasn't it. Jack might think he needed time alone, but that wasn't best for any of them. Jack hadn't responded to Abby's gentle requests. Maybe what Jack needed was something more forceful.

"No, I think I'll go downstairs and have a drink." Sam turned for the door.

"Samuel," Jack barked, getting out of his chair. He stood with his feet apart staring at Sam. He pointed at the door to the bedroom. "You will get your ass in there and take care of our wife."

Sam shrugged. "Why?

"Because she needs you."

Sam tried to give off a negligent air he didn't feel. "So? I need you. She needs you, too. It doesn't matter what we need. You're going to pull away. You're going to leave us. Oh, you'll be here in body, just not with your heart or your soul. You'll get pissed off enough at some point to see us again, and the process will start over." Now Sam felt a kernel of anger leap to life. "Tell me something, Jack. When did you get to be such a pussy?"

Sam ducked as the glass flew past his head and smashed into the wall. It hadn't really come close to him. Jack hadn't thrown it at him, but there was no small amount of rage in the act.

The bedroom door flew open and Abby stood there watching

them. She'd been crying and it pissed him off even more.

"What the fuck are you so scared of?" He practically yelled the question. He walked straight up to the man who had been his whole world for almost twenty years. "Are you so scared of losing her that you'll push both of us away? Would you rather be alone than have to deal with the possibility of losing her?"

"You will not talk to me that way." Jack's face was red, and Sam knew he was getting to him.

He had a desperate desire to smash through that wall Jack kept putting up. Being back here was reminding Sam of a few things. He was reminded of exactly why he could never have had a relationship with Julian. He could never be satisfied being admired and, in some ways, worshipped. Julian treated his subs like little dolls to be taken care of and played with. Sam wanted more. He wanted to be loved and he was done waiting for it. He finally understood.

A real sub was smart enough to know what he wanted and brave enough to ask for it.

He held his ground as Jack stared him down. There wasn't anything to be afraid of. He'd almost never fought with Jack before, and each and every time he had, he'd backed down. He wasn't going to do that this time. This time, he was going to win. It was the only acceptable outcome.

"You will not throw me away again," Sam returned just as passionately. "You will not toss me to the side because you know I'll always be your fucking lapdog. You can't only love Abby. Maybe it's not fair of me to change the rules after all these years, but there it is. You're worried about losing Abigail? Worry about losing me, Jack, because if you pull the same shit you've been pulling for the last six months, then I'm walking. If you don't want me, I'll find someone who does."

Sam turned to walk away. He knew he wouldn't get farther than the bar downstairs, but he couldn't watch as Abby soothed Jack and tried to convince him to see things their way. He just couldn't.

His hand was almost on the doorknob when he was hauled back. Every muscle in Jack's body seemed tense and ready for violence as he pulled Sam close.

"You think I only worry about Abby? How can you say that?

You think I don't worry about how impetuous you are? I built a whole fucking bar so I'd know where you were at night. I changed the course of my life because I knew if we stayed here, you would get hurt. Every decision I have made has been with you in mind. Don't you dare say I haven't loved you."

He was shocked as Jack's mouth slammed down on his. There was a moment of stunned motionlessness before he grasped Jack's shoulders and held on for dear life. Jack's mouth was a force of nature. He was inside and dominating Sam with his tongue and lips. Jack's big hands wound into his hair to hold him still. He didn't have to. Sam wasn't about to fight. This was everything he'd wanted.

Jack wanted him. Jack loved him. Jack was passionate about him.

His arms wrapped around Jack's waist, and he let his hands explore. He ran his palms down the strong planes of his back to cup his ass. Every muscle was perfect. Even through Jack's jeans Sam could feel his heat.

Jack came up for air. His face was magnificently savage to Sam's mind.

"Knees, Samuel," he ordered.

He fell to his knees and immediately went to work on the fly of Jack's jeans. That hard cock sprung free, and he was swallowing it down as he pushed the denim aside. He couldn't wait to get that rigid flesh inside his mouth. He loved the sweet way Abby tasted, but he craved the saltiness of Jack, too. He wanted the best of both worlds. He grunted as Jack's hands twisted in his hair. The nip of pain was sensational. He liked the bite and the warmth that pain left in its recess.

Jack fucked his mouth ruthlessly, thrusting hard in and out. Sam ran his tongue around the rock-hard cock, sucking down the liquid dripping from the tip. He opened his mouth wide and gave Jack just the edge of his teeth. All at once it was over. Jack pulled out, his erection still huge and unsatisfied.

"I'm going to do a lot more than get a blow job," Jack growled. "Take those fucking clothes off and get on the bed."

Jack stalked toward the bedroom. Abby tried to move out of his way. She was biting her bottom lip in a way that let Sam know she was nervous. He could practically read her mind. She wouldn't want to get in the way. Sam wanted to tell her that she could never be in the way. She was the center of their world. Jack got to her first.

Jack reached out and grabbed her. He shoved her against the wall and held her there, pinning her with his body. He kissed her with every bit of ruthlessness he had used on Sam. Sam watched them as he tossed his clothes aside. Jack hadn't bothered to zip up, preferring to leave his erection on display. That made it easy for him to pull Abby's hand down to stroke his cock. Her hand ran up and down his erection, a truly beautiful sight. The head was thick and deliciously purple. Sam's dick throbbed in anticipation.

Jack tore open the robe Abby wore and threw it aside, leaving her gorgeous body naked. With a hard tug of his hand, he pulled her close, letting his cock grind against her as their mouths melded together again. Watching them made Sam's body heat until he worried he was going to go up in flames. He was going to be between them soon, and that was where he'd always longed to be.

"Get your ass to bed, too." Jack groaned as he let her down. He walked into the bedroom without a second glance.

Abby turned to him, worry evident in her eyes. "Sam, I don't want to come between you."

He pulled her naked body close to his. Her nipples rubbed against his chest. He kissed her briefly, skimming her waist and hips with his hands. She was like silk against him. "You won't. I'm going to come between you and Jack. It's my night to be in the middle, baby. Don't you dare walk away."

It wouldn't be the same without Abby there.

"But Jack—"

"Needs to work out some of his fears," he replied, knowing deep in his heart that this was what Jack needed. "He loves us. He doesn't understand that he can be weak sometimes. We have to show him it's all right. Give him what he needs."

Abby nodded, emotion in her eyes. "I love you, Sam."

"I love you. You're my woman," he said with a grin. "Now let's go get our man."

Chapter Sixteen

Jack paced the room, impatience warring with the sick feeling he'd had ever since that moment that he'd realized it was happening all over again. He kicked off his boots and shucked his jeans to the side. What the hell was taking them so damn long? Did they think this was fun for him?

Every minute they weren't with him sent him further into his head.

In his mind, he saw the gun Leo had picked up off the floor. The Dom had tried to conceal it, but Jack hadn't missed the glint of metal. It had been shoved against Abigail's stomach. It could have just as easily been Sam. If Sam had been whipped first, he would have been down there, waiting to be Slater's victim.

That fucker had put his hands on Abigail. He'd treated her like she meant nothing at all, like she was some kind of fucking pawn to be used and discarded. Rage screamed inside him, seeking an outlet.

He shoved his fist through the bedroom wall.

"I'm sure Julian will appreciate your renovations, Jack," Sam snarked.

He and Abigail stood in the doorway watching him. There was no judgment in their eyes. It was as though they were simply waiting for him to be done with his fit.

He wasn't done yet. "I should have killed that fucker. I should have put my hands around his neck and squeezed until his eyes popped out. How could I have let him walk away?"

"You didn't, baby." She strode straight up to him and put her arms around him.

He started to step back. The idea of her putting her hands on him when he was so angry made him nervous. It was like he was too dirty to have her touch him. But then he could probably be covered in another man's blood with a knife in his hand, and she would put her arms around him and ask if he was hurt. Sam would be there, too, only he'd probably be offering to wash the knife and help him hide the body.

"He didn't walk out," Sam continued her thought. "He was kind of dragged along, crying the whole way. He's probably being tortured even as we speak." Sam's face got serious. "It's over. It happened and we survived it. Put it behind you. We won't let you shut us out again."

But Jack was on a roll. He was sick to death of being afraid. The terror rolled in his gut, but it was nothing compared to the anger he felt. "And I swear, I'm going to beat the shit out of that Leo guy if he so much as looks Abigail's way again. The same goes for Julian with Sam. I am sick of people questioning my rights to my subs. Abigail is my wife and, damn it, you're my Sam. I won't let other people try to take you away from me."

"After what you did to my back, I seriously doubt anyone's thinking like that, Jack," Sam said.

"And from now on, I decide the punishment. Julian can go to hell. I am not living by his rules. I make the rules for this household. I do not have to live by his dictates. I don't have to follow some goddamn handbook on how I live my life. And the two of you are not allowed to fucking die on me." He reached down and pulled Abigail up. "And neither one of you is allowed to leave me. Is that understood?"

"Yes, Jack," she replied.

He looked at Sam, who had his hands on his hips. Jack tossed him a questioning look. They were going to have to work on Sam's obedience.

"Fine, I won't leave. I wasn't going far anyway. Can we fuck, please? This is getting painful." He indicated his massive erection. "We can work through your angst later."

"He's going to be the death of me," Jack whispered to his wife. He looked between his lovers. "I was afraid I would push you away with my demands. I can see now that the only way I can push you away is by holding you at arm's length." He opened his other arm, and Sam walked into it.

Their bodies pressed together. Something deep inside Jack loosened and broke free.

"You can push us to do some crazy stuff," Abigail admitted.

Laughter welled inside him, banishing the darkness. "Then I'll have to come up with some creative torture." His eyes met with Sam's. "I love you both. I won't check out again. I promise." He leaned over and brushed his lips against Sam's and then Abigail's. When he was done, he looked at his wife. "Get on the bed, baby. We're experimenting tonight."

She was on the big bed before Jack could say another word.

"Sam, I believe our wife would like some attention." Something relaxed deep inside Jack. He was in control again. It was exactly where he liked to be.

A decadent smile spread across Sam's face as he dropped to his knees in front of Abigail. "Spread your legs, baby. I need something sweet."

He pushed her knees apart and shoved his face in her pussy. He had a glimpse of how wet and perfectly aroused she already was. It didn't matter. Sam could lick her all day and she'd just make more. He'd never had a woman get so wet for him, want him so badly.

Abigail didn't need lube, but Sam was going to. Jack pulled the lubricant out of the dresser. He spread the lube in his hand. He enjoyed watching Sam lick at their wife as he stroked his erection, making certain he was nice and slippery. He was hard as a rock at the thought of what was about to happen. It had been forever since he'd fucked a man, and he'd never been with one he loved. Tonight he would be fully and completely with Sam and Abigail.

It was perfect.

"Abigail, move back," Jack ordered. "Sam, you're going to get inside our wife and then wait for my instructions."

Sam pressed her legs open and seated himself. He groaned as he pushed his erection in. She tilted her hips up to take him all the way to his balls. Sam wasn't one to wait. He started thrusting in and out, his head falling back.

Jack didn't stop him. Sam could thrust like that for a really long time.

"Does she feel good?" he asked, his voice low and husky as he continued stroking his cock.

"God, yes." Sam twisted his hips, making her moan. "You know how tight she is. She fits me like a glove."

He groaned slightly at that thought. Sam was going to be tighter than a glove. Suddenly he couldn't wait. He was done holding himself back. It was past time to join them. Hell, he was always going to join them from now on. He ran his hand up Sam's strong back, pushing him forward lightly. "Spread your legs. I need room to work."

Sam shuddered as he spread his feet apart, though it still didn't make him miss a thrust. Abigail was pushing back against him now. Her thumb was stroking her clit. He could hear the sweet sound of flesh slapping against flesh.

Sam's fingers joined hers. "Come for me, baby. That's right. I'm going to make you come all night long."

That wasn't going to happen until he was ready. "That's going to have to wait a minute. I need you to hold still, Sam."

"Damn it," he cursed but stopped and leaned over. He planted his hands on either side of Abigail's head. She didn't complain at all, even though it was apparent she'd been seconds away from heaven. She held still and let her hands drift into Sam's hair. Jack could hear her whispering to Sam. She told him how much she loved him. Abigail looked up at Jack, and he saw the love shining in her eyes. His heart clenched. This wasn't sex, not even close.

This was making love.

He smiled in return and moved between Sam's legs, letting his hands cup the muscled cheeks of Sam's ass and pouring out more lube. He spread those cheeks and started to work the lube into the tight rim of his ass. The plug they removed earlier in the day had opened him up a bit, but he was still tight as a drum.

"Relax, Sam." He gently pushed his middle finger in, working the lube around. Sam pushed back. "Patience."

"I don't have any." Sam laughed as he groaned. "I never did, man. Come on. I want your cock, not your fingers, Jack."

He sighed. Later, he would probably spank the hell out of Sam for that, but now he was just as impatient. He lined his dick up to that tight hole and gently started working his way in. Tight, so tight, that ring of muscles fought him, fought to keep him out. "Press back against me."

It was so fucking good. He wasn't even past the rim and he was fighting orgasm.

Sam flattened his back and pushed out. Jack steadied himself. He put a hand on Sam's abs. They were tight in anticipation. Jack tunneled in as carefully as he could. When his hips were flush against Sam's backside, he held still. He could feel the nub of Sam's prostate rubbing against his cock.

"Fuck," Jack muttered because there was no way he could last. It was too tight, too hot, too good.

"Yes, fucking would be nice," Abigail said a little desperately. "I'm so close."

Sam laughed, and he could feel it all along his cock, the sensation threatening to send him over the edge. He was done playing. Jack pulled out almost to the rim and thrust back in. Sam's head came up.

"God, yes," he yelled. He pushed back, forcing himself onto Jack's dick, then shoved forward into Abigail.

Jack gripped Sam's hips and set a brutal pace. He dragged his cock in and out, the heat and pressure making him crazy. Sam's body fought to keep him inside. His tight hole sucked at Jack's cock, tighter than anything he'd felt before. She heard Abigail cry out as Sam got her to come. Then Sam's head fell forward, and he was the one shouting as he filled their wife.

Jack felt his balls tighten and a tingle at the base of his spine. He pushed as far as he could into Sam's body as the orgasm took him. The hand on Sam's stomach tightened, and he pressed forward. He hissed as the orgasm squeezed his balls, shooting them off like it would never stop. He dragged air into his lungs as he thrust in little bursts, unwilling to leave the hot clasp of Sam's body. He finally slipped out and let gravity pull him forward.

They landed in a heap of arms and legs.

"Are you okay?" Jack asked when he could breathe again.

He felt Sam's hand wind around to land on his hip.

"Never fucking better, man. I like being in the middle. Though not to sleep." Sam got up suddenly and pulled Abigail between them. "She's softer than you and doesn't give off as much heat. You're like a furnace."

Sam settled back down, cuddling up to her, his head resting happily on her chest.

Jack went up on his elbow. He wondered what he'd been so upset about before. It didn't seem to matter now. They were together. That mattered. Abigail was looking up at him with dreamy eyes.

He laid a kiss on her forehead. "You okay, baby?"

Her lips curled in the sexiest smile. "I want to watch next time. It's like my own private movie."

Sam's head came up.

"No, we're not taping it." He had to be stern on that point or Sam would start up a new hobby.

Sam let his head fall back down with a pout. "You want to watch? You know what that makes you, Abby? That makes you a pervert."

"No, it doesn't," she insisted, snuggling down between them. "It just makes me Abby."

It made her perfect. It made them perfect.

* * * *

"Is she going to sleep all morning?" Jack asked as Sam walked into the room. He stopped and really looked at his longtime friend.

Sam wore a pair of boxers and scratched his stomach. His hair was wet from his shower. There was a cozy intimacy between them now that hadn't been there before. They had been friends, the closest of friends.

Now they were more. So much more.

Sam yawned and stretched. "Well, she went through a lot. Can you blame her? She got whipped, and then some guy tried to kill her, and then we did the whole crazy three-way thing four times in one night." He stopped and a grin covered his face. "Maybe we should wake her up with sex."

Jack shook his head and laughed. Naturally that's where Sam would go, but he had other plans. "I like how you think, but there's no time for that this morning. I want to be out of here in two hours. We're going home."

"Where we can have going-home sex to relax after all the vacation sex, right?"

Oh, they would definitely have going-home sex. He wanted them there, in the house they'd provided for Abigail. So much had happened that all he wanted was to get home to assure himself it was real. His thoughts were cut off by the knock at the door. When he opened it, Julian himself pushed through a large elegant tray. Sally followed behind him. She was bright and fresh faced. The moment Julian had the tray where he wanted it, Sally began pouring coffee into the china cups on the table.

Julian was already dressed for business in a three-piece suit that looked all elegant but made Jack think of a cage. "Good morning, Jackson, Samuel. I wanted to make sure you enjoyed your stay. Breakfast is on the house this morning."

"Thank god," Lucas said, walking in from the hall, one hand on his stomach. "I'm starving."

So much for his intimate morning plans. He would have to get used to it. The tight circle of people he trusted and gave a damn about was getting bigger by the moment. His younger brother looked over the food with an eager glint in his eyes. He downed the cup of coffee Sally handed him. Next month, Jack would have Lexi at the house for Easter. His heart did a little flip-flop as he thought about it. Two more people to take care of, to think about when he made a decision.

This was his family. Years he'd gone without, and now they were here.

"Hey, don't you eat all the bacon," Sam complained good-naturedly. "If you're anything like your brother, we're going to need to tell Benita to double the grocery order."

Julian stood apart, his eyes on the table where the younger men were arguing over the pancakes now. His gray eyes were surprisingly warm as he looked up at Jack. "You and Sam seem fine. I worried a bit that last night might bring back bad memories for you."

So many bad memories, but he'd realized that the way to deal with the bad ones was to make new memories, precious ones, loving ones. "Sam and I are very happy. So is Abigail. Don't worry about us, Julian. We'll be fine and we'll be back. I think my subs won't accept anything else."

"I can't tell you how glad I am to hear that. I've missed you, old friend." He pulled a small envelope out of his pocket and turned to Lucas. "But this is for a new friend. In case you need to blackmail your father. I know it's a family tradition."

Lucas's eyes went wide as he pulled out the contents of the envelope. "Wow. These are disturbing. I don't think I want to see my father in fetish wear. He let her spank him? Damn."

He flicked through the pictures, his face glazed with shock. Sam snuck a peek and shuddered.

"Jack, your dad looks like you, but his dick isn't anywhere close. Papa's got a tiny package."

"I must take after someone else," Lucas murmured. Jack nearly laughed out loud when his brother flushed. Lucas stood up straight and handed the photos back to Julian. "Thank you, Mr. Lodge, but I'm out of the blackmail business. I have better things to do with my time."

"Like punch cattle," Sam supplied.

"I have to punch them?"

Pride swelled in Jack. His brother was going to be okay. He needed time and patience and a family who loved him unconditionally. That was all. Luckily, that was something Jack was damn good at.

Julian handed the photos to Sally, who tucked them into the pocket of her suit. Like Julian she was all business this morning.

Julian took a cup from Sally. "Very good, Lucas. I'll keep them in case you need them later. Know you're always welcome here. Jackson, Samuel, don't be strangers. Sally, come to the office when you're done serving breakfast."

Julian shook hands with him and left quietly. As soon as the door closed, Abigail walked out of the bedroom, looking like a rumpled kitten.

"I need coffee," she said.

Sam already had the situation in hand. "Here you go, baby."

"Oh, good, breakfast." Abigail's eyes lit up and he worried maybe they would have to order more.

Sally held out a hand, gesturing to the tray. "I have a variety of breakfast favorites. There's pancakes, bacon, eggs, danishes, and fruit."

Abigail looked down at the small buffet. Her smile faltered and she went stark white. With shaking hands, she managed to set down the coffee mug before she darted back into the bedroom.

"Abigail?" Jack ran to keep up with her. Sam was hard on his heels.

She was on her knees in front of the toilet throwing up everything she had in her stomach.

He sank down beside her and pulled her hair out of the way, giving her the only support he could. They would have to rethink their plans if Abigail was sick. He patted her back and made sure she had an anchor.

Her whole body shook and he looked back at Sam. His partner's face was pinched with worry. She'd been so sick for the past month, but she'd seemed to be coming out of it. Was she relapsing? Getting worse?

"Darlin', are you all right? Do I need to call a doctor?" They would stay in Dallas and see a specialist.

Lucas looked in. He slapped Sam on the arm. "Dude, is she pregnant?"

Her head came up. "No. No. I'm almost thirty-eight. I can't be pregnant."

Sally stood in the doorway. "I think Lucas is right. I had a friend. The smell of bacon made her puke when she was pregnant. It was funny. Not the puking part. Sorry. She was really psycho about taking her birth control pills, but then she was on antibiotics and they canceled out the pills. She was pissed."

"Oh, my god," Sam breathed, his eyes wide as saucers. "We're going to have a baby? I think I'm still a baby."

Jack shot his brother a stare. "Lucas, go with Sally and ask Julian for a pregnancy test. I'm sure he has them."

Lucas nodded and walked out with the blonde.

"I'm too old to be pregnant," Abigail said, glassy-eyed.

"I'm too young for her to be pregnant." Sam looked equally shocked.

"Is Sally right about the antibiotics?" Jack ran a soothing hand along her back. She'd been on three different antibiotics trying to get rid of the infection in her lungs and they had not started using condoms. It hadn't occurred to him at all.

She nodded. "Sometimes antibiotics counteract birth control." She seemed to search her brain. "It's definitely possible. I'm a nurse. Why didn't I think of it?"

Because she'd had other things on her mind. Because she'd been worried about her marriage. "There's no blame, darlin'. None at all. Let's get you cleaned up."

Jack got her in the shower and helped her brush her teeth and then they waited for Lucas.

Twenty minutes and one pregnancy test later, Jack stared at the plus sign. Sam looked over his shoulder.

"Damn, Jack, what are we going to do with a kid?"

"The normal things a family does with a kid." Jack was surprised at his utter calm. Abigail was pregnant. She was going to have a baby. He was going to be a dad. He searched deep inside for some level of fear and panic and couldn't find it. A deep sense of satisfaction was the only thing inside him. That and an anticipation that made him smile like he hadn't in forever. Their future was right there, growing inside his wife. "We'll play baseball with him, teach him how to ride, stuff like that."

"I have a twenty-one-year-old daughter," Abigail said, still in shock.

"She'll make a good babysitter." Jack kissed the top of her head, pulling her close.

He and Sam were going to be dads.

"He's going to be a cute kid," Sam said. It was obvious he was calming down, too. "We gotta be careful. He's going to be awfully good looking. He'll probably have my hair and my build. I'm okay with him having Abby's eyes. They're really pretty."

Jack snorted. He felt unaccountably light hearted. He didn't care who'd actually fathered the baby, but couldn't help playing. "What makes you think it was your sperm? My sperm is obviously the dominant sperm. My sperm told your sperm to get to the back of the line. The boy will have black hair and green eyes."

Sam shook his head. "I bet my sperm listens to your sperm about as good as I listen to you. My sperm is also very impatient. It ran to that egg. Little Sam is gonna be a handful."

Abigail burst into laughter. "Holy shit. If this doesn't get me on a talk show, nothing will. And this one is a girl. I just know it."

She put a hand over her stomach, and there were tears in her eyes that had nothing to do with sadness.

Jack put his hand over hers, and Sam's fell on top, too.

"I don't think I can handle a female me, Jack," Sam said seriously.

Jack swallowed. He didn't think he could handle it, either. After a moment, he got up.

It was time to take his family home.

Chapter Seventeen

9 months later

Jack stared down at the sleeping infant, the world seeming to slow until there was nothing in the world except the two of them. His heart threatened to explode every time he saw that baby. Her tiny mouth moved, suckling on something in her dreams.

It was far worse than anything he could have dreamed up. The baby didn't look anything like him. Oh course, she didn't look anything like Sam either.

"Is baby girl asleep?" Sam yawned as he stepped into the nursery. "Or is she hungry again?"

"She's finally out for the count," Jack whispered, not wanting to risk waking her again. It was one in the morning and Abby was exhausted. Infants were a lot of work even when three parents were involved.

He made sure their three-week-old baby girl's swaddling was in place. Olivia Barnes-Fleetwood was a master of escape. Every time he made her into a tiny baby burrito, she wriggled until her arms wound their way out with a triumphant cry. It had become his favorite thing in the world, watching her get her way.

"God, she's so pretty." Sam's blue eyes studied the daughter they shared.

She was beautiful, and that was the problem. She looked exactly like her mama. She had pretty red hair and alabaster skin. Jack had to pray she wouldn't have her mama's figure, but he didn't hold out much hope. He was going to have to kill a bunch of teenage boys one day. No doubt about it. Little Olivia wouldn't be allowed to date until her father was dead.

"She's beautiful," Jack agreed, watching her breathe. He loved to watch her sleep. He adored all the faces she made while she dreamed her baby dreams.

The last nine months had been a revelation for a man who thought he'd never have a family. Now, everywhere he looked his life was full of people he called his own. His wife and Sam were always there, the cornerstones of his world. He'd watched his brother become the type of man he was proud of. Lucas had worked hard and earned his place on the ranch. Unfortunately, he was leaving soon. His brother was starting law school at the University of Texas in Austin a bit earlier than they'd planned, but it was time. He was surprised at how much he knew he'd miss his brother.

Lexi had moved home for the summer to be with her mom. Now she was home for winter break to help with her little sister. Lexi was well on her way to becoming a lovely woman. She was open and kind. She'd also gotten awfully close to Lucas, and that was a problem. She had a boyfriend, and a serious one at that. Jack was worried Lucas was getting in over his head. It was easy to see the way Lucas lit up when Lexi walked into a room. But Aidan O'Malley was someone Jack liked despite his own misgivings. He didn't see Lexi leaving him any time soon. In fact, he rather thought those two would get married one day and it would break Lucas's heart.

He had his eye on that situation. He was surprised at how much he loved his stepdaughter. His heart was a huge thing, he'd found. It was capable of all sorts of love.

"Come to bed," Sam urged, taking his hand. "She's asleep. We have to take advantage. It's the only time she's not in charge."

"Baby girl is always in charge, and I don't want to wake up Abigail." His gorgeous wife was being supermom. It was tiring her out. Between their baby and the clinic she was about to open, she was one overworked mama.

Sam's mouth lifted into a brilliant and incredibly sexy smile. "Abby is not asleep. She's awake, and she's frisky. You need to talk to her. The doctor told her to take it easy for six weeks. She's rubbing all over me, telling me she feels fine. She's making me crazy. I haven't been inside her for a month. I can't stand the teasing."

He bit back a laugh. His subs were misbehaving again. He pulled Sam into the hall. "Well, we have to fix that, don't we?"

He opened the door to their bedroom. Abigail was sitting on the bed pouting. She looked beautiful wearing nothing but one of his T-shirts. He knew she was worried about the baby weight, but he thought she'd never been more lovely. "Sam tells me you're horny, darlin'."

She smiled his way, that hot expression that let him know what she wanted. "Sam is a tattletale."

Unfortunately, she wasn't getting exactly what she wanted tonight. "No sex, Abby. The doctor said no intercourse for six weeks. But that doesn't mean we can't put on a show."

She sat up straighter, clapping her hands together. "My own personal porn stars."

Sam was out of his pajama bottoms in a minute. It was a talent of his. Sam was on the bed, kissing their wife, asking her which scene she wanted to jump to. He looked up at Jack.

"Here you are, Jack, performing on command," Sam noted with a smirk. "What does that make you?"

"Happy," Jack replied. He jumped on the bed to Abigail's playful squeal.

He jumped in the middle, and that was a good place to be.

* * * *

Julian Lodge and the whole Texas Sirens gang will return in *Siren Enslaved*, coming spring 2018.

Author's Note

I'm often asked by generous readers how they can help get the word out about a book they enjoyed. There are so many ways to help an author you like. Leave a review. If your e-reader allows you to lend a book to a friend, please share it. Go to Goodreads and connect with others. Recommend the books you love because stories are meant to be shared. Thank you so much for reading this book and for supporting all the authors you love!

Sign up for Lexi Blake's newsletter
and be entered to win a $25 gift certificate
to the bookseller of your choice.

Join us for news, fun, and exclusive content
including free short stories.

There's a new contest every month!

Go to www.LexiBlake.net to subscribe.

Away From Me

By Lexi Blake writing as Sophie Oak

Coming February 6, 2018

Re-released in a second edition with updates.

Shattered by the loss of his wife, Callum Reed is a man surrounded by rules designed to protect him. He rebuilds his life with careful discipline, but can't deny what he feels when he meets the lovely Gabrielle Sullivan. She's everything he wants in a woman, but he views all relationships as contractual. Despite her misgivings, Gaby signs his contract and becomes his perfect partner. Until the night she breaks his cardinal rule.

After three years of perfect obedience, Gaby declares she wants love and she isn't settling for less. Love isn't in their contract, so Cal lets her go. But Gaby has a secret reason for leaving. When Cal discovers the truth, nothing will stop him from following her.

On a secluded island paradise, Callum will do anything to prove he's the perfect husband for his defiant love.

* * * *

"Hello, Cal," she said evenly. "How are you?"

He looked her up and down, his dark blue eyes showing absolutely no expression. Those eyes assessed her, roaming every inch of her body in a decidedly clinical fashion. "I've been perfectly fine, Gabrielle. How have you been?"

His hand was suddenly on her elbow. Her skin tingled where he touched her. He didn't pull at her, merely squeezed gently, and she let him lead her. Yes, that was a force of habit, too, but perhaps her Irish friend was right. If they had any hopes of being comfortable around each other, they had to talk. They began walking slowly away from the pool.

"I'm well." That could have come out a little stronger. She sounded like a scared rabbit and that wasn't at all the impression she wanted to make on Cal.

"That's nice." Naturally, his voice sounded perfectly even. He could be negotiating a deal rather than talking to an old lover. "From the evil glances I'm getting from some very old friends, I would think I had tried to kill you."

"I'm sorry, what?" This wasn't the way she'd expected their first meeting to go. She'd kind of avoided thinking about it.

His jaw went tight. "I'm talking about all my friends looking at me like I'm some kind of criminal. I'll admit I haven't exactly been social lately, but I didn't expect to walk into a party and find myself completely unwelcome. The only thing that's changed is the status of our relationship, so I'm wondering what's been said about me."

Damn Heather and her big mouth. It was supposed to be a secret. She smiled brightly and slipped her arm through Cal's. Yes, she needed to handle this. She'd never intended to make anyone hate Cal. He simply hadn't been able to love her.

She had no interest in the two of them becoming a focus of gossip. If she seemed comfortable with her ex-lover, perhaps the other guests wouldn't talk about them. She tried to look nonchalant. "I have no idea why. I haven't seen any of these people since I left town ten months ago. Maybe it's me they're wary of."

"I doubt that, pet," Cal said, all silky and smooth. His voice had a direct line to her soft parts. "Even my oldest friend seems to have turned on me. Greg barely spoke to me this evening. His friendliest words were to tell me to leave you alone. I swear, Gabrielle, if he didn't need me to broker his deals, he might not talk to me at all. Now I wonder why that is."

Gaby flushed, guilt flooding her system. She truly hadn't meant to hurt him, but she didn't want to rehash the end of their relationship. She'd kept the secret this long. There was no reason he should know about it now. "I don't know. I have never spoken to Greg about us."

"I'm sure Heather talks enough."

Gaby felt her heels sink into the grass as they left the deck. The evening grew darker as the lights from the torches got further away.

211

The gazebo in the distance seemed to be Cal's destination. She followed willingly. If they were going to talk, it was best to do it in private.

"I can't control Heather's mouth. That's supposed to be Greg's job. He's her husband, after all."

Cal helped her up the gazebo's steps. He was always solicitous. It was one of the first things to attract her. He was a Dom of the first order. Gaby had been looking for someone like Callum since the day she realized there was a whole world out there for people like her. She'd gone through a couple of men who claimed to be Doms but really just used it as an excuse to be selfish. A real Dominant was someone like Cal, who always took care of her, even if he didn't love her.

"Well, as it was pointed out to me so recently, a Dom only has as much control as his sub allows him." His deep blue eyes were almost black in the moonlight and there were lines around his eyes that hadn't been there before. There was a weariness to his frame that called to her. She fought the urge to smooth down his tie and snuggle in his arms. He wasn't hers to take care of anymore. He turned to her. "So what have you been up to since you left?"

Her hand unconsciously went to her breast, thinking of the pain that centered there. "This and that."

He leaned back, staring at her as though trying to decide something. "I never could figure you out, Gabrielle. I didn't know if you were simply content to be kept or if there was some ambition lurking under the placid surface."

The darkness was a welcome ally as she felt herself flush. If they'd been under even the soft lights of the party, he would have known how much that hurt. "Well, you weren't interested in my ambitions."

He shrugged. "I just wondered what you did all day."

Her laugh was bitter and without an ounce of humor. "I ate bonbons and watched soaps. I counted the hours until you got home." She turned away from him and looked out over the yard. In the distance, her friends mingled and laughed. She still seemed so far away from them. Maybe she would always seem far away now.

Distance had given her some perspective, especially when it came to her old Dom. "You weren't interested in who I was as a person, Callum. You were interested in who I was as a sub. My submissive self was docile and sweet. That was what mattered to you. I didn't ask questions or make demands. It was a D/s relationship. It wasn't a love affair."

She knew the difference now.

His fingers ran across the exposed skin of her shoulders and she held on to the railing of the gazebo. The spaghetti straps that held her dress up offered little protection against his gentle assault. She shivered at the touch.

"And you don't want that anymore, do you? You don't want a man to dominate you? You don't want a man to take charge?"

Oh, there were certainly parts of her that did. His hands ran down to her waist, settling on her hips. Push him away. Do it now or this is going to go poorly. You are not capable of handling this.

But she'd waited too long. When he pressed his groin against her backside, she could feel the hard ridge of his erection, and she knew she wasn't going to walk away.

It was only sex. Sex with Callum had been mind-blowingly good. There wasn't any reason she couldn't enjoy it again as long as she held herself apart. It had been so long. And tomorrow morning, she would be on a flight back to her island, where she was surrounded by gorgeous men she couldn't fuck because they were either an employee or a guest. She was starting over. Shouldn't she honor her past with one last nice night?

Yeah, her girl parts were super stupid and they were firmly in control.

Cal pressed his hard dick against her and her brain no longer mattered. That dick had been the best she'd ever had and her whole body reacted. It was like her body knew what it had been through in the last ten months and was demanding payment. That big, hard dick was payment for all the pain.

She could handle it. Hell, after what she'd been through, she could handle anything.

Siren Enslaved
Texas Sirens Book 3
By Lexi Blake writing as Sophie Oak
Coming Spring 2018

Re-released in a second edition with updates.

Julian Lodge has everything a man could want. He's rich, successful and owns the most exclusive club in Dallas. But something is missing.

Finn Taylor has worked his way up in the world from humble beginnings in Willow Fork, Texas. The only thing he still loves in his hometown is Danielle Bay. He never told her he was actually bisexual, and he never confessed his love for her. Now she's getting married, and Finn is sure he's lost his chance with the only person he'll ever love.

Julian's vacation to the Barnes-Fleetwood ranch brings them all together. After Dani jumps into Julian's car while fleeing her wedding, Julian knows he has to have her. But nothing is easy in Willow Fork. A danger from Julian's past threatens them all. Julian will have to convince both Dani and Finn that being his will be the best decision they ever made.

About Lexi Blake

Lexi Blake lives in North Texas with her husband, three kids, and the laziest rescue dog in the world. She began writing at a young age, concentrating on plays and journalism. It wasn't until she started writing romance that she found success. She likes to find humor in the strangest places. Lexi believes in happy endings no matter how odd the couple, threesome or foursome may seem. She also writes contemporary Western ménage as Sophie Oak.

Connect with Lexi online:

Facebook:
https://www.facebook.com/pages/Lexi-Blake/342089475809965
Twitter: https://twitter.com/authorlexiblake
Website: www.LexiBlake.net

Sign up for Lexi's free newsletter at www.LexiBlake.net.

Made in the USA
Middletown, DE
03 May 2018